AT HER FEET

By the Author

Better Off Red: Vampire Sorority Sisters Book 1

Blacker Than Blue: Vampire Sorority Sisters Book 2

The Fling

At Her Feet

AT HER FEET

by

Rebekah Weatherspoon

2013

AT HER FEET

ISBN 10: 1-60282-948-9
ISBN 13: 978-1-60282-948-0

THIS TRADE PAPERBACK ORIGINAL IS PUBLISHED BY
BOLD STROKES BOOKS, INC.
P.O. BOX 249
VALLEY FALLS, NY 12185

FIRST EDITION: SEPTEMBER 2013

CREDITS
EDITORS: CINDY CRESAP AND SHELLEY THRASHER
PRODUCTION DESIGN: SUSAN RAMUNDO
COVER DESIGN BY SHERI (GRAPHICARTIST2020@HOTMAIL.COM)

Acknowledgments

Thank you to Meghan O'Brien and Andrea Bramhall for encouraging me to write this story.

Thank you to Kasey Dickerson for being the Liam Fey of my dreams.

Thank you to Radclyffe for signing off on this story when I was a little afraid she wouldn't.

Thank you to Cindy Cresap for hugging it out with me.

Thank you to Sheri for all the pink.

And lastly, thank you to Tecora and Steph for believing in me when I wanted to throw in the towel for the two-hundredth time.

Dedication

To Summer Youngblood.
Our next place will have a room just for you.

Chapter One

It's a little after eleven p.m. My TV's on, but I'm sitting at my desk. I'm bouncing back and forth between Twitter and a few gossip sites, waiting for my porn to load. I'm at that point in my life—twenty-seven years old, employed, but pathetically single. I've been burned by my sexual escapades. Not physically. I'm squeaky clean, and I never approved of fire play, but I've had a piece of my heart charred to a nice black. I'm social enough, but too picky and too developed in my tastes to go for something casual or meaningless, so it's me and my hand for the time being. I mind. I can't pretend I don't. That burning still hurts a little.

I note the time and the fact that I'm already wet just waiting for my porn to load, and I decide to check out my kinklife account. After Laurel, I almost abandoned my profile. At first, I kept it to spite her, and then I kept it in the hopes that I'd find something new. I gave up on that months ago, though. Now I go look out of curiosity. Laurel's since deleted her account, so I'm not worried about that 160 x 160 pic of her leather-clad breasts, but I think of that picture just for a moment as I glance at the word SINGLE next to my own 160 x 160. I ignore the lines below, the declaration of my patheticness. I know what it says. Looking For: *Mistress, Mommy, Teacher, Long-term Relationship.*

I'm a member of forty-something groups on kinklife. I cover ground from anal play to spankings, and a few more colorful things in between. Some I've learned from Laurel, some I've learned on my own. I look at the events and updates. The *Lesbian/Bisexual* group in Sherman Oaks has a spa day planned for the weekend. I don't respond to the general invite. I can't do groups. There's a seminar on puppy training at the dungeon in Pasadena. I'll be skipping that, too. DirtyJenna celebrates her first time with photographic proof in the *Squirty Girls Club*. Been there, done that.

DomNick, a nice man I met a few months ago at a rope-bondage class, has posted pictures from his weekend. He's offered several times to take me in. Nothing official, he's promised, but he likes me and hates that I don't have a Dom looking after me. He *is* nice, but I'm just not interested. I like a few of his pictures and leave a comment that says I'm glad he had a good time but leaves no illusion that I wish I'd been there.

I click on *Lesbian Mommies and little girls*. There's no plan here. I just click the link.

I found BDSM between the pages of a book, but it wasn't the scenes of bondage that captivated me, or even the juiciness of the sex acts themselves. It was the relationship between the Dominant and the submissive that moved me. They weren't strangers brought together by a need to exchange pain, though over the years that scenario has appealed to me. It was the way the submissive felt about her Dominant. The way she yearned to give up her control to him, and the way, at every turn, he met that surrender with sensual challenges and respect. They were lovers, partners, in every sense.

I'd never come close to that type of relationship before, but I understood that yearning. I'd searched for it in my previous relationships, though not in the same terms, and not with such transparency. I wanted to give myself to someone. I still do. I didn't find that opportunity until I met Laurel. And with Laurel I found that with giving there has to be some sort of getting. That's why they call it erotic power exchange, not erotic power life suck. But that's what happened with Laurel.

I followed her blindly, anxiously down a certain path. She taught me things, showed me a way of living and fucking I'd never experienced before. I gave her my submission, and she got my loyalty, and my obedience, and my body when she needed it. I gave and I gave, and she got. Luckily, I was able to see that she was draining my well dry. I needed more for myself. I think that's what attracted me to the idea of the Mommy or Daddy Dominant and the submissive, adult-little girl relationship. The title itself caught me off guard at first. There's so much to a name at any given moment, so much meaning to what you call someone so close to you, but the more I talked to other submissives, who not only prided themselves on being labeled a little girl but knew the power it carried, owned the level of intimacy that came with such a name, the more the idea of being someone's little girl grew on me. I've read and discussed different philosophies on the matter, and the differing opinions only highlighted how many kinds of Dominant/submissive relationships there are.

In some instances, the title of Mommy or Daddy turned submissives off, for obvious reasons, but when it came to identifying with others, or slapping a name to the situation, that's where the couple would fit. What they actually called each other was for their ears only. For some it was about age role play and age regression. For others it involved relinquishing a certain sense of responsibility to your Dominant while giving in to their sadomasochistic demands. But I always saw a common theme: an affection that went beyond tending to your submissive after a physically or emotionally demanding scene. There was also a level of protection that seemed to be bound to a genuine sense of possessiveness on the part of the Dominant. This is my little girl, and I will protect her not because she is my submissive or even my property, but because I love her. I think all Dominants care, the good ones anyway, but this was more than that.

Pieces stuck with me, and when I finally approached Laurel on the subject, I had a sense of what that type of relationship meant to me. I work hard. Overtime at the office isn't unusual for me. I'm responsible and giving, at times to my detriment. I was happy to submit to Laurel's hand, or flog, or paddle, but I needed more. I needed her affection with my subservience. At the end of the day when I felt my job weighing me down, and after she'd used my body until I nearly lay limp, I needed her care.

The other submissives I interacted with bragged shamelessly about the love they received from their Daddy Doms. One little girl I chatted with briefly online had an entire blog dedicated to her love for her Mommy Mistress. The sadistic side of Laurel, that I did enjoy, was present in those blog posts, but their relationship was so much more. More pampering and spoiling, more patience, more rewards for submission given freely. I mean, they cuddled. Pictures of her pinkened ass, glowing after a thorough spanking, graced the pages right beside photos of her Mistress stroking her hair. I wanted that sort of love in my life.

The more I thought about it, the more I wanted it, but that meant Laurel had to give. So I told her about those Dominants and their submissive little girls. She knew all about them, but she humored me. Flogged me all night when I was done arguing my case, and then she said she'd try. It wasn't her style, but she said she would try. She couldn't. She didn't really want to. Things ended, and that's putting it nicely. I moved on.

And now I try to be patient while I wait for the right thing. The right person and the right situation. The right type of submission for me. I mean it when I say I'm not "actively" looking. Still, it's the third post that catches my eye and sends a small spark of excitement over my skin.

Mami looking for her little girl—Los Angeles, posted by Mami-P.

Beside the post title is a small photo of a gorgeous Latin woman. Her lipstick is bright red, and her hair is up in white curlers. The picture only features her face, but that's enough for me, and clearly, it's enough for others. Kinklife.com caters to a worldwide audience. Little girls from all over are begging for a Mommy to take care of them. A few Mommies had listed in a strange cluster in the UK. I'd seen one post for San Diego, but not L.A.

That small spark, the pinch of hope that tightens my chest, quickly fades once I look at the date. This post has been up for four days and has twenty-four comments. That means only two things:

our Mami-P has up to twenty-four offers, twenty-four little girls vying for her attention. Or our Mami-P has had a few offers, but a conversation thread has sprung up between her and a special little girl.

I'm curious to see who has beaten me to the punch even though I wasn't really looking. I click the link and find it's a mixed bag. Eleven little girls seem to be doing the virtual shove to the front of the line. Two state that they are from L.A. The others beg for an online relationship. Mami-P doesn't give clear responses to any of them. The rest of the posts are an exchange between Mami-P and Mommy4LilBit. M4LB seems to be trying to unload her little girl on Mami-P. She's not into any of it. I look at her initial post again.

Mami looking for special adult little girl for serious long-term relationship. No games. Sorry, but no infants or toddlers, and no incest play. Must be local.

I read it three more times, and then I click her profile. Her status matches mine: single.

She's about as active on kinklife as I am, but I'm not looking for her friends or groups. I go right for her pictures. There's only three. I look again at her profile picture. She's very beautiful; that hasn't changed. The other two photos pique my interest even more. In one, she's caught by some onlooker as she observes a conversation. She's sitting in a lawn chair, and she's knitting. A woman with a skill is always nice. The third picture actually makes me wet.

Mami-P posed for this portrait beside a vintage sewing mannequin. She's in full '50s garb: a calf-length red dress with white polka dots, and black heels. She's wearing makeup, and pearls, and a killer smile. My imagination jumps ahead. I'm in her kitchen and she's lecturing me about proper etiquette. I'm nodding, soaking it all in. I'm in awe of her knowledge. I want to learn what she has to teach me, but really I'm waiting patiently for her to bend me over the counter and fuck me.

I click the private message link below her profile name and type Hi! in the subject line. I give her my real name, tell her I'm local, and ask that if she hasn't found someone already, if she wants to talk. I hit send and remind myself that it might be another four days (or never) before I hear back from her, but that doesn't change the fact the spark is back. My body is buzzing. Hope. Anticipation. I've been guarded and cautious, but when it comes to something or someone I want, I'm an optimist. It's led me to a great job, this positive thinking, and some great friends. It also led me to Laurel, but Mami-P is ten times hotter than Laurel, so I'm willing to let myself get a little excited about this. The worst thing she can say is no.

I check Twitter again.

My porn's loaded, but I'm not ready yet. I open another tab and search for another video to watch. When that's done loading, I'll watch them both. That'll give me enough of a distraction.

I'm clicking links like crazy—news, gossip, Twitter, back to news—and nothing's sinking in.

An alert box pops up at the bottom of my screen. New e-mail from *P.Castillo*. I open it and find just two lines.

Hello there, sweetheart.
Would you like to chat?

Beautiful and she e-mails in complete sentences, which is truly a rare thing these days. Do I want to chat? Yes. Yes, I do.

Our conversation over ychat is short. I've wasted my wank time, and we both have to get up in the morning for work, but we do cross some important ground.

Her name is Pilar. I tell her to call me Suzy. She works as a wardrobe stylist, and she lives in Miracle Mile. I tell her about my apartment in Koreatown and my job in digital marketing. I tell her straight off that I think she's pretty. I ask if she wants to see my picture. She does. Her approval of my looks seems genuine. She asks if I am mixed, politely, thank God. I get this question all the time, but some people don't know how to ask it without making me sound like a circus freak.

My mom's Jamaican, which accounts from my brown skin, and my thick hair, and my butt. My dad's Korean, which accounts for most of my face and my last name. I confuse people, trust me. People say I'm pretty, but I attract the exotic fetishist that just wants a mixed girl on their arm or under their gag for the novelty of it. My 160 x 160 is a picture of a white kitten for that exact reason.

She asks me how old I am because I look like a baby. I tell her I'm twenty-seven. I tell her she looks really, really old. I add a smiley face. She tells me she's thirty-nine. I tell her she doesn't look over thirty, which she really doesn't. She says she likes younger women who know when to lie.

She tells me she's second generation from Mexico. Her parents live in Long Beach. She asks me what I'm doing up so late. I tell her about the porn. She asks me to send her the links. She sends me a smiley face and tells me she likes my taste in X-rated material. By this point, I'm yawning, and I know I can't fall asleep during our client presentation tomorrow.

I ask her if she likes me so far. She says yes and asks for my phone number. She says she was serious in her post, reminding me that she's looking for something fun, but monogamous and long-term. She says she'd like to talk soon. Online play isn't her thing. Thanks to Laurel, it's not my thing either. I tell her to call me when she's free in the next couple days. She says she will.

Before we log off, she tells me not to stay up too much longer. This simple command is sweet, and I find myself smiling behind my clenched knuckles. I tell her I can't wait to talk to her again. She says the same. I say good night, and she says sweet dreams. I skip the porn and get right in bed. I fall asleep thinking about Pilar in her polka-dotted dress and her smile.

Something needs to change at work. My job isn't hard when it's running smoothly. I execute digital marketing campaigns. I don't have to code. I don't have to design creative components. I'm like that closer lady on TNT; I make sure the websites, and contests, and banners, and apps we've sold to the client get done. But here's the problem: I have too many accounts, and we don't have enough producers to help me out. I manage accounts for a theme park, a candy company, and a national optical chain. These are pieces of cake, especially since the theme park's marketing pushes are only in the spring.

But we've recently taken on a major account for a fashion company, 21 And Up, that caters to older teens and young twenty-somethings. I was psyched about this acquisition for like five minutes, until Valerie put me in charge of their mobile app. The work is easy. The client is a nightmare.

I'm on the phone now with Katie, our account exec. She's only across the office, but we're a social bunch. If I get up, I'll face a gauntlet of conversations—and Mitch's magic tricks—before I reach Katie's desk. And that's if I don't run into Liam. My best friend and I have no business working in the same office.

"They told me they sent out the press release last week," Katie says. I'm pissed that I've just found out that the launch of 21 And Up's mobile app has been pushed up.

"Okay, but we're not the media. They have to tell us these things before they send out press releases. Josh didn't approve the budget for the overtime." I'm thinking of telling our coder, Leah, that she's about to have a long week. She's a good sport, but I hate to do this to her.

"I'll talk to Valerie about this," Katie says. "I know you have Clear Vision to deal with."

"We can handle it, but I just need to be in the loop. I can't do my job if they don't share this information with us."

Katie laughs. She's just as annoyed as I am.

I look over as an alert pops up on my screen: *Emergency meeting for 21 And Up* from Valerie. I open it and see she's scheduled it for noon. The note attached reads *I'm buying lunch.*

"Do you see this?" I ask Katie.

"Yes." She sighs, and I'm almost positive I hear her bang her head on her desk. "We'll just wait and see what Val has to say, and then I'll let her know about this fabulous lack of communication."

"That works for me." We hang up and I go back to my e-mails. I open the latest from Grand Adventure. It's June. Their site is perfectly updated with promotions and attraction highlights. Their account guy is asking about a new banner ad. I close my eyes and shuffle it through my mental calendar. I don't get very far because my cell phone rings. I don't know the number, but the area code is 310.

"This is Suzanne Kim," I say in my most professional voice.

"You told me to call you Suzy."

"Oh my God. Hi," pops out of my mouth first. I'm shocked, but pleased, and that overwhelms much of my brain. I laugh, embarrassed at myself, then give my greeting another try. "I meant, hi."

"You know who this is?" I can hear the smile in her raspy voice along with a slight accent.

"Yes. It's Pilar."

"Can you talk for a few minutes?"

"Yeah. Give me one sec." I get up then and book it for the side exit. I can't keep my cool at my desk.

Our building is an architectural spectacle on the south side of West Hollywood. I find a seat on the glass benches that overlook the gardens that line the back entrance, and then I take a deep breath.

"Okay," I say. "Hi."

"Hello. Did you sleep well?"

"I did. And you?"

"I was thinking about you for a while, but eventually, I slept very well."

Her words make me giddy, and I find myself tapping my heel on the side of the bench. Her voice is pure sex, I think to myself at this point. I'll never get tired of hearing it.

"What would you say to meeting me for dinner tomorrow night at The Grove?" Pilar asks.

I say yes. "It's on my way home." I instantly regret that. "I mean I'd meet you there if it wasn't on my way."

"That's nice to hear." Her laugh is just as sexy. "I want to e-mail you a little list. It's not a contract or anything. I just want to give you a clearer idea of what I'm like, and what I expect, and then there's a questionnaire for you."

I like her approach with me. She's flattering and sweet, but she's setting guidelines and expectations early. I need that.

"That sounds good. Send it over."

"I'm already fighting the urge to call you 'baby,'" she says.

I almost dissolve into a Suzy puddle. "You can," I say without hesitation. That's wrong and I know it. We need to come to some sort of agreement first, but I already like what I know about her. And I want her to like me. I want her to call me baby.

"Go over the list tonight, and if anything freaks you out, call me. If not, answer your questions, and we'll talk about it tomorrow night."

"Okay." We agree on seven p.m. at a restaurant called The Barn. They have delicious mac and cheese. "I'll go over the list," I reassure her.

"Okay, baby," she says. And I die right there. "You get back to work."

We say good-bye, and I almost twirl all the way back to my desk.

❖

"Joshua quit."

Several "Whats!" and gasps come from around the conference room. Beside me, Liam curses and bites his fist. Josh is straight, but Liam was trying really hard to test that theory.

"He quit when?" I ask.

"This morning," Valerie says.

"Well, that explains why he's been out," Mitch says. "He wasn't sick, he was interviewing."

"Did he tell you that?" Valerie is very cool and level-headed, but her face turns a little pink.

"No, no," Mitch says frantically. "But it makes sense." He's been working here three years and he's never used a sick day. Suddenly, he's out sick something like six times in the last month."

"Does make sense," Liam says. "That beautiful fool."

"What did he tell you?" I ask Valerie. Joshua runs the bulk of the 21 And Up account, not to mention an account for Dylon Motor sports. I look at Mitch and our other producer, Daisuke, and we know we're fucked.

"He just said he was taking time to evaluate a life change. Either way, he's gone. Mitch, I want you to take on Grand Adventure and Clear Vision. Daisuke, Bee's Candy will become your responsibility. Suzanne..."

I hold in my groan and fight the urge to vomit. "I want you dedicated one hundred percent to 21 And Up."

I curse to myself but say okay.

"I'm going to bring on two more producers as soon as we hear back on Dylon, but I just need you guys to hang in there with me."

We all agree. No one in the room is to blame. I can't even blame Josh. He hated marketing, and I'm proud of him for getting out. The guys grab some food. Valerie asks me to her office. I plan to meet with the guys that afternoon to pass on the projects. Liam promises to save some lunch for me, and I follow my boss out of the room.

I like Valerie. I've worked for women before that I just didn't mesh with, but Valerie seems to understand all of us. She only pushes us so far before she pushes the client back, and she always shows gratitude when we finish a project. She's a little inappropriate at times. Liam loves that about her, but she has a wealth of quality dirty jokes at the ready that help balance out the occasional awkwardness.

"How are you?" she asks once I close the door.

"I'll be fine." I tell her about the mobile app and the press release, though. I'm not complaining, but I need her to know what I'm dealing with.

"I know," she says. "Joshua had similar complaints. But I have faith in you, Suzanne. You're my best producer. Let's just get through this and then we can talk promotion," she says with a smile. "Oh." I can feel my eyebrows touching the ceiling. "I—thank you. That would be great."

Valerie comes back around her desk and puts her hand on my shoulder. We walk toward the door. "Get the boys rolling on Clear Vision and Bee's, and I'll help you cover 21 And Up for the next couple days. Joshua at least left me a thorough explanation of where his projects are."

"At least there's that."

Part of me wants to kill Josh, but if things go well, I might be thanking him for a nice little raise.

Liam's waiting for me at my desk. He hands me a soda and a chicken wrap. "What did Val want?"

I wipe a small smudge of eyeliner from his left eye before I plop down in my seat. "Just a pep talk."

"I'm so sad Josh is gone. His ass. It was perfect."

"You're so lucky he never went to HR about you," I say.

"He's too butch for that. Besides, it was all in good fun."

"You gays with your double standards."

"Well, I have to tell you what I told Josh. I've come up with some amazing creative designs for that account. Don't fuck it up."

I scowl at Liam, but he has a point. He designed the components of the new website that convinced 21 And Up to sign with our agency. If we lost the account it would land on my shoulders.

"Don't worry. I got this. I *do* want to know why Josh left."

"Facebook him," Liam says with a shrug.

"Good call."

"So tomorrow night—"

"Oh, shit. Whatever it is, I can't."

"But why?" Liam whines.

"I have a date thing." Liam knows about my kinks. He was there for me when I broke up with Laurel, but I'm not going to talk about it in the office.

"Oh! Tell me!"

I lower my voice and crook my finger for him to lean closer. "Sexy, *sexy* woman. A little older than us. I hope she makes me her bitch."

Liam leans even closer. "Are you going to let her finger bang your mouth?"

"Oh my God! You're gross."

"I know. Well, fine. I'll ask Gary if he wants to go."

I laugh. "Why do you hate your boyfriend?"

"I don't. He just never wants to go out."

I love Gary. He's very sweet. He's also one of those gay guys that some people think doesn't exist. For those who don't understand that being gay isn't a way of walking or a fashion statement, it's that he acts so straight is the only way to explain it. People are always shocked when he introduces Liam as his boyfriend and not his outrageously gay little brother. Gary likes sports and beer. Liam likes drag shows and anything that ends in *tini*. They're complete opposites, but seeing them together would make a lot of people jealous. They love each other that much.

"Tell him if he goes out with you tomorrow, you'll go to that fight in Vegas with him."

"What? No way." Liam pauses. "Wait. That might work. I love hotel sex."

"I know you do. And you can squeeze in some Cirque du Soleil between the hotel sex. Where are you going tomorrow, anyway?"

"My mom surprised me with tickets to *The Best of Broadway* at the Bowl."

"Oh, yeah. You're taking him to Vegas."

❖

I work dumb late, but at least I'm not alone. Mitch and Daisuke are with me. Valerie takes off at her usual time, but she tells us to order dinner and bill it to the company. We bulk up on Thai food, which is a horrible idea. I'm ready to pass out right after we eat, still I couldn't ask for better company. Mitch and Daisuke make me laugh as we plug away. We're caught up by nine thirty, and finally, I head home.

It's ten o'clock by the time I get to my apartment and shower. Another thirty minutes before I'm settled in bed with my laptop. I go right for my e-mail. The notification has taunted me all afternoon. It's still there, of course, when I sign in, pushed to second place by an e-mail from Jeep asking me if I'm ready to trade in my Wrangler for bonus incentives. I know the layout of the banners will hurt my eyes, so that's going in the garbage. I torture myself a few moments more, and then I open Pilar's e-mail.

Hello Gorgeous,

It was lovely to hear your voice today. Like I said, take your time with this. If there's anything you don't understand or want to discuss with me tomorrow, that's completely okay. I just want to get to know you better, and I want you to know me. Call me if you need anything.

—Pilar

I think about her saying these words to me in person; I think about her calling me baby. I want to call her right now, before I read the rest of her terms, before I even look at the questionnaire, but that eagerness has bitten me in the ass before. This isn't like a regular relationship. It's up to me to do as she asks, which I want to, but I have to proceed with a certain sense of caution. I have to consider what's in my best interest first, and not let my imagination run with the fantasy before Pilar and I come to an agreement. I am giddy still, and eager, but I'll be patient.

I open the document and look at her list of terms. I worked through a similar list with Laurel, but this is a little different. There's less focus on sadistic and masochistic practices. Actually, there's almost no mention of either, only that she will use spanking for both discipline and pleasure. For the list of sex acts, she clarifies from the start that she is open to both vaginal and anal intercourse. She's only interested in being the recipient of the former. Any and all water sports are completely out, and if I have desires of diaper play then I need to look for another Mommy right now. We're on the same page there, so I keep reading. She includes light bondage, but expresses that she has no interest in gagging me. I take that as a good sign. I like to be vocal.

The rest of what she details are the facets of her role as a Mommy Dominant. She wants a sense of structure and routine when we're together. I'm to mind my manners and my language. At the same time, she wants to spoil me, cook for me, bake for me, pamper me. I have no objections to any of these things. Her portion ends there. I assume we'll talk more about her over dinner, over time.

I wanted to print out the questionnaire at work, but knowing my luck, we'd have a system error or a paper jam, and the first thing the printer would finally spit out in the morning would be the details of my sex life in black and white, right into the hands of someone like Katie or Valerie. I read through the questions once and am pleasantly surprised. I grab a notebook and a pencil off my desk and start to answer the questions.

She wants to know what sex acts, points of bondage, and submission I'd like to include. Nothing really differs from her responses, but I do note that I am a fan of giving and receiving oral sex, and I like to be tied up. I include my fondness for mutual masturbation. It's been a while since I've done anal, but I mark it off as a can-do. Pilar strikes me as someone who would be incredibly gentle. I note that face slapping, in my book, is an invitation to a fistfight and one of my hard limits. She asks if I know the age of my inner child. This stumps me. I've thought about this a lot and only got as far as thinking that maybe this part of me doesn't have an age, just a younger, more innocent frame of mind. I tried to work on this with Laurel, but we didn't really get anywhere. She called me needy and annoying, and that was the beginning of the end.

Next is the part I really like. She asks what my favorite movies are, if I like to play dress-up. She wants to know if I ever had a favorite teddy bear or any pets. She wants to know what my favorite color is. She asks if I like to play any games. She wants to know what's my favorite way to relax and if I have any food allergies or anything I just refuse to eat.

Finally, we'll decide on a safe word together, in person.

It's almost one before I finish. I'm exhausted but anxious. I want to skip work tomorrow and get right to our dinner. I want to call her. Instead, I send her a text. *Good night* is all it says.

She texts back almost right away. *Sweet dreams, sweetheart.*

Day from hell, but I still go to sleep with a smile on my face.

CHAPTER TWO

The next day of work is excruciating. Valerie does her best to get me up to speed on 21 And Up, but every five minutes we're interrupted. A call from Daisuke about Bee's. Mitch showing up at my desk with questions about Clear Vision. He comes back three more times, then four more times for Grand Adventure. I text Pilar a couple more times to tell her I'm stuck at work. Finally, at seven thirty, I leave and make my way over to The Grove.

I brought a change of clothes with me, but I'm too, I don't know. I'm too worn out to scramble into a bathroom to ditch my blouse, my tights, and my heels for something a little more comfortable. More me than my work clothes. At least the bow tie I have on looks cute. I check my makeup in my poorly lit car and fix the few strands of hair that have escaped from the high, messy bun piled on my head before heading down to the escalator to The Barn. Sometimes I wish my hair wasn't down to my waist, but it's too curly to pull off any shorter styles. I'm fiddling with it as I try not to run down the escalator. The Grove is packed. By the time I make it through the mass of tourists taking pictures in front of the singing fountain, I'm flustered all over again. I tell the hostess I'm meeting my party, and she directs me right to a small corner booth in the back.

I see her, Pilar, and I forget all about work. I forget about how I was thinking about tracking Josh down and punching him in the crotch for ditching me with 21 And Up. Pilar stands when she sees me. I'd held on to the image of the red polka-dot dress in my mind these last couple days, but the real thing is perfection. She comes around the side of the table and thanks the hostess, but she keeps her eyes on me. I know her face matches mine. Or maybe I'm smiling more.

Everything about her is round and plump, from her cheeks to her large breasts to her hips. Her whole body is inviting. I'm not short, but she's taller than me, fuller, but in the best possible ways. Her smile is her dominant feature. She has a wide mouth and full lips, but her brown eyes are very expressive. She's only wearing the slightest bit of makeup, but I'm willing to venture she'd look just as beautiful without any on. She has on a blue pinstripe shirt-dress, cinched below her chest with a wide, brown belt. The belt matches a pair of knee-high slouch boots. Her long, thick, black hair is down, but her bangs are held back, though pushed slightly forward by a matching brown headband. She looks so good.

"Hi," Pilar says brightly. I say hello back, and as she hugs me, I feel protected and cared for. I'd even venture to say loved in that moment. We're doing it backward, I can already tell. Like how she already calls me baby. The hope of trust and the affection is already there before we've made anything official, but I can't change the way I feel.

"Come sit down," she says.

I slide into the leather seat beside her. She's wearing a rose perfume I haven't smelled in years, but I remember instantly how much I love the scent. I move a little closer. "I'm so sorry I'm late."

"Don't worry about it. I'm glad you made it."

Pilar already has a glass of red, but our waitress is back in the next moment, so I order a glass of white. I need it after the half week I've had. "I brought the questionnaire," I say as I dig through my purse.

Pilar chuckles a little. "Just relax. We have plenty of time for that," she says, but I'm already unfolding the papers. She takes them, but she's still amused. "You want me to look at it now?"

"Yes." I reply with a cheeky smile.

"Okay." She unfolds the light-green paper I tore from my notebook, then slips her arm around my waist. I don't think; I just put my head on her shoulder. She takes her time reading over my responses. My wine comes, and I almost finish it before she puts my papers down. We order. I get the mac and cheese and the grilled-chicken salad. She gets the short ribs. She's so my kind of woman.

"So," she says as the waitress walks away. "How did we end up here?"

I look up at her. "What do you mean?"

"How did you end up in my inbox? How did you end up on kinklife?"

I let out a short breath and tell the truth. "My ex-girlfriend, Laurel, introduced me to the community. We met in a book club."

"Really? Was it a kinky book club?"

"No, but one of the other women was sick of reading Oprah recommendations so we decided to try an erotic romance about a woman who finds her true love through bondage."

"And this intrigued you."

"It did. I kept talking about it, and finally, Laurel told me she was into things like what we'd read in the novel. She asked me if I was interested in learning more."

"I'm interested in how she became your ex," Pilar says. I liked her forwardness. This was a good question. How someone ends a relationship is indicative of how their next relationship is going to start. Laurel is the villain, that much is true, but what I say next might paint me in a different light. Still, I tell the truth.

"She trained me very well, for her needs. But I have my own mind, and I still had free time. I talked to more submissives. I read more. I joined kinklife, and I started seeing all of these other fetishes that I wanted to explore. So I told her."

"And she didn't want to be a Mommy to your little girl." Her hand slides up my back, then back down to my waist. I hold in a slight shiver.

"She said she wanted to at first, so I went with it, but after a while she just, I don't know, she became less and less responsive, and eventually, she rejected my younger persona outright. I would come to her wanting to play and she'd tell me to grow up. Or say how obnoxious I was acting. One night she took me to a play party and introduced me to another woman who was supposed to be my new Mommy. She also decided then to tell me that she'd taken a job in Phoenix. She wanted to stay together, but she thought this other woman could take care of my other needs better. I was so livid, I broke up with her on the spot."

"Good for you," Pilar says.

"Yeah, I was proud of myself until my cab showed up, and I realized I was in a leather skirt and pasties." I laugh, still thankful for the cab driver who waited outside my building until I was inside safely. "I've only been with a few other people since, but I was more honest with myself about what I wanted. I was able to walk away before things got too complicated."

"Do they feel complicated now?"

The waitress shows up with our food, and Pilar asks for more wine. I ask for a water. We both start to eat before I answer. Our meal gives me time to consider how I want to respond to her question. I settle on the whole truth, but I'm not sure how to phrase it.

"I have trust issues, and I know that's the main thing a submissive needs to give to a Dominant."

Pilar corrects me. "Well, a submissive's trust is the most precious thing a Dominant can earn."

"You're right, but I didn't understand that with Laurel. I thought the trust was deserved. I feel like I can trust you, but I felt like I could trust her. But I recognize now that this is a different situation. You're a different woman. I wanted to be taken care of. I wanted to be *pampered*. I wanted to let myself go, but she kept reminding me that those were things I could do for myself. She'd just tell me to go to a spa and get a massage, but when she needed the release of whipping the shit—" I remember Pilar doesn't like foul language. "Sorry."

She strokes the side of my hair. "It's okay. Go on."

"She was very sadistic, and I was there to play into those needs, but she didn't think our street needed to go both ways. And in the end she just tried to pass me off. No discussion about where we were as Dominant and submissive or as a couple."

"Hmm," is how Pilar responds.

"Too much baggage?" I ask. I'd rather know now if she's not in the mood to deal with my shit.

"No. That's not what I was thinking."

"What are you thinking?"

"I'm thinking how we all need to work on things in relationships, and with you I want to make sure I work on my communication. And I want to make sure I listen to you."

"Did you have communication issues in the past?"

She's quiet for a moment before she answers. "In a way I did. My first little girl couldn't reconcile her sexuality with her beliefs. I tried to be there for her in every way I could, but eventually, we had to end our relationship. I saw glimpses of our breakup along the way, but I thought my support would be enough. It wasn't."

"Were there others?"

"Yes, there were, baby, but just one other little girl. She was a complete brat. I don't work well with brats. I will discipline you when I have to, but I don't need my buttons pushed every day. And there's just certain behavior I don't want to tolerate from anyone: children, adults, or adult children. I passed her on to another Mommy who is more than willing to deal with her tantrums. They are very happy together." She smiles and I believe everything worked out for the best there.

We finish our dinner, and even after the dessert, we sit close in the booth, talking and touching. Eventually, Pilar asks me the question. "So what do you say?"

I think a moment more before I answer. "I'd like to give it a try and see how it goes."

She leans forward and kisses my forehead. "I'd like that too."

We decide to start clean on Friday. I'm to spend the weekend at her house. Pilar gives me permission to give Liam her address and phone number. She promises that I am more than free to leave at any point if I'm feeling uncomfortable, but she hopes I will talk to her before it gets to that point. I'm to go to her house straight from work. Friday is another late day, a day made worse because I spend nearly every minute thinking about what my night with Pilar will be like. I wonder how strict she will be, what she really means by "structure." I'm out by seven, and I make my way over to her house. It's easy to find. There's room for my car in her driveway. I pull in behind a black Acura SUV. After a few breaths, I grab my bag and walk to the front door.

Pilar meets me at the door with a hug and a kiss on the cheek. As soon as she lets me in, I'm surrounded by her rose perfume and whatever delicious Italian dish she's making in the kitchen.

"I'll show you to your room first, and you can get settled. And then we'll eat."

I follow her through her living room and down a short hall. We pass a room filled with fabric and sewing materials and stop in the middle of the hall. She opens the door for me, and I almost have a stroke. It's a little girl's dream bedroom. Everything is pink and white: the floral bedding on the white iron daybed, the tea set in the corner. Even the little desk complete with stationery and pink-and-white office accessories. There's a Hello Kitty TV above the bureau. The bed is covered in stuffed animals centered around a giant, fluffy white bear. On top of the comforter is a pair of white panties with pink stripes and a matching nightshirt.

She lets me look around, and when I turn back to her, I'm speechless.

"Do you like it?"

"I love it." I told her my favorite color was pink and that I liked Hello Kitty, but I never imagined this. I tell her so.

"I'm glad you like it. A friend of mine is a set designer. She helped me out a little."

"No, I—I love it." There's no other way to describe my feelings.

Pilar squeezes my hand. "Why don't you get washed up and change for dinner." She nods toward the pajamas on the bed, then to a door beside the dresser. "There's a bathroom right through there."

"Thank you. I'm pretty quick. I'll be right out."

"There's no rush," she says.

I rush anyway.

❖

I'm standing in the bathroom, and I'm nervous. I tug my nightshirt down another inch and decide the pigtails I've gone with are completely appropriate. I find Pilar in the kitchen. She's still dressed from work, in jeans and a polo shirt, but she's wearing an apron. I like it.

"Do you need any help?" I ask.

"Nope. Dinner's ready," she says with that beautiful smile. I walk to her side and take the plate of lasagna and salad she hands to me. She pours me a glass of milk and grabs herself a glass of water, then joins me at the table. I'm still nervous. I don't know what to say. I want to do so many things with her, but I don't know where to start. I don't know if I can start. So I ask her about her day at work.

"Thank you for asking, baby. It was good."

"What show do you work on? You never told me," I reply.

"I style for *Cliques*. It's on the CW."

"Oh, my God. I used to do the marketing for Mallor Entertainment. *Cliques* was my last project." The ship over at marketing division of Mallor started sinking just as the first season of *Cliques* wrapped. We were way understaffed, but instead of long-term solutions, people were demoted and given more responsibility. Liam found me a position at Reach Advertising, and I made my escape.

"It's a small world, isn't it," she says.

"It is." I don't know what to say then, and it becomes obvious that Pilar isn't in love with the sound of her own voice. We finish dinner in near silence. I help load the dishwasher, and then Pilar tells me to go pick out a movie from the rack beside the TV. Before I leave, she grabs my hand.

"You're doing fine," she says. "I want you to relax and be yourself. I don't want you to perform."

I nod before I scamper away.

Nothing beside the TV has anything above a PG-13 rating. I'm guessing she's hiding the R stuff in her bedroom. Her selection is awesome, though. I snatch *Curly Sue* from the rack and put it in the

DVD player. Pilar is still in the kitchen so I go back to my bedroom and grab a stuffed golden retriever off the bed. It's super soft with floppy ears. I slept with some sort of stuffed animal all the way through college, but when I moved this last time a box full of stuff, along with my bear, was lost. I never replaced him. This floppy puppy seems like the perfect cuddle partner until I figure out where exactly Pilar and I stand.

She joins me on the couch with a cup of coffee for herself and a cup of juice for me. She puts both on the coffee table, then pulls me tight to her side. I feel better once her arm is around me. I love how soft and warm she is. I love the swells of her breasts. I hope she lets me play with them. She lets me start the movie, and then I wiggle until my head is in her lap.

I don't remember falling asleep, but when I wake up, Pilar is guiding me back toward the bedroom. She tucks me in with my stuffed puppy—I have to give him a name—then kneels beside the bed.

"What should I call you?" I ask, yawning.

"What do you want to call me?"

"I don't know yet. Pilar feels right, but so does Mami."

"Either is fine with me. Sometimes I'll call you Suzy and sometimes I'll call you baby." She tickles my stomach. I giggle and shuffle under the sheets. Her hand moves lower and she strokes the striped panties between my legs. I swallow and my clit tingles. "We'll play tomorrow, okay?"

"Okay."

"Good night, sweetheart," she says before she kisses my cheek. I want her to kiss me on my lips, but I'm too scared to say so. Instead I say good night.

I lie awake for a long time. I can hear Pilar moving around the house. I'm wondering what she's thinking and what she's feeling. I wonder if she's wanting me like I want her. I stop thinking about her and let my eyes wander the room dimly lit by a heart-shaped night-light in the corner. Beyond traveling for random family and Liam-related events, it's been a while since I slept in a strange bed. Or maybe it's that I know Pilar is still awake and I want to be with her. I've decided to call my stuffed puppy Frank. I hug Frank close to my chest and start to wiggle my leg. It's something I've always done to help me fall asleep.

Eventually, it works.

❖

The next morning, I wake to the smell of cinnamon. I'm hungry and Frank is only good for bedtime comfort. Half asleep, I lumber down to the kitchen. Pilar is standing at the stove when I walk in. She's still in her pajamas—a pair of boxers and a T-shirt. Her hair is up in a ponytail. She's not wearing a bra. Her breasts sit a little lower and her nipples poke through her shirt. I wonder when she'll let me touch them.

"Good morning," she says in her perfectly sexy voice.

"Good morning," I reply. I sound like I swallowed a Brillo pad. I walk over to inspect what's in the pan. She's making pancakes.

"How did you sleep?" she asks.

"Okay. Can I have a kiss?" I ask bluntly. She's in charge, but I feel a little cheated about having to sleep alone. I've also wanted to kiss her since the moment we met.

"Of course you can," she says. She sounds happy with the request. She leans down and pulls me closer with a firm hand on my butt. Her lips are soft and her breath smells like fresh coffee. She kisses me sweet and slow, teases me with her tongue. Her mouth makes me wet, and I want to rub myself against her apron-covered thigh, but the pancake is burning.

She pulls away and tosses the burnt flapjack.

"My, you're a sinful little distraction for Mami."

"Do you like the way I kiss?" I ask.

She smiles just a little. "Yes, baby. I do."

I look around the kitchen, then back at the stove clock. It's eight thirty. I never really sleep in on the weekends, but if I'm home, I find myself passed out on the couch by four thirty in the afternoon. I wonder what Pilar has planned for the day and if a cup of coffee for myself will be necessary. I wonder if she'll let me have it.

"What are we doing today?" I ask.

Pilar flips the next pancake, then pulls me back under her arm. "We're going to run errands, then we're going to have lunch, and then we're going to come home so you can take a nap." She asks me to hand her a plate. I grab one off the counter, then watch as a heart-shaped pancake is placed gently on the dish. It's thick and smells like heaven.

"What will you be doing while I nap?" I know it's only Saturday, but I feel the lacquered claws of the 21 And Up account scraping at the back of my neck. It'll be Monday before I know it, and I want to spend as much time with her as I can.

"Go sit down, baby."

I do as she asks and set up my pancake with the warm butter and syrup that are already on the table. She pours me a glass of water and places a bowl of chopped-up strawberries beside my plate.

"I'll be doing Mommy stuff, like cleaning and making dinner," she says as she joins me with another cup of coffee. I assume she's already eaten. "What's wrong?"

I realize I'm picking at my pancake. "Nothing. I just thought we'd do something more fun."

Pilar's mouth quirks up at the corner, but there's a twinge of hurt in her eyes. I realize how ungrateful and bratty I sound. "I didn't mean it like that," I blurt out.

"I know. This is new, and you were hoping for some excitement. There will be excitement, but as I recall, you've worked late every night this week. From the tone of your texts and even your voice on the phone, you need some downtime. I told you I like to nurture and pamper. I don't think it would be very nurturing of me if I whisked you off to Tijuana for the weekend only to drop you on your doorstep hungover and under-slept."

I feel horrible now. She's completely right. I asked to be taken care of, and that's exactly what she's doing, and on day one I'm acting as if she's not doing enough. It hasn't even been twenty-four hours and I'm blowing it.

"I'm really sorry. Will you forgive me?" My stomach sinks, and I feel the tears threaten to rise. I scan her face for genuine acceptance of my apology.

"Come here." She scoots her chair back and pats her lap. I join her without hesitation. Her arms are around me, and instantly, I feel better.

"I just want you to think about why you're here. I promise we will have fun, but it's not in my nature to return you back to your straight life feeling worse for wear. I want every moment you spend with me to be joyful and fun and relaxing."

"I know. I want that, too." Boy, do I *need* that. "You've just wowed me so much already with your amazing cooking and the room. I think a little part of me was expecting some sort of spectacle."

"Well, this is something I want you to work on, management of your expectations." She rubs my back and kisses my chin. "But at the same time, in the ways I've promised, I know I will exceed them. Okay?"

"Okay." I kiss her, this time on the lips. When I pull away she's smiling.

"Finish your breakfast and then we'll get ready."

I stand in front of my new closet. Pilar's filled it with cute dresses and rompers. She's instructed me to pick out an outfit, but if I'm not comfortable with anything she's purchased I'm to tell her and we'll discuss where to go from there. But as I sift my way through the hangers, I see why she's running a wardrobe department. Every piece is cute, girly, and youthful, but not in a way that will draw negative stares. However, it's June in Los Angeles. I could walk down the street in a bra and hot pants, and no one would blink.

I decide on a sleeveless dress with a white top and a pink floral skirt. There are several pairs of shoes for me to choose from. I grab a pair of brown sandals. In the bureau, I find pair after pair of lace and floral panties with bras to match. I pick a white lace set, then get dressed. I want Pilar to do my hair. I find her in her bedroom. She's dressed and just putting on the last of her makeup.

"You look very pretty, baby." I admire her black peasant skirt and her low-cut turquoise shirt. I have to get at those boobs.

"Thank you. You look very pretty too, Mami." It doesn't feel right to call her Pilar, especially after how I behaved at breakfast. "Would you please help me with my hair?"

"Of course." She pats the foot of the bed, and I hand her my brush and the hair ties and ribbons I found on the makeup table in my room.

"I really like all the clothes. Thank you."

"You're very welcome."

"How did you know my size?"

"Just part of my job, baby. I've been eyeballing measurements for a long time now."

"Oh, right." I laugh at myself. Clothes are literally her thing. "Should I call you Mami in public?"

"There. Done." I look down as she flips the braids over my shoulder. My hair is so long and wavy and thick I expected to be waiting and wincing for a while. I turn to face her. "You look adorable," she says. "In public you may call me Mami or Pilar. Whatever you want, but here's what I want from you today. I want you to be on your best behavior. *Please* and *thank you* everywhere we go, to everyone who helps us."

I know it sounds a little strange that she's giving me this lecture, but it only fosters my feelings for her even more. I like that Pilar wants me to be polite to people. Who likes an asshole?

"Best behavior." I nod with a smile. "Got it. I mean, yes, ma'am."

"You're a silly girl, my little Suzy. Give me a few more minutes and we can go."

❖

I was wrong. It's not a trip to Mexico, but we have our own little adventure. Pilar takes me all over Los Angeles. First, we go downtown to the fashion district. The streets are packed with people and vendors. It's hot as hell outside, but I don't mind because Pilar holds my hand. We stop at a few different stores where Pilar picks up more fabric. She lets me select more ribbons, and at this interesting button shop she lets me buy a pair of fairy wings. They're flashy and impractical, something you'd wear only on Halloween, but they catch my eye, and Pilar lets me have them.

After, we go to Toys 'R Us, where she lets me pick out one game and a stuffed animal of my choosing. I admit that I'm content with Frank. Then I have to explain who Frank is. I grab some sidewalk chalk and a pack of Hello Kitty UNO cards. We stop for lunch at a place called MILK that serves a wide array of grilled sandwiches and milkshakes. I finish my lunch before I ask for some ice cream. I get two scoops of peaches and cream in a cone. It has actual chunks of peaches in it. It's delicious. Pilar treats herself to a milkshake, and we sit outside and have a quasi-adult conversation about summer blockbuster movies. Quasi because I'm a little more animated than usual and doing most of the talking, but Pilar doesn't seem to mind.

On our way to the grocery store, she tells me she never leaves the house on Sunday unless it's a special occasion. "That's my day off." So we grocery shop for dinner and food for the next day. In the store an old woman tells me she likes my dress. I say thank you, and Pilar rubs my back as we walk toward the checkout.

By the time we get home, I'm exhausted. I help put away the groceries. Then Pilar tells me to go change out of my dress. I slip out of my bra and into another T-shirt, then grab Frank. Pilar puts on a soccer game on Univision, then lays me down on the couch with a throw blanket she's pulled off her bed. It's four thirty and I'm out like a light. Just like any other Saturday, but this time I'm with Pilar. And Frank.

CHAPTER THREE

I wake up slowly. I've kicked the throw blanket off, and Frank is under my head. I don't remember my dreams, but they were strange and perverted. I'm wet. I stretch and, without thinking, slide my hands between my legs.

Pilar is sitting across the room in her big armchair, knitting.

"Hello," she says sweetly.

"Hi," I say, but it comes out more like e*yeeee* because I yawn. And then I pout. "I'm horny." It's been a week since I've gotten off, and being with Pilar only jacks up my sex drive. Something about her working the needles turns me on, too. She looks so matronly and authoritative. Her hands seem so skilled. I like the way she's looking at me so I don't move my hand.

"You can touch yourself," she says. I think for a second about how I want this to go down. I love the idea of masturbating for her, but I really want her to touch me, and if I don't say something now, I know I'll be kicking myself later.

"I want you to help me. Please."

"Since you were such a good girl today." Pilar puts down her knitting needles and sits on the edge of the couch beside me. She admires my body before she runs her fingers over my panties and along my pussy. I bite my lip and hold still.

Her hand slips lower, and she rubs me in earnest.

"It takes me a long time to come," I tell her.

"That's okay." She pulls my panties off nice and slow. I don't wax, but I do trim, and she doesn't say anything about that. She just strokes my clit, making me wetter.

"You have a very pretty pussy, baby."

The dirty word coming out of her makes me shiver.

"Thank you."

"Do you want me to put my fingers in your pussy?" she asks. She's still rubbing me. I close my eyes and open my legs wider.

"Yes, please."

She pushes two fingers deep inside me, making me groan. I open my eyes, and I watch her as I start to move my hips. She focuses on my body and I focus on her. I want her. More of her touch, more of her naked.

I reach forward and rub her breast. She continues to finger me, but she glances up, then down at my hand. She doesn't tell me to stop. I feel over her bra, over her shirt; the size of her breast is more than enough to fill my palm. I squeeze as she fucks me harder. She pumps in and out, uses her other hand to stroke my clit. I can feel how wet I am. I moan and let out a slight whimper. I rock my hips faster. I'd almost forgotten how good it feels to have someone inside me.

She pulls her fingers from my cunt and holds them up to my mouth. I sense she's changed her mind about something.

"Will you fuck me?" I ask.

"Yes, baby. I plan to." I lick her fingers clean then.

She makes me stand and pulls off my shirt. From that position, I watch as she shucks off her skirt and pulls her shirt over her head. Her black bra and underwear are next. She shifts the throw under her, then beckons me forward to straddle her lap.

I still love the fullness of her body, but seeing her bare skin makes it so much more delectable. Leaning down, I cup her breasts and suck one of her dark nipples into my mouth. She groans then and relaxes further into the cushions.

I smile up at her, then continue worshipping her breasts. She makes deep noises of pleasure and holds my head in place. I move to the other nipple. I tease it with my teeth before I suck it between my lips. I take as much of her into my mouth as I can. I suck harder, then rub the flat length of my tongue over the tip.

Pilar curses under her breath. Her hips squirm under mine.

Finally, she's had enough. Her finger is under my chin, and she encourages my lips to hers. We kiss for a long time, and as we kiss, she grasps my butt and pulls me tighter to her body. She's shifted lower on the cushions so my pussy grinds against her pelvis. I break our kiss and grip her shoulders. I ride her as hard as I can, setting a vicious pace.

"That's it. Good girl. Ride me just like that," she says, and I know the pace suits her.

I'm close. I'm going to come any second. Pilar turns us suddenly, and I'm pinned to the couch. She leads the charge now, her slit directly on mine, our slickness mixing. She comes first with a sharp grunt. I kiss her as she's coming down and keep rubbing myself along her hip.

I don't know how it happens for me. I think about her weight on me, and I'm getting hotter and hotter. Her hand slips between us, and she tweaks my nipple. I hold her hand there, enjoying that unique pleasure that I never associate with pain. My hips slow, but I force myself up, and that pressure, my Mami's tongue in my mouth, her fingers' grip on my breast, it all makes me come. It's one of these deep orgasms, so concentrated in my pussy that it becomes the focal point of my whole body. I ride the aftershocks, still kissing Pilar, still rubbing myself lightly against her skin. We move so I'm more on top of her and not the other way around.

"You're a very good girl, Suzy," she says, her voice sleepy. I smile and snuggle closer. I want to play with her nipples some more, so I do, lightly running my finger over the tip. She doesn't stop me. I think she likes it.

Saturday night, Pilar makes some steaks, and we eat in front of the TV. There's a Harry Potter marathon on, and Pilar admits she hasn't seen any of the series yet.

"I was waiting to read the books," she tells me.

I turn in my seat and glare at her. "Do you really think you're going to read all of the books? Be honest with me. Be honest with yourself."

Pilar bursts out laughing. "You're right, baby. Let's watch them."

By the time *Chamber of Secrets* is over, I'm sleepy again.

"It's only ten. I have no idea why I'm so tired," I say as I yawn.

"You're letting your body rest. There's nothing wrong with being tired. Why don't you go take your shower, and then I'll tuck you in."

I realize she means for me to sleep alone again, and I'm disappointed, but this time I keep my mouth shut. I dig Frank out from the crack in the couch and go back to my bedroom. The adjoining bathroom is nice. I take my time in the shower. When I come out, Pilar has changed for bed as well. She's sitting in the rocking chair, flipping through a catalog. She's put another nightshirt on my bed, but no panties. I'm not sure what that means.

"I just need to put on some lotion," I say.

"Would you like some help?"

For practical reasons, this is a good idea. There's always a spot on my back that's a pain to reach, but I'm thinking more about having Pilar's hands all over me, so I say yes.

I grab the lotion off my bureau and hand it to her. She works faster than I expect, taking the practical approach. She does my whole back, down to my feet in under a minute. She's gentle, and her hands are so soft, but she doesn't even linger on my butt. What's the point of lotioning up your naked plaything if you're not gonna linger on the butt?

She turns me around and squirts a little into my hands so I can do my face while she gets the front of my legs. Again with clinical application, she moves up my body. She rubs lotion over my stomach and between my legs. To my continued disappointment, she lingers there long enough to spark my arousal, and then she's heading back up to my chest. My breasts and shoulders are done in nearly the same swipe, then my arms. I sit on the bed on my towel, and she does my feet.

I make sure I'm smiling when she looks up at me.

"There," she says with a bright expression. "All done."

I thank her and slip the nightshirt over my head.

We repeat the same routine as the night before. She turns on my night-light, then kneels beside the bed. "Did you have a good day?"

"Yes, I did. Thank you."

"You're welcome. I'll see you in the morning." She leans over and kisses me on the lips. I want her to shove her hand into my crotch, but she keeps everything aboveboard. She says good night and leaves me alone with Frank and the rest of my stuffed-animal menagerie. I don't know why I'm upset. We had a great day, and the couch sex was fantastic, but still I want more. Maybe this is why things went sour with Laurel. I was never satisfied. My need for attention was just too much. I wonder if Pilar feels that way. I wonder if she's the type of woman who needs a little space now and then. I feel like I should ask, but I don't want to push her. But then again, I'm lonely. And horny again.

I'm awake for what seems like hours. I check the clock and it's only been forty minutes. My mind has already decided twenty minutes ago that I'm not spending the night in this bed, but finally my body catches up. I take Frank with me. Pilar sleeps with her door open. I knock lightly on the frame.

"What is it, baby?" She lifts her head up, but in the dark I can't see her face.

I chance it, praying I don't piss her off. "Can I sleep with you?" I ask. I sound pathetic and helpless, but it's not an act. I don't want to sleep alone. Pilar sits all the way up now, and I can see her face in the dim light from the hallway. She squints, but she doesn't look annoyed. Sympathetic and a little pleased, actually

"Yes, you may. Come here." She moves from the center of the bed to make room for me.

I crawl into the sheets beside her. Pilar pulls me in close and tucks my head under her chin. I nuzzle her breast, and I close my eyes, but still I can't sleep. It's that buzz of electricity from being close to her. She brings me comfort, but she also tantalizes me. I take another chance and slide my hand to her breast. I roll the lush weight under my palm and hear her let out a short breath through her nose.

My heart is pounding now. I'm excited because she's not stopping me. I slide my hand under her shirt, but as I move up her belly, she sits up and pulls the cotton over her head. Pilar lies on her back, and I feel another change between us then. She's letting me be in control. I kiss her breasts, then neck, and then her chin. I find my legs spread over her stomach and take a moment to ditch my nightshirt. We kiss, and this time she seems eager. She lifts her head, urging me to kiss her. I'm not sure where the confidence comes from, but I do more than kiss her. As our tongues move together, I slide my hand between her legs. She shudders as I stroke her clit. I like drawing a response from her. I move down her body. I skip her breasts and go straight for her pussy. Gently gripping her lush thighs, I lick her slowly. I love her smell and the way she tastes. I love the thickness of her lips, how slick they are. I slide a finger inside. Her fingers slide along the back of my head.

A noise I can't control bubbles up from my throat. She grips my hair tighter and lifts her hips. I stop licking her clit and proceed to suck the hard little tip. Pilar is breathing harder. I love how turned on she is. I love that *I'm* turning her on, but I want to kiss her when she comes. I barely move a full inch back up her body, and her hands are hooked under my armpits. She pulls me up, and we are kissing again. I love her lips, but I miss the little bit of control she's given me. I reach for her hands again, and she lets me pin them above her head.

My body is secure in the cradle of her hips, rocking us both up toward the headboard and back down into the sheets. I lose track of any sense of time, not that I even want to mark it now that I'm with her, but I lose all sense of everything that isn't the skin between us.

All I can think about is her breasts against my ribs and our slits connecting.

I think it's some sort of miracle that I come first. I haven't let go of her hands, and I know I must be pinching her fingers, but she keeps equal hold on my palms as I whimper out her name. But it's "Oh Mami," this time. "Oh, Mami. Fuck." I can't help it. Not that I want to. She tells me I'm a good girl, and I come again.

It's her. I know it. Sadly, with Laurel, I had to learn when to block the other person out. I had to find orgasms on my own, especially when I felt her slipping away from me. I had to pretend it was Laurel making me come and not my own determination. My own self-preservation.

Now, though, it's Pilar. Her skin. Her voice. She wants me and I can feel it. I want to please her.

Her hands slide down my back, and she holds me close as she continues to rub against me. I kiss her neck and her lips. When she comes she doesn't say a word, but I feel her breath on my cheek. Afterward, when she's holding me, she says my name, then something unintelligible, but it sounds sweet. Either way, I shift closer, and she holds me tight.

Sunday, I don't know what's wrong with me. I'm hyper. Really hyper. I wake up alone in Pilar's bed. It's late, almost lunchtime. She's put Frank in my hands before she left. I hop out of bed and power walk to the kitchen. Frank's legs are dragged against the wall. I'm sure he's glad just to be a part of something. Pilar is in a tight camisole and some sweats. She's whisking eggs.

She glances at me over her shoulder with a smile. "Morning." Then she goes back to her eggs. I creep up next to her and sink down to the kitchen floor on my knees. Mind you, I'm still naked.

Pilar puts down her bowl and looks at me. She's fighting a smile as she lightly takes my chin in her hand. "Is there something I can help you with, baby?"

"I know you said Sunday is your lazy day—"

"I said it was my day off."

"I'm sorry. Today is your day off, but I was wondering if we can play outside today?"

She doesn't say anything at first. She just does this little thing with her lip. One side juts out and the other side is under her teeth. I wonder if later I'll realize that this is her tell. This is the face she makes and the thing she does with her lip when she's about to say yes.

She runs the knuckle of her forefinger over my cheek. Her hand smells like nutmeg. I realize that something's baking in the oven.

"You got me that pretty sidewalk chalk and there's so much sidewalk out there."

"There is a lot of sidewalk. Come here." I stand up, and then she grips my waist and hoists me up on the counter. She steps between my legs.

"My butt's near your eggs," I say.

"That's fine with me. I like having you naked in my kitchen."

"You do?"

"Yes, I do. We can go outside today, but dress light. It's already warm out."

"You don't want me naked on your sidewalk?"

"I wouldn't mind that one bit, but there are kids in the neighborhood. We don't need to give them that sort of education."

"But we can go outside?"

"Yes. After you eat. And put on some clothes."

"Fine," I say, pretending to pout before I smile. "Thank you. You'll have the best-looking sidewalk on the block. "

"I'm looking forward to it, baby." She kisses me then. I'm into it, but I still yelp that she pinches my nipple.

After I put on some clothes—a pink romper with thin straps and frilly trim—we eat a little brunch. Pilar makes omelets and coffee cake, and there's fruit. It's all delicious, and I'm reminded that even though my parents taught me to cook a ton of different things, I've been living off crap and meals for one for ages. I help clear the table, and then she sends me outside. She says she'll be there in a few minutes.

I take that time to run and draw something by her car—a heart and a little love note. Hopefully, she'll see it before she goes to work. Pilar comes outside eventually, with a magazine, her knitting setup, and her iPod doc. I'm in front of the house drawing an elaborate series of vines and flowers up her walkway. I forgot how much this chalk gets all over your hands. She puts on some hip-hop, but the guys are singing in Spanish so I have no idea what they're saying. Still, I like the beat. The next song is Jay-Z. I sing along. Luckily, it's the clean version so I don't have to skip the swears. When I glance up, Pilar is looking at her magazine, but I can tell she's grinning at my ridiculousness.

I'm baking like a potato by the time I make it to the street, but I'm having so much fun just letting my mind wander. I'm getting dirty and it's no big deal. The woman I belong to is watching me, and she doesn't seem to mind that I don't want to sit around and talk about "serious" shit.

I move a few times for the occasional pedestrian and dog, but later in the afternoon, I have company. Two little girls, maybe nine or ten years old, show up to admire my work. "Can we draw?" The shorter one asks. She's Korean and her friend is black. I'm already in love with their friendship.

"Sure," I say before I look around. "I'm almost out of pink though."

"That's okay. I have more." The little Korean girl turns and bolts back to the house next door.

"I'm Suzy," I say to the girl who's been left behind.

"I'm April and that's Joanna."

"I grabbed the whole bucket," Joanna screeches as she comes tearing around the corner. She's towing a small beach bucket full of sidewalk chalk. There seems to be a variety of pink. She doesn't ask me my name, but plops down on the grass beside me.

"I think we should go to the beach," Joanna announces.

"The beach?" I have one of those moments of panic where I'm genuinely trying to figure out what the hell a child is talking about.

"Yes." She points down the street. "We start down there and draw Venice. Then we come back here to Santa Monica, and then my house is Malibu."

"That's a lot of beach," I say. The girl has mapped out a good thirty yards of sidewalk.

"We've got a lot of chalk," Joanna replies. "What's your name?"

"It's Suzy," April replies for me.

"Cool. Suzy, you've got sand and water. April, you take the sky. I'll do landmarks. It'll take awhile to get the pier just right."

I'd like to double-check that the neighbors don't look like the gun-toting kind, but a slight nod from Pilar tells me it's okay. So we go down to the next house and start on Venice. Free-drawing vines is fun, but the details of sand and waves are all business. I stop periodically and watch Joanna, in shock at just how accurately she's capturing the VENICE sign and the little shops that line the water.

"You're black, right?" Joanna asks me suddenly.

"My mom is," I tell her. "And my dad is Korean."

"That's awesome. So you're like both of us." This is the first time April's perked up all afternoon. I don't think drawing the entirety of the California coastline is her idea of a good time.

"I am. A little of both."

"Are you Ms. Castillo's girlfriend?" Joanna asks, moving right on to the next important topic. I panic for real this time. It's not like I can tell this kid the truth.

"What makes you ask that?" I say, keeping my tone light.

"My mom told me that Ms. Castillo only likes girls, and you were here yesterday, too."

"It's gay," April says. "When a girl dates girls it means they're gay. My uncle's gay, but he dates boys." I smile at the adorable giggle she lets out.

"I know it's gay *or* lesbian," Joanna says. She won't be shown up in this conversation. "I just want to know if they're girlfriend and girlfriend."

I glance at Pilar, but she actually seems to be focused on the article she's reading. Another chance, I take it and pray I'm not fucking things for Pilar with her neighbors.

"I am her girlfriend. Her new girlfriend."

"Ooooh," Joanna says, clasping her piece of chalk under her chin. "Do you guys kiss?"

April is suddenly appalled. "That's rude, Jo. You're not supposed to ask that. And she's not supposed to kiss and tell."

I want to high-five April, but I don't. Instead I say, "That's gross. Of course we don't kiss."

"Well, you're supposed to. She's your girlfriend," Joanna replies, but she lets it go.

We're moving on to Santa Monica when I hear "Joanna!" from over the hedge.

"Mom. I'm right here!"

Joanna's mother comes around the corner. She's pretty, but not as pretty as Pilar. "They aren't bothering you, are they?" she asks.

"No," I say, and I mean it. "Suzy. I'd shake your hand, but..."

"I know. That crap gets everywhere. At least it comes out easily. I'm Karen. Only a few more minutes, girls. April's mom is on her way."

Both girls groan, but Karen isn't paying attention to us anymore. She waves to Pilar then, and walks up to the porch to say hello. I don't know how well they know each other, but I do watch their interaction out of the corner of my eye. They both disappear into the house.

They're back a few minutes later with lemonade for all of us. April's mom shows up just as she's downing a second cup.

Once April is gone and Joanna is corralled back over to her side of the hedge, Pilar tells me it's time to go inside. I collapse on the couch. It's been a long time since I spent a whole afternoon in the sun.

"The kids asked me if we were doing it," I say.

"They did?"

"Well, Joanna told me her mom told her you're gay, and she asked if I was your girlfriend. I said yes. Is that okay?"

"Of course, it's okay. Her mother's been flirting with me for years. She probably had some explaining to do," Pilar says. "Don't worry, baby. I'm not into her."

I believe her, but it's hard not to be a little possessive. She leans down and kisses me. "I only have eyes for my little girl." That does the trick.

❖

We have pizza for dinner and watch TV for a while. But suddenly at eight, she turns the TV off.

She turns to me. "I want to have a little straight talk." I'm a little nervous, but I say okay. Pilar takes my hand. "I've enjoyed having you here. I want to know how this weekend has been for you."

"It's been great. I really like spending time with you."

"Moving forward, I'd like you to spend weekends with me. If I have a weekend engagement, I'd like you to accompany me. Depending on the situation, we'll decide how we should present ourselves."

"Okay. That works for me."

"If you have somewhere you need to be, let me know in advance and I'll make adjustments."

"My weekends are usually pretty dull, so I doubt it'll happen, but okay."

"I'm going to want to see you during the week, if our schedules allow it. How do you feel about that? And I want you to be honest with me. I don't want you rushing around town if what you really need is a night's sleep in your own bed."

I try to control my excitement. I hadn't thought this was an option, but it's what I want. The idea of going five days without her is brutal. I practically forgot about my apartment. But I tell her honestly how I feel.

"I would love to see you during the week. If I have a bad day at work, being with you will be exactly what I need."

"About work. There's one thing I want you to do. Every day you'll have a different pair of panties to wear. I want you to find time during the day to send me proof that you're wearing them."

"You mean send a picture to your phone?"

"Yes. I want to see your pussy in my panties every day."

"I can do that," I say. "Um, what if we can't see each other, but I want to call you or text you?"

"You can call me whenever you want, but just text me first."

I try to hide my giddiness again with a simple okay. Laurel had so many rules, and one of them was that I was never to call her. I was to wait for her to contact me. Looking back, that wasn't the best arrangement.

"Good. Every week we'll talk like this, but if something comes up, you don't have to wait for this time." I think for a moment, wracking my brain for some question or concern, but I can't think of anything. Pilar asks me one more time if I have anything I want to discuss, but I assure her I'm good to go.

"Sunday night you'll have your bath and then it's early to bed." I sense she's back in Mami mode so I don't question her plans.

We go to the bathroom and she undresses me as the water runs. I expect the same professional-like attention she paid me before with the lotion, but I'm wrong. She helps me out of my romper, and as she slips the fabric down my belly, she kisses my breasts. Several kisses to the top of each and a few soft kisses to each nipple. As she moves lower, she kisses my belly, then the top of my slit.

When she stands, I'm anything but disappointed. I recognize this look in her eye. She wants to touch me. She's just getting started.

She helps me into the bath and starts washing me with a rose-scented scrub. It smells like her perfume. She moves slowly and talks to me as she goes. She tells me how pretty I am and how well I behaved today. When she moves to wash between my legs I ask her to kiss me. She does and I'm happy. The bath does the trick. Though I'm turned on by her caresses, I'm relaxed and a little drowsy. The idea of going to bed a little earlier than usual has its appeal. After I'm toweled off and lotioned up, she tells me to wait in my room. She's gone for a few minutes. When she comes back, she's naked.

She has a set of pink padded wrist cuffs and a long strapless dildo in her hand. I don't ask what she has planned, and she doesn't offer an explanation. She lets me watch as she slips the short end of the dildo into her pussy. My mouth starts to water. Then she secures the cuffs to the back of my bed frame. I see how she wants me, but again, I wait for her instruction. I feel myself slipping into complete submission. I want her to take this as far as my body can handle. I want her to be in complete control.

"Yellow if you're uncomfortable. Red if you want me to stop."

I nod, unable to find my voice. She doesn't demand a verbal reply, and this makes me trust her even more. She understands where I'm at mentally. I let her arrange me, bent over the bed with my feet on the floor, and then she secures my wrists. The leather is soft and the padding a nice addition. I let my head hang and wait for her to put the dildo inside of me.

But that doesn't happen.

She's behind me, maybe on her knees, and she's spreading me apart. She's looking, maybe, or maybe she's about to take me with her mouth. I don't know, but I don't have to wait long. With a downward stroke, she smacks my right cheek. It's not painful, just shocking. I yelp and jerk forward. She pauses just a moment, then smacks the same cheek again. Then her mouth is on me. I feel her whole face pressed between my legs. She's sucking my lips between her lips. She's driving at me with her tongue. And then she pulls away. She smacks my other cheek.

This goes on for a long time. She warms my ass with a controlled spanking and makes my pussy swell with every stroke of her tongue. I'm squirming and moaning. I'm not begging for anything, but I'm calling her Mami and she's breathing hard. Soon, she stands. She grips my waist hard, and I know she's about to fuck me and she's going to be rough doing it. I'm primed for her dick. It's long and thick, but I take every inch. I lean back into it. She pounds me, each thrust sending me forward, but her hands digging into my hips hold me in place. She varies her pace as we go, faster then slower, but each bit of contact is forceful. I love the way it feels, and when she adds her fingers on my clit, I'm nearly screaming. She stops the movement of her hips and I find myself riding back on her dick, fucking myself at my own pace as she continues to finger me at my front. My pussy latches on to her, squeezing and convulsing around the cock. I'm coming so hard, I'm cursing and saying her name, "Mami," this time. It'll always be "Mami" when she makes me feel this good. I feel myself ejaculating, but her cock is buried so deep, my release has nowhere to go.

She doesn't bring me down softly. Instead, she flips the catch on the cuffs and I'm free of the bed frame. She pulls out and throws me on my back. I can feel my come slipping down my thigh. She ditches the dildo altogether and straddles my stomach. She holds her lips apart with one hand, and with the other, she's viciously stroking her clit. I grab her hips.

"Fuck, Suzy," she says. "Oh fuck, baby. I'm gonna come." We make eye contact and a violent shiver runs over my body. Her eyes squeeze shut and she starts to come. She's rubbing her clit so hard, I wonder if it hurts, but she doesn't stop. Finally, she collapses on me. She's panting hard. I suck her breast.

"Oh, that feels good, baby." I move to the other and pay it just as much as attention, but she stops me.

"It's time for bed." She stands and seems to regain her composure, but her eyes are still a little wild. She takes the cuffs off me and puts them on the floor by the dildo. She helps me under my sheets.

My lights are turned off and my night-light is turned on. She kneels beside my bed and I expect a simple kiss good night, but she slips her hand under the covers. Our eyes hold each other the whole time she fingers me. This has always been a part of the fantasy. She can leave me wanting more or she can take. I want her to take. I want her to sneak into my room at night and do this to me. I think about that and I'm clenching my sheets as she finishes me off.

I want to say I love you, but I don't. It's tricky in a situation like this. I love her dominance. I love her affection. I love the way she's touching me, but we're not in love yet. And I know in my head, if I say those words I'll be creating another level of attachment for myself, one she may not return.

I say good night instead and accept her tongue in my mouth as she kisses me one more time. Her parting kiss on my forehead seems final. I'm meant to stay in my bed tonight. I dig up Frank and curl up on my side. I miss Pilar already, but sleep finds me quickly. I'm too worn out to dream.

CHAPTER FOUR

Monday morning comes like a punch in the face. I shower quickly. I have my come between my legs and traces of Pilar's on my stomach, so I use her rose scrub to wash it all away. When I come out of the bathroom, I spot a pair of pink panties with yellow ducks on them next to my work clothes. Next to the underwear are two wrapped boxes. The larger one is filled with my underwear for the week. In the other are two white bow barrettes.

I pack up my stuff and find Pilar in the kitchen. She kisses me quickly, then hands me a cup of coffee and a plate of eggs. I realize I'm actually running late. I scarf down my food, but before I bolt out the door, Pilar takes me by the waist.

"Have a good day and drive safe," she says.

"You, too." I pause, looking at her ample breasts between us. "I really like being with you."

"I like being with you, too. Do you want to take Frank home?"

I wince a little and nod toward my things. "Yeah. I already grabbed him. Is that okay?"

"Yes, baby. The stuffed animals are yours. He can stay with you when we're apart." She kisses me and then it's really time for me to go. I'm glowing on my way to work even though my e-mail alerts are already going off on my phone. The minute I walk into the office, my joy is dashed. Back to the real world.

❖

By one, it's a wonder I still have any hair on my head. Valerie and I survive a two-hour meeting with 21 And Up, where they suggest we've gotten the launch date for the mobile app wrong. I keep my cool and insist they check the e-mail that I re-forward as we are speaking, clearly outlining the launch of the mobile app for the middle of July. They argue that the tenth is the middle of July, even though I told my guys the fifteenth. Valerie promises we'll get it in on time. After we hang up, I promise not to quit, even though she's just committed us to more overtime.

Clear Vision is still including me on their e-mail chains even though Daisuke and I have both told them I'm no longer on the account. I want to scream and yank my hair out. I don't. I decide I should eat something first, then pitch myself off the top of the building. Liam grabs us lunch and we hide in an empty conference room. I need a break before someone gets an office supply to the head.

"Tell me about your weekend," Liam says.

"Oh, shit." I jump up and grab my phone. "Be right back." I ignore Liam's confused look and make right for the restroom. The stalls are empty, so I pick one and quickly hike up my skirt.

Pilar's been in the back of my head all day, but quickly she comes rushing to the forefront. I stick my fingers down the front of my panties and take a few pictures with my phone. One comes out the way I like it and I send it to Pilar along with a text. *Luv, Your Little Suzy Girl.* I hate that with that one image sent the fun is over. I head back to the conference room where I find Liam eating my chips. I steal his garlic fries.

"What the hell did you just do?"

I unleash a devious smile. "Nothing."

"Oh, you did something. Tell me."

"No. How was your weekend?"

"Fuck that. Lemme see." Liam reaches over and snatches my phone.

I stare in horror for a moment. Then I play it cool. If I panic, he'll think he's got something juicy in his hands. "There's nothing on there."

"Like this picture of some ducky underwear and your…Your fingers! You nasty bitch, and you sent it to someone. You sent the duckies to? Who is Mami?" I feel a little better because I know he's grossed out by vagina. Still.

"Give me my phone back," I say.

"No way. You really call her 'Mami'? That is so hot. I have to meet this woman." He tilts my phone and looks closer at the picture. "The duckies are cute, but you need a wax, girl."

Suddenly my phone starts to ring. "Give it to me."

"Oh my God! It's her. It's Mami."

"Give me the fucking phone!" I actually dive over the table at this point and lunge for my phone. Liam bobbles it and then tosses it into my hands. I look at the display. It's Pilar.

I crawl off the table and straighten my clothes. I take a deep breath while giving Liam the finger, and then I answer. "Hello?"

"Hi."

"How are you?"

"I'm good, baby. We're on lunch right now. Thank you for the picture."

I know I'm blushing and grinning like an idiot, so I turn around. "Did you like it?" I'm toeing the carpet like an idiot too, but that can't be helped. I channel my happy down to my feet.

"I loved it. I loved the doodles you left me as well. Unfortunately, I don't think I'll be able to see you tonight, but I miss you. And I'm thinking about you."

"You are?" I know I sound ridiculous, but it's like I'm a meth head and her words are the goods.

"I am."

"Can I call you tonight?"

"How about I call you and tuck you in over the phone?" Her rules, right.

"I'll be waiting."

"In your duck panties."

Liam's chewing extra loud to get my attention. I keep my back turned and lower my voice. "In my duck panties. I promise." God, I want her so bad.

"I'll talk to you later, then."

"Okay," I reply. It comes out super breathy and flighty, but I don't care. We hang up and I spin on Liam.

"Shut your mouth. Right now."

"This. All this happened over one weekend?" he asks.

"All what?"

"You should see yourself. I'm waiting for those ducks on your underwear to fly out of the room. You're like Disney-princess happy. You need to sign me up for that bondage matchmaking service you're with. I want to be this hung up on someone after three days."

"Are you kidding? You were trying to lock Gary down after an hour."

"I know, but he doesn't ask me to send him dirty pics from work." Liam pretends to cry for a moment before he sags back in his chair with a sigh. "Well, I'm glad you're happy and not in pieces in her garage, but I was hoping to get a frantic call from you saying she tried to get you to fuck the tongueless gimp in her basement." He stares at the ceiling with a dreamy expression and says, "And I did envision you running down the street naked, screaming for help."

"Thanks. That sounds lovely."

"What? You tell me you're taking up a new dominatrix for the weekend, a boy's gonna daydream."

"She's not a dominatrix. She's—"

"Whatever she is, I'm glad you're happy. And since you're so happy, I have some news."

"Gary finally agreed to that threesome you want?"

"Pssht, I wish. No, I want to take this moment when your spirits are extra high to tell you that Andre told me 21 And Up is going to launch a new paper-doll function on their website."

"Okay," I say cautiously.

"You'll be able to mix and match outfits on a model that looks nothing like you."

"Sounds fun. What's the problem?"

"They want it ready for back to school."

I laugh because it'll be at least two weeks before this project gets to me through the proper channels, three weeks considering the way 21 and Up hates to follow the proper channels. That puts us right smack in the middle of July to start building a site option that should be launching in the middle of July. A site option that could take two to three months to build, beginning to end.

I close my eyes and think of a happier place, where 21 And Up's main offices mysteriously explode overnight. And then I remind myself there's only so much my team can do. If 21 And Up wants something so major in so little time, they'll pay for it. And even then they still might not get it on such short notice.

I pound my first on the desk and curse louder than I've ever cursed before. Liam calls it "The FUCK Heard Round The World." Mitch comes running to see if I'm okay.

❖

I'm watching crap TV, hanging off the side of my bed. Frank's with me and he's not judging me for my bad taste in television. I called home and talked to my parents. I ate a somewhat healthy dinner. I'm sleepy, but I want to wait for Pilar to call. I wake up drooling, in the most uncomfortable position. I pull Frank from under my neck and roll over. It's two a.m. and Pilar never called. I'm upset. Still drowsy, but upset. I look at my cell, which I find under my stomach. No missed calls, but there's a couple texts.

Sorry, baby. My nephew had an accident. He's okay, but I'm with my sister. I'll call you in the morning.

Now I feel shitty and I'm wondering what happened to her nephew. And I'm wondering if Pilar is okay. I text her back and tell her I'm thinking about her. I have to pee so bad, so I handle that. After that, I turn off my TV and try to go to bed on purpose. It takes a little while, but finally, I fall asleep. Frank's in my arms. Not under my neck.

❖

The next morning starts with almost two-dozen e-mails, followed by a conference call. No one from 21 And Up mentions the paper-doll site. I decide to give Katie a heads-up so she doesn't think she's about to pass on a piece of information that I might wring her neck for. I'll tell Valerie, too.

I steal some gummies from our stockpile of Bee's candy and head for Katie's desk. On my way, I stop mid-stride by a rather large bouquet of flowers on my desk. Liam, who can smell intrigue, appears behind me.

"Are these from…" He lowers his voice. "Are these from your Mami?" He reaches for the card. I slap his hand away.

"I don't know who they're from," I say.

"Well, then, look at the damn card."

"Go away first."

"What the fuck? No. I want to see what dirty things she has to say."

"No."

"I hate you." Liam snatches the bag of gummies out of my hand but doesn't budge another inch.

"I'm going to look at this card and you're not going to say a word. I don't care what face I make. I don't care if I giggle like a schoolgirl. You say a word and our friendship is over."

"I'm gonna laugh if they're not from her," Liam says.

"Oh, God. That would suck."

He rolls his eyes at me. "Just open it."

I snatch the little envelope open and read the handwritten note.

I think I owe my little girl more than a phone call.

I'm a Suzy puddle again. It's not even the miniature garden she's had sent to my desk. We've really just met, and it's the way she says certain things that has me desperate to make her happy.

"What does it say?" Liam asks.

"Nothing." I hold the card behind my back. "I'm a very busy person with very-busy-person stuff to do. Was there something else I could help you with?"

"Uh, no, ho. You asked me if I wanted to go out and grab a sandwich."

"Right. I need to get out of here. I'll talk to Katie when we get back."

"You gonna drop the bomb?" Katie, the account exec for 21 And Up, the person who is supposed to come to me with these projects so I can estimate a timeline and a budget, still doesn't know about the new paper-doll portion of the site, and the asshole client wants it in a matter of weeks.

"Yup." Was I ever gonna tell her? After lunch. "Let's go."

I text Pilar as we walk to Hearth Cafe. The sandwiches are like forty-five bucks apiece, which is typical for the stretch of commercial real estate between West Hollywood and Beverly Hills. Just as we reach the front doors, Pilar calls me back. I take a few steps back to the sidewalk and answer.

"Hello."

"Good afternoon, baby."

"How's your nephew doing?"

"He's much better. His mother just called me. I'd love to tell you all about it tonight. When you come spend the night with me."

"You want me to come over?"

"It's been a long day and a half. I need my little girl with me."

The way she asks for something while keeping her tone so confident is extremely sexy to me.

"I'd need to go home and get a change of clothes."

"Get here whenever you can."

I tell her I will.

Thank God we hang up before I do something crazy like confessing my absolute infatuation with her. It would make me sound like I'm in love.

I manage to focus on work for the rest of the afternoon. Still, it's hard. There are the flowers on my desk that everyone wants to know about. Plus, even though she sent me the large bouquet, that doesn't excuse me from the daily task I'm to complete.

After I share that little nugget of wisdom with Katie and talk her down from cursing out her contacts at 21 And Up, I sneak off to the restroom.

Someone is in one of the stalls, but it's not a big deal. Today I'm wearing a pair of light-pink panties with little white hearts on them. I slip my dress pants down just enough, then snap a few quick pictures.

I come out of the stall and find Valerie is washing her hands at the sink.

"That was some pretty stealthy peeing there." She chuckles a little.

"False alarm," I reply, like having a trick bladder is better than explaining to your boss that you were taking pictures of your underwear for your mistress. She follows me out of the restroom but doesn't question me further about my weird behavior. But I'm not completely off the hook.

"Those are some serious flowers you've got there," she says as we reach my desk. "New boyfriend? Wait." She pauses with a look of false recollection. "New girlfriend."

"Neither," I lie. And I'm glad I shoved the card into my purse because my reflex smile that seems to pop up whenever I think of Pilar is showing. "Just an apology from a friend."

"Geez, there must be a story there." Her smile tells me she wants to hear more.

Luckily, my office phone rings and saves me from further humiliation. I like Valerie, but not enough to even hint around about my sex life.

❖

I make it to Pilar's around eight thirty. She's waiting for me in a black satin robe.

Once we're in the living room she says to me, "Do you need some time to wind down?" She wants to know if I need a few minutes to find my Suzy space. She wants me to leave Suzanne Kim at the door, but I'm fine. Seeing her and hearing her voice are enough for me to let certain trappings of adulthood slip away. I shake my head like the docile little girl she needs me to be. Pilar seems happy with my reaction. She leads me to her bedroom.

"I picked up some dinner, but I wanted to relax with you first." In her bathroom there's a larger tub. It's filled with water and bubbles. Large candles line the sink. I turn back to her, to say something like "Thank you" or "wow," but she starts to undress me. I hold still as she unbuttons my blouse. She slowly gets me out of my pants.

We get in the tub together and Pilar wraps me in her arms. Her legs shelter my thighs, and her breasts press against my back. This is exactly where I want to be.

"How's your nephew?" I ask. Talking is the only thing distracting me as her hands glide over my nipples.

"My sister said he won't stop talking, so that's a good sign."

"May I ask what happened?"

"You know those fixie kids who terrorize the city?" she says playfully. Everyone does. There's a large underground culture of teens and twenty-somethings that ride fixed-gear bikes all over town. At first I was baffled by the phenomena. I don't understand riding around L.A. in circles at night, but it really is something to see a hundred or so bikes coming down Wilshire Boulevard into Koreatown in wave after wave of strobing wheels and blinking lights. When they're stopped and posted up in front of my building they seem like a nice-enough bunch, and they obey traffic laws better than most L.A. drivers. I know Pilar is only joking. They baffle a lot of the city, not terrorize it.

She goes on. "Some drunk driver plowed through a group of them in Culver City."

I spin around as much as I can to face her. "A drunk driver? Who the fuck gets that wasted on a Monday night?"

Her face grows stern and she lightly taps my lips. "Language, baby."

"I'm sorry," I say as I shrink back a little. Her hand stroking down my back calms my anxiety, though.

"It was some producer's kid. He's already offering to cover all medical bills, but my sister said she's suing if his daughter doesn't go to rehab. My nephew just wants to get back on his bike."

"How long will it take?"

"A while. He took the brunt of the impact. His legs are pretty beat up."

"That really stinks. How many nieces and nephews do you have?"

"Twelve. My brother has eight and sister has four."

"I bet they love you."

"I am a favorite aunt. What about you, baby? What's your family like?"

"I have a twin brother, Thomas. He's my exact opposite, but I love him. There is a girlfriend, but no kids."

"And where is he now?"

"The Big Apple. He's a money guy. I think my parents were such hippies he felt he needed to go in the other direction. They run a pot dispensary up in the Bay Area."

Pilar laughs. Most people do. I just shrug. My parents are lovely people. Unconventional, but lovely. "I know. They love their pot. They love their kids, but they love their pot."

"That's amazing. My family does a little bit of everything. Motorcycles, movies, food trucks, medicine, teaching. We're all over the place."

"Sounds like a big family."

"It is."

"You're worried about your nephew, aren't you?"

"I am, baby."

The position is awkward, but I hug her and she hugs me back.

"You can talk to me about him, if you want," I say quietly. She doesn't reply, but she still holds me. "What's his name?"

"Felix," she says, and then she sighs. "I just want to hold you."

This was something I learned a long time ago, not from Laurel, but from another sub. Sometimes our mistresses need more from us than our obedience. Sometimes they need our comfort, our support, and sometimes they need it in very specific ways. Laurel wasn't like that. She never needed me unless she was in the mood to tie someone up. Or if she didn't want to go to the movies alone. But she never needed me to hold her. If my Mami wants to hold *me*, she can hold me all night.

We stay in the bath a little longer. We don't speak, but we kiss and we touch each other. After, she tells me there's food. But I'm not really hungry. We get in her bed, and we kiss and touch some more until I fall asleep.

At one, I wake up again and I'm starving. I don't make it out of the bedroom before Pilar is out of bed as well. She puts me in one of her T-shirts. It's too big and it smells like her bedroom. I love it.

We eat rotisserie chicken standing up by the fridge. She asks me about work, and once I start, I'm rambling. She asks questions even though I'm throwing out so much information. She won't remember all of the names or the things we do. It's not like you can teach someone everything about digital marketing over chicken. But she's listening to me and she's asking me questions.

Back in bed, I realize I left Frank at home. I'm fine because I'm with Pilar, but I hope he's okay without me.

The next morning, Pilar comes to my room just as I finish getting dressed. She's carrying a wooden paddle. She won't look at me as she rotates the handle in her hand. I swallow and straighten my shoulders.

"Last night in the tub, I said a bad word." I come out with it because I remember immediately.

"Yes, you did."

"And you told me I'm to watch my language."

"Do you know why?"

Even though I have an idea, I don't know the exact reason so I shake my head. She's still not looking at me, but she sees.

"When I take you out, your behavior reflects on me. When I have a little girl beside me who can't mind her manners or watch her language, I look like I don't care how people perceive you. I look like I don't care about *you*."

"I understand."

"Drop your pants and bend over the bed." I do as she asks, and as soon as I brace myself on the bed, I realize I'm shaking. I'm scared. Laurel blurred this strange line between punishment and her pleasure. The way she made me feel emotionally, especially as things started going south, I could never tell if I was being punished because I was doing something wrong or because she was beginning to hate me. I know Pilar doesn't hate me. She's talking to me and that's big enough. She's been perfectly clear why she's doing what she's about to do, but I'm still scared.

"Are you ready?" she asks.

Of course I'm not. She has a paddle in her hand and I'm not naked. She's not behind me eating me out. She's got a paddle in her hand, and she's waiting for me to be ready for an actual punishment that I earned.

"Yes, Mami. I'm ready."

It comes in stages. The first strike sends me forward. The first impact is the contact on my ass and then the sudden burn as she pulls away. The pain travels up to my chest. And then to my throat. It comes out as a stunned screech, but I clench my teeth to keep some part of it in. The second strike comes quickly. This time I hold my scream all the way in.

"Pull up your pants," she says.

I do as she tells me, and miraculously, I manage not to cry. Two tears escape, but I don't consider two tears to be the same thing as crying. Pilar puts the paddle down on the bed, then wipes my face. I straighten my shirt. My butt hurts, but my feelings hurt more.

"Do you need more time before we eat breakfast?"

"No. I'm fine."

"Why are you crying?" she asks. Her tone is serious, but not condescending. She wipes my face again because three more tears break loose.

"I don't want to disappoint you."

"Did I say I was disappointed?" I shake my head. "I'm trying to teach you the way I like things, and if you don't like the way I want things, you need to tell me so we can talk about it. I don't want you to hold things in."

I shake my head again. "I just don't want to disappoint you. I like the way you do things, and I like that you want to talk to me."

She leans forward and lays the softest kiss on my cheek. "I am *not* disappointed. You're learning. We're learning together. Okay?"

I nod. The tears have stopped. She lightly pats my butt. It doesn't really hurt at all anymore. "We're having waffles and some strong coffee."

We eat, and Pilar doesn't do something weird like force me to talk. She touches me, my face and my hair, while I eat my waffle. She waits for me to say something. Eventually, I ask her how the show is going. She tells me it's going just fine. They're almost done shooting, and they've already been renewed for another season. She might try to book a movie during her hiatus. She hasn't decided yet. I like listening to her talk.

She walks me to my car. It's early still, but it's already warm out. I open my car door, and when I turn to say good-bye, she takes my face in her hands and kisses the hell out of me.

"Trust me," she says. "I'm far from disappointed."

I can't see straight and birds are singing in my ears. My butt feels great.

CHAPTER FIVE

It's Friday again. My week has been a mix of the lowest levels of marketing hell and the highest peaks of Pilar-related bliss. Katie and I have joined forces. I slap 21 And Up with a ridiculous budget for the paper-doll site. Then I tack on a bunch of money for the overtime they're demanding for the new deadline on the mobile site. Valerie backs me up by assuring the client that I'm completely on top of all projects and that the money they spend will be well worth it. It will. I'm confident of my abilities. Liam's art design is gorgeous, and our web architect, Felicia, will work around the clock as long as she's getting paid. We're going to finish these stupid projects, and then I'm going to take my vacation days.

In the meantime, though, there's Pilar.

We don't spend another night together before the weekend, but we talk every night. I send her pictures from work, and at night I send her dirtier pictures. One night she sends me one back. She can put her whole nipple in her mouth. When I see that little skill, I almost fall off my bed.

I come up with an idea. I want to give her a fantasy on our Friday night. I ask her politely if we can play a game. At the Century City AMC 15. I explain further that she's my teacher. I know the school year isn't over yet, but I'm eighteen now.

She's particularly quiet for a few moments.

"Mami?" I say.

"What if people see us?" she finally says. I bounce on my bed, then regain my composure.

"Um. Well. That AMC has assigned seats. I could buy us tickets. Leave one for you at the guest-services counter and you could meet me inside. It'll be dark and no one will see us." She's quiet again.

"I'll wear a skirt?" I suggest. "A short one. And I'll surprise you with the underwear."

"Pick a nine o'clock movie and I'll buy the tickets."

"Do you care what we see?" I ask.

"I won't be watching the movie and neither will you. Good night, baby."

She hangs up before I can say anything else. She is that excited. Horny and a little flustered. I got to her. I did that all by myself. I bounce on my bed again and squeal. Then I call Liam. He's a night owl. I know he's awake.

"You're naked in a cage on the side of the freeway, and you need me to come save you." That's how he says hello.

"Close. I need a schoolgirl outfit. A good one. By tomorrow." Liam has useful connections and a knowledge of Los Angeles that only a native to the city would have. I can point you to a few Starbucks; that's about it.

"Oh, God, yes. Thank you for letting me be a part of this."

"Uh, you're welcome, weirdo. Will you help me?"

"Yes. Text me your dress, shirt, and shoe size. I'm taking an extra long lunch tomorrow. If anyone is looking for me, you tell them I think I have warts on my dick and I have to get it checked out."

"You really want that around the office?"

"Can you think of anything more gross, but not life threatening, than warts? Warts get me missing. Life threatening gets Val checking up on me Monday morning asking if I need medical leave."

I laugh. "Warts it is." Though I'll probably just tell people he has a regular doctor's appointment.

"Good. I'll enjoy my lunch and you'll look like a barely legal Catholic-schoolgirl tramp."

"Realistic, not trampy," I whine.

"I know. Text me your shit. Bye." I'm still bouncy when I get off the phone with Liam.

❖

I'm buying Liam a car, or a nice bike, or a puppy. I'm in the bathroom at AMC theaters and I look perfect. A few women look at me. Well, they all look at me. I'm clearly in my twenties and wearing a Catholic-school jumper. It's a little longer than I imagined the night before, but it's the real deal. He found it at a thrift store, ran it home, dropped it off with Gary. He washed it for me and brought it to the office before five thirty. I owe them both a puppy.

I go for it full with my hair: braided pigtails and all, with ribbons. I have on knee-high socks and Mary Janes. Finally, a woman flat-out stares.

"I'm going to a costume party," I say. She looks embarrassed, and then she smiles before she remembers she was washing her hands.

I put my brush in the backpack I dug out of my closet. My work clothes are in there along with my heels. I look like I'm about to be in a porno because there's no fucking reason in real life for me to be in the school uniform. But this is my awesome sex life where I get to do seemingly ridiculous but incredibly hot things with my Mami.

I grab a soda and some candy and wait for the last of the cleanup crew to come out after the seven p.m. show. Once they're done, I'm the first person into the theater. There's that awesome movie-theater radio playing. I text Liam to thank him again. He texts back demanding reaction pics of Pilar's face. I tell him I love him and there's no way in hell.

The theater starts to fill up. Pilar comes in when it's about thirty-percent capacity. She's nearly the last person around the carpeted corner, wearing dark slacks and a button-down shirt, and a tan jacket that looks very adult. Her hair is up in a tight bun and she's wearing glasses. I look forward and stop myself from bouncing in my seat.

She slips past a few guys at the end of the row and makes her way to me. She doesn't say a word when she sits next to me. I take a sip of my soda. And then I turn to her. It's over the top and a little obnoxious, but I've been planning this all semester.

I grab her forearm. "I can't believe we're doing this," I say. My voice is close to a whisper, but it's not quite there. "My parents think I'm studying with Katie."

She looks down at my hands. "Not yet."

I turn back around in my chair. "I'm sorry, Ms. Castillo. I—I'm sorry."

"Don't be sorry. Just be patient."

So I'm patient. I wait through the weird commercials they show before movies now and an hour of previews. We're watching the most recent release from Marvel Studios. It's already been out for a month so the theater isn't full. There's a lot of explosions, so many that the audio should cover my moans, if we ever get down to business.

I grab my candy and shove a few pieces into my mouth. Pilar doesn't move a muscle. Something on the screen blows up. I think about tipping the whole box of candy into my mouth.

Pilar holds out her hand. I think she wants the candy, so I put the box in her palm. She takes out one piece and holds it out for me. The way her hand is, the hand that's closest to me, it looks like she's thinking about scratching her head. I shift around so my feet are under my butt, then prop myself up on the armrest. I take the candy from her fingers with my mouth. She holds out another like she's waiting for me to do something specific. This time I suck her finger and she watches me. That seems like the right thing. We do this again and again until her fingers are sticky.

She reclaims her hand and licks the sugar and my saliva off. It's crazy sexy to watch. She takes her coat off then, and then she unbuttons and unzips her pants. She reaches for the armrest, and when it's out of the way, she puts her arm around me and pulls me close. I put my head on her chest and look at the screen. She takes my hand and guides it into her pants. She's wearing this stretchy satin underwear. I wonder what color it is as I run my fingers over the smooth fabric.

Pilar's wet. My fingers part the trimmed hairs over the height of her slit and find her clit. My fingers slide lower and she covers my arm with her jacket. She's soaked. Her underwear is wet, too. I go to town. I rub her slow. I rub her fast. I manage to slip two fingers inside her pussy for a time before I pull them back out and finger her clit some more. She holds on to me, doing her best not to moan. She's huffing air out through her nose instead. I know she's going to come soon, so I don't stop.

The guys at the end of the row are watching us, but they can't see anything, and even when the screen lights up the whole room, they can only imagine what's going on under her coat. They have no idea just how swollen and wet my Mami is and how I made her that way. They have no idea that she's figured out she can reach my right breast from the way we're sitting. They can't see that she's squeezing everything around my nipple, and they don't know how wet it's making me.

Pilar grits her teeth and rests her head on top of mine as she comes. She squeezes my breast even harder and I want her inside me so bad. As she's coming down, she takes me by the back of my neck and she kisses me.

"I'm going to take care of you when we get home, little girl. What I want to do to you we cannot do in public," she says.

My hands are still in her pants. "Okay," I whisper. I wiggle my fingers and she kisses me again.

The movie is pretty good even though I'm confused about one guy till the very end because I wasn't paying attention when he was introduced. Pilar holds me and I keep my fingers where they are. Toward the end she moves her hips again and I realize she's good to go, again. So we go again.

People are watching us as we walk through the parking garage. Pilar is holding my hand. She has the strap of my backpack and her jacket draping over her other arm. We pay our three bucks apiece for parking. Well, Pilar pays for mine because she doesn't want to wait for me to dig through my bag for my money when she already has her wallet at the ready. She walks me to my car, and once my stuff is in the backseat, she turns to me. She's all business. Eight ways of business. It's only been a little while, but I've never seen this kind of focus on her face.

"You are going straight to my house. Don't speed. You're going to beat me there anyway. Drive safely and wait for me in your car. When I get there, we're going straight into my bedroom, and I'm going to fuck the shit out of you."

I smile a bit. "You said a swear."

"I'm in charge. I'm allowed to swear." She's still all business and I think she's becoming more aroused. "Go home right now. When I get there, we're fucking."

"Yes, Mami." She kisses me, then practically puts me in the car. I drive slowly, slow enough. It's L.A., I can't go that slow. I do get there before her, but only by a minute or so. I grab my backpack and Frank, then hop out of the car the second she pulls up behind my Jeep. She goes straight for the front door and holds it open for me. I go right for her bedroom as I hear the front door close. I hear Pilar dropping things like her keys and her purse. I hope she doesn't drop-kick her phone. I put Frank and my bag in her rocking chair and wait patiently by the bed.

She's a tornado when she comes into the room. Her clothes go flying. Her dildo comes out, but she tosses that on the bed. She orders me to sit on the comforter. Once I'm on her bed, she starts pulling off my shoes.

"I don't have time for it now, but at some point I'm getting a picture of you in that uniform," she says. Still all business. She leaves my socks alone, but her hands shoot up my skirt and she almost rips my underwear off my legs. They get caught up in the tornado. My undies go flying across the room and my legs go over Pilar's shoulders. I bite my tongue so I don't curse again. I feel her tongue on me and her hands on my hips. I love the way she's making me feel, the way she's making me writhe on the bed, but I start to get hot. I barely manage to sit up. Her face is still buried between my legs.

"Mami, can I take this off?"

"Yeah. Let me get you out of that thing." She stops immediately and helps me stand. I'm sweating already by the time we unzip my jumper. When I turn around, I see how patient she's being. Her eyes are all fire and lust. She wants to devour every inch of my body, but she wants me to be comfortable. She's being patient for me. I shuck my jumper and then I kiss her. My hands are between us, unbuttoning my shirt, but our lips are tugging at each other. I can taste myself on her tongue. When I'm naked, she grabs my waist and nearly tosses me on the mattress. She's on top of me, kissing me again, grinding me into the bed. Her lips move to my ear.

"I want you to fuck me, baby. With the cock. You think you can handle that?" She pulls away so she can look me in the eyes when I answer.

"Yeah. I can do it." Even though I don't expect this request from her.

"Good girl." She reaches for the strapless dildo and gently inserts the short end into my pussy. She rubs my clit as she eases it in. Then she situates herself on top of me and sits on the longer end. Her eyes close as the length fills her. I moan as her weight causes the other end to rock against the muscles inside me.

She rides me. I rise up to meet her, but she's guiding us. She's directing both of our pleasure. I see exactly why she likes this toy. I feel like she's fucking me with thick, blunt strokes. Her arms come down on either side of me and we kiss again.

I come. My body has been ready for hours. I orgasm hard with my head digging back in the pillow and incomprehensible sounds coming out of my mouth. My Mami lets me ride it. She reads me well and lets me ride the peaks until I start to come down. She leans back then and starts to ride me even harder. Her large breasts hang over my mouth. I grip them both and rub my lips over her nipples. She makes a deep whining noise as she continues to work her hips.

I keep at her breasts, trying to ignore the shock waves that are still pulsing between my legs. If I think about where we're touching and how, even though there's an artificial length between us, I can feel her skin everywhere…if I think about those things, I know I'll come again. When she takes the cock in deep, her juices smear on my skin. I can smell her. I can taste her. She's moaning louder the more I suck on her breasts. Suddenly, she freezes, and then tremors begin to rock her body. She's coming and I love to watch.

I reach for her face and press my lips to her forehead. She lets me. Her eyes are still closed, but all traces of strain start to leave her face. She is still rocking against me, but slowly now. I want to tell her I love her, but it's the lust talking, the infatuation and the endorphins. I keep my mouth shut.

We have to separate for a moment. Pilar climbs off my lap and slips the cock out of me. It goes somewhere, but I don't see. When she's back, she rolls me on my side and wraps her body around mine. Her fingers come between my legs and she's fingering me for the closeness, not to make me come. Soon though, I find my hips moving, my ass rubbing against the curve of her hips. She rubs me with purpose now, kissing my neck and my ear. I knew we weren't done yet. I want more and so does she. Her other hand is on my breast and I cover it, urging her to squeeze harder.

We're rubbing against each other, her fingers stroking me and her pussy coating my butt and my thigh. We both become frantic at some point, another rough thrust and stroke. She pinches my clit and I'm done. I roll my head on the pillow, arching into the sweet pain as my pussy quakes. But she does her best to hold me still. Her leg comes over my hip and she fucks herself on my skin. I'm still shaking and she starts to come on me again. Her leg stays draped over me for a while. My head is fuzzy and I like the weight of her, so I don't mind. Eventually, she pulls the sheets over us and we sleep.

We need to plan our fucking and our eating a little better. It's two and I'm starving, but I want something good. Not something twenty-four hours and fast. Pilar is sound asleep, or so I think. I touch her belly.

"Mami?" I say.

"Yes, baby."

"I'm hungry."

Her eyes blink open and she stretches. "So am I."

"Can I take you somewhere?"

She scowls with a hint of confusion.

"There's this great taco truck near my place. They're out there till five a.m. Please. They make the best food."

"You're telling me where I'm going to find the best Mexican food."

I giggle. "I understand now how foolish that sounds, but—"

"Get dressed. My baby wants tacos, my baby gets tacos."

Pilar drives. There's nowhere to park on the street so we park in my garage, then walk a block to the truck. The owner recognizes me, and he and his wife both wave through the truck window. I eat there a lot. When Pilar asks me what I want, I feel a little cheated at first. This is my truck, my find, my treat. Still, I tell her what I want. She orders our food in Spanish, then talks to the owner for a little while as I wait.

"What did you say to him?" I ask once we're out of the line. There are chairs and a folding table on the sidewalk, but we stand and wait.

"I told him my baby wanted tacos so here we are. I also told him about my brother's truck. He said he'll prove his tacos are better."

When our food is ready we say good-bye and I ask Pilar if she wants to eat in my apartment. She does. We key into my place, and I find myself going on and on about how much I love the building. Pilar likes it too, which means a lot to me.

I show her around even though it's only a one-bedroom.

"This is where I was sitting the first time we chatted," I say as I point to my desk.

Pilar smiles.

"It's nice to have a little context," she says.

We eat on my couch and when we're done, I turn to Pilar. "So?"

"My mom, and brother, and my niece make better tacos, but these are good." I start sulking and she laughs. "Let's go back to my place," she says. "You can sleep in my bed." At this point, I forget all about the tacos.

❖

The next morning, Pilar lets me sleep late. She's in the kitchen when I crawl out of bed. She's made chocolate-chip muffins. I take one and steal a kiss. She pats my butt.

"Did you enjoy my game last night?" I ask, even though I know the answer.

"I did. We should play games like that more often. Today, my friend Bizzy is coming over and she's bringing her little girl, Holly. You two are going to have a play date." She leans forward and wipes a bit of chocolate off my mouth, which I realize is hanging open in shock. "What is it?"

"Uh, nothing. I—" I don't want to share her. That's the truth, especially after the night we had. I hate being away from her during the week, and the idea of having to split my weekend time with her drives me nuts, but I can't say that. I can't be that disobedient.

"Listen, baby. Bizzy is a good friend of mine and her relationship with Holly is new, too. I think it would be great for you to have another little girl to talk to."

I consider this for a moment. Pilar might be on to something. I can tell Liam anything. Even Gary will listen to me judgment free, but it would be nice to have another submissive little girl to use as a sounding board. It might even be fun to have someone else to play with.

"Wait," I say. "When you say play date, do you mean play board games or play oral-sex exchange?" Laurel made me fuck other subs for her amusement in the past, but I never liked it, and it took me a long time to finally voice that opinion. If anything, I need to tell Pilar I'm not comfortable with that idea.

But she just laughs, surprise lighting her expression.

"No, baby. Bizzy and I are going to talk, and you and Holly can play in your room or play outside."

"Okay," I say. The relief in my voice is genuine, but she's captured my interest. "Do you know a lot of Mommies and little girls?"

"Not a lot of little girls, but I know a nice handful of Mommy and Daddy Dommies."

"Do you guys have a knitting gang?"

Pilar gives the tip of my nose a playful tweak. "No gangs, baby. We do get together sometimes, though. I think today Bizzy and Holly will be enough for you."

"Yeah, I think so."

"I think so, too." Pilar leans over and kisses me, ending the discussion.

We eat breakfast, and after I shower, Pilar helps me lotion up, and then I put on a baby-blue romper with yellow dots. When Pilar finishes my hair I look downright adorable. Pilar looks gorgeous. She's pulled out a navy-blue, fifties-style halter dress. She pins her hair up in big, thick waves. She looks amazing and I'm so happy to call her mine.

Holly and Bizzy arrive just in time for lunch. Bizzy is an older white woman, a fiercely sexy butch. She's in a leather jacket and jeans. Her gray hair is short and styled handsomely. She's tall and in great shape. Under different circumstances, I'd have a hard time resisting her. Beside her is Holly. I don't like Holly from the moment I lay eyes on her. She's pretty, with blond ringlets bouncing around her face and pink pouty lips. Her outfit is fantastic: a poofy pink-and-white dress. Shirley Temple would be jealous. But it's the sour look on her face I don't like, and something in her green eyes is altogether evil. She actually glares at me when Pilar lets them in, and I can't help feeling like I should glare right back, but I hold a smile on my face.

Pilar does the introductions. I fold my hands behind my back and smile up at Bizzy. She touches my cheek. "Pilar, she's beautiful."

"Thank you. So is this precious little thing," Pilar replies about Holly, but I realize instantly she doesn't mean it. It's a pitch in her voice. She sees the sour, too. We both say hello to Holly. She doesn't say anything to either of us.

We have lunch in the dining room instead of the kitchen. Pilar made finger sandwiches, but tons of them. There's fruit and lemonade. She offers Bizzy a beer, which she takes. I enjoy listening to them talk. Their conversation is keeping my mind off Holly's terrible table manners.

Bizzy, who has Holly call her Daddy, is an attorney. She's considering firing her secretary. When Pilar asks about the lawsuit involving her nephew's accident, my ears really perk up. "I would definitely see what the judge says first. He might rule to cover the hospital bills, but if not, your sister is well within her rights to sue," Bizzy says. "The girl's family will settle if they don't want it to become more sensationalized to the public."

"You can get more if your nephew never walks again," Holly says. My neck almost snaps as I jerk back in surprise. A strained smile touches Pilar's lips. "Thank you, Holly. I'll take that into consideration." I glance at Bizzy. She doesn't say anything. She just feeds Holly a grape.

Bizzy asks me about my job, and I politely tell her I'm in digital marketing. She tells me Holly is a high-school teacher. I glance at Holly with her napkin tucked under her chin and crumbs all over her face, and I almost choke. People trust their children with this person.

Once I'm full, I sit quietly and wait for Pilar to excuse me from the room. This doesn't happen until Holly decides to pass the time by kicking Bizzy's chair under that table, harder and harder each time.

"Why don't you show Holly your room?" Pilar suggests. "I have fudge pops for you girls later." I say okay, even though I don't want Holly's fudge-covered hands near any of my stuff. I stand and she follows me to my room.

"This is cool. Bizzy doesn't have a room for me," she says. This is good, I think. We're talking at least.

"Where do you sleep?" I ask.

"In a crib at the foot of her bed." Her eyes seem to harden. "She likes me close by." I want to smack the tone right out of her mouth. As if Pilar doesn't like having me close by. Holly walks around my room, sure to touch everything she passes. I almost pounce on her when she starts touching my Hello Kitty tea set. Even I don't touch it, I love it so much. I hear a little snapping noise and my throat squeezes closed. I run to her side and see that she's broken off the handle on one of the teacups.

"Oops." She looks up at me before she sets it down. I might cry. I really might cry, but I remember this is Pilar's guest, and no matter how intentional and vindictive she might be, accidents do happen.

"How many Mommies have you had before?" she asks as she opens my closet. "Too bad you're not my size. I'd steal all this stuff." Holly is fatter than me. Yeah, *fatter*, so I ignore her comment and answer her question.

"I had one mistress before, but the Mommy aspect didn't sit well with her."

"That sucks. Bizzy's my first Daddy. My last Mommy thought I needed more structure, but I just needed someone more sadistic. Daddy's perfect for that." I have no response to this information, not that Holly is looking for one. She keeps talking. "I've heard a lot about Pilar. She's fucking hot. I might have to look her up if things don't work out with Daddy."

I'd punch her in the face, but she might like it. Instead, I keep my mouth shut. But she goes on. "You know, your Mommy made me this dress."

"Did she now?" I can't help being snarky this time.

"Yep. Fits like a dream. She makes a lot of dresses. Did she make you that jumper?"

I look down at my clothes. "No. She bought this."

"That's a shame."

I watch Holly as she walks over to my bed. I'm prepared to dive for Frank, but then I remember I left him on Pilar's bed. My breath of relief is short-lived, though, as Holly grabs the over-sized white bear from behind my other animals, causing most of them to tumble onto the floor.

"What are you doing?" I almost shout. She has Sir Bears-Alot by the ear and she's dragging him to the center of the floor. She drops him, then reaches up her dress and yanks off her underwear.

"Don't tell me you've never fucked your teddy bear before," she says as she straddles Sir Bears-Alot. By the time my brain catches up with what my eyes are taking in, it's too late. Holly is humping my bear. Her naked vagina has made contact with his plush white fur, and she's humping him with wild abandon. I'm frozen. I don't know what to do. She's violating my bear.

"Stop that," I say, but Holly is happily getting off. She's not listening to me.

"No. Come here," she gasps. "Get on behind me. This feels so good. We can fuck him together." She stops just long enough to unbutton the top of her dress so she can pull out her breasts. "Hop on," she says. "I'll let you touch my tits."

I'm done. Fuck polite. Fuck hospitable. Fuck sharing your toys. I grab Sir Bears-Alot by the head and yank him right out from under Holly. She sprawls on the floor, her legs wide open, giving me a view of her pink, wet pussy. I look down at my bear and there's a wet spot on his stomach. "Look what you did."

She snarls at me, then spider-scoots across the floor before landing a solid kick to my shin.

"Ow!" I grab my leg, covering the throbbing skin. "What the hell is wrong with you?" I hear chairs skidding across the floor, and I know Pilar and Bizzy are coming. So does Holly. She instantly starts to cry, real tears. She's some actress.

Pilar gets to us first. Bizzy is right behind her. We're a sight. I'm clutching my leg, which hurts like it's broken, and Holly is sobbing with her breasts out. Her underwear is across the floor.

"What happened?" Pilar asks.

"She made me take off my undies, and then she made me open my dress, and then she made me hump the bear," Holly says.

"No, I didn't!" I reply.

But Bizzy is too preoccupied scooping Holly into her lap to listen to me. "Daddy's got you," she says.

"Suzy," Pilar says. She's scolding me. She's actually scolding me.

"She grabbed the bear, dropped trou, and then put her nasty skank lips on the bear. And then she kicked me. I didn't touch her."

Holly sobs even louder. "She's lying. She said she wanted to compare boobies."

"No, the fuck I didn't." I've always been the kind of person to own my errors. I'll admit when I'm wrong, but there's nothing

I hate more than being called a liar. Bizzy holds Holly even closer, *shhing* and rocking her. Pilar's face is red, but I don't care. I didn't do anything wrong.

"I think we should go," Bizzy says.

"Yeah, that might be for the best," Pilar replies.

I sink to the floor then and examine my legs as Bizzy gets Holly back in some presentable order. She keeps sobbing the whole time. I glance up when they walk out the door, but I don't say a word. I hear muffled voices as Pilar lets them out, but I can't make anything out. I don't care what Bizzy has to say. My leg is swollen and my bear is going to need therapy.

I look up again and Pilar is standing in the doorway.

"What do you have to say for yourself?" she says.

I know I should bite my tongue, but I'm pissed. This isn't about Suzy behaving herself anymore. It's about Suzanne defending herself. I let loose. All of it.

"Are you kidding me? You thought I would want to spend time with that little monster? She comes in here, insults you, insults me. She tore apart my room and then she fucked my bear. Go ahead. Smell him. She wiped herself all over him."

Pilar swallows and her nostrils flare. "First thing, young lady, this is my room. Not yours. You are a guest in my home just as they were guests in my home. And we treat guests with respect."

"I didn't do anything! All I tried to do was rescue Sir Bears-Alot and I got myself kicked."

"Suzy—"

"No." I quickly stand up. "You lecture me on good behavior and your friend, *your friend,* brings this spoiled little bitch into your house to talk back to you and kick your furniture and break my things. I'm sorry. *Your* things. She basically accuses me of trying to molest her, which you know I would never do, and you're asking me what I have to say for myself? I'm saying I don't want to hang out with Holly again. She's not the kind of submissive little girl I want to spend time with."

"You're going to sit in here and think about the way you're speaking to me. And when I come back, you'll be punished."

"For what? I didn't do anything."

"That TV stays off and give me your cell phone." My face drops. She can't be serious, but she is. "Fine." I dig through my bag and give her my phone. Looks like I won't be calling Liam to pass the time. "You can take Sir Bears-Alot with you, too. I'm not touching that thing until a HazMat team is done with it."

I see the anger flash in Pilar's eyes before she storms out of the room.

She leaves me alone for hours. I'm mad at her so that suits me just fine. We could have had a great Saturday. I was still high from our movie date and the amazing sex afterward. I would have followed her on a million errands just so I could hold her hand and make her laugh, but no. We had to spend the day with Bizzy and her little brat.

The thought of Holly pisses me off even more. I grab Sir Bears-Alot and throw him out in the hallway. He's forever contaminated. I should have punched Holly anyway.

I fall asleep at some point. When I wake up Pilar is standing in the doorway. She has the paddle.

I groan and roll over to face the wall.

"You want me strip?" I mumble.

"It won't matter either way. You're not going to want to sit when we're through here."

"Fine." I roll over and sit on the edge of the bed. I won't look at her, and when I speak, I couldn't sound more bored. This is bullshit. "You're punishing me for talking back to you, for talking back to you in front of company. For being rude to a guest and for using bad language. And you probably think I tore Holly's panties in twain and ripped her heaving bosom from her dress that you made her."

"Stand up and bend over the bed."

I do as she asks.

My mother believed in spanking, except we called them beatings, because in the real world spanking implies some sort of mock punishment; it's a reminder. You get beat when your parents want to rearrange your thinking. I got one beating in my whole life.

It was Thomas's fault, come to think of it. But after that, my parents just had to look at us and we got right back in line.

When Pilar spanks me with that paddle, I realize my mom was taking it easy. Pilar kicks my ass. There's no other way to describe it. She's had time to calm down so she's in the zone and focused. She swings that paddle with centered, hard strikes and I try not scream. It hurts. A lot. She stops when she knows she should and not a few strokes after. A couple tears run down my face. I wipe them away quickly as I stand up. I'm trembling, but I ignore it.

Pilar doesn't look at me as she says, "Get changed for bed. When you're ready, you can have your dinner in the kitchen."

I don't say anything. She leaves the room.

I'm determined to change, so I do even though my ass is on raging fire. The pain is throbbing down my thighs, and I realize my shin still hurts. I get a good look at it in the light, and a dark ring has formed where Holly kicked me. My lower body is such a sad case. I bite the inside of my cheek to keep from saying certain things out loud.

I make my way to the kitchen. I think Pilar is surprised to see me so soon, but that's her issue. I take a seat at the table, concentrating on the throb of the pain instead of the burn as my weight settles on the wooden seat. My ass will be bruised for sure, but I'm too angry to care about it at the moment.

Pilar puts a bowl of spaghetti in front of me, but she withholds the silverware. She sits next to me. I still won't look at her. Her hand is on the back of my chair and she leans closer. I expect her to growl at me in some menacing tone, but her voice is calm.

"I am upset that you yelled at me and that you cursed at me. I am also upset that Holly kicked you and accused you of those awful things. And I'm also upset with Bizzy and myself. Bizzy was my first mistress. I met her after my mother got cancer. She groomed me and she helped me through a really tough time. Once I got through that period in my life, she saw that I was not a submissive, so with kid gloves, she taught me everything she knew about being a Dominant. She is a good person and an excellent teacher. I don't know what Holly's problem is, but Bizzy matters to me. She is more than my friend. She is my mentor. I wanted her to see how lovely you are. I wanted her to be proud of me for picking such an amazing little girl.

"You should have come to me right away, as soon as Holly's behavior was getting to be too much for you. You should have come to me, and Bizzy would have dealt with Holly. Instead, you cursed me out and accused me of things that you know aren't true. In front of my mentor. Holly is a brat and I do not like her. And she has been with Bizzy for a week. Bizzy will train her or Bizzy will toss her, but either way, you should have come to me."

I keep silent. I don't know what to say. "If I am asking too much of you, you need to let me know. But I don't think I am. Eat your dinner and then it's the time for bed."

"Yes, ma'am," I say. My voice is rough.

"I didn't make Holly that dress. I made it for my first girl, Crystal. Holly and Crystal are the same size so I gave Bizzy the dress." She hands me my fork, then leaves the room.

I need to eat. My stomach is rumbling, so I eat, but it takes effort to swallow every bite. When I finish, I wash out my dish and put it away. When I go back to my room, Sir Bears-Alot is gone and my phone is back on my bed. I toss it on my bureau.

I start to cry. It's not one thing. It's everything. I hurt Pilar and I embarrassed her. She's mad at me and I'm still a little upset with her. Still, deep down I know the issue is that I'm starting to love her. This situation between us isn't cut-and-dried. I think about what I said and who I said it to, how pissy I was after my timeout. I was a brat. I was rude to Pilar. I think I love her, and I took out my sore shin and my sexually tortured bear on her. I think about loving her and I'm even more upset.

I can't trust that love because it's wrapped up in submission, and pretty rompers, and ducky underwear, and pink roses, and bubble baths. She's giving me the fantasy right in the middle of my dull reality, and I don't know what to do with it. I don't know how to tell her that I don't want to share her because I love her so much. I don't know how to say that I'm this needy. Laurel was right. I'm needy and annoying, and when I don't get my way, I become no better than Holly.

I'm needy, and if I don't get it under control, Pilar will get rid of me, too.

When Pilar comes into my room, I'm sobbing uncontrollably. I think I'm on the verge of a panic attack. She picks me up and carries me to the couch. I had no idea she was so strong. She sits me down across her lap, careful not to put pressure on my ass, and I can't stop crying.

She rocks me. She whispers sweet things.

"I'm sorry," I manage to say. "Please don't get rid of me. I'm sorry."

"Shh, baby. I'm not going to get rid of you. Just calm down."

"I didn't mean to swear at you."

"Oh yes, you did." Pilar laughs a little. "But I'm not going to get rid of you. I'm stuck on you, my little Suzy. I'll spank you again if I have to, but I won't get rid of you." She pulls me closer, and I wrap my arm around her waist and bury my face in her chest. Sooner rather than later, the tears start to slow. She rubs my back. I nuzzle closer.

"That wasn't a spanking," I mumble. "You tried to kill me."

She laughs. "Quiet now, my Suzy girl."

I don't know when it happens, but I fall asleep. When she wakes me up, I'm still in her arms.

Chapter Six

Pilar wakes me up around ten. She slides me to the other side of the couch, then leaves the room. When she returns, she has lotion, a washcloth, some water, some ice cream, and Frank. She's wearing her pajamas and directs me over her lap so she can put the lotion on my bottom. It's a soothing lotion, and even though it doesn't take the pain completely away, it helps a lot. Once I sit up, she wipes my face, and then she pops open the ice cream. We share a spoon.

"Tell me what's really bothering you," she says.

I think about what I should have said at breakfast, when she asked me what I had on my mind the first time. I think about what I said instead of the whole truth, and I think about Laurel. I can change certain things, but I can't change who I am.

"I'm too needy."

"That's what your old mistress called you. Is that what you think now?"

"Yes." Pilar wipes my face again as a few leftover tears escape.

"Why do you think you're needy in relationship to me?"

"This morning when you told me Bizzy and Holly were coming over, I was angry. I wanted to spend the day alone with you. You gave me a great week. The flowers, and the midweek overnight, and the phone calls. You let me play my game last night, and then after…I want to spend as much time alone with you as possible. I still want more."

"You understand I have to keep you wanting, don't you? That's part of this. If you don't want anything from me anymore, then we're done. That's when *you* don't need me anymore."

"I didn't think of it that way."

"That's how I think of it all the time. When you don't want to see me alone, I'm in trouble. Do you understand?"

"Yes."

"What else is on your mind?"

"I didn't like being blindsided by their visit. I know you make the plans and the rules, but that caught me off guard in a bad way. I know you told me to manage my expectations, but I didn't think you'd have guests."

"Hmm." Pilar thinks for a moment. "That's fair. Is there anything else?"

"I do want to meet other little girls. I liked the idea of getting to know Holly before I actually met her, but—"

"She's horrible. I would never make her a dress, baby. I'd stab her with the scissors before I even finished measuring her."

I snort and swallow a bit of ice cream too fast.

"I'll make some calls and see what I can do. This isn't a game to me, and I don't want you to think I don't care about your feelings and your well-being. I want you to be happy with me, and I want you to be happy and feel safe with anyone I introduce you to. How's your leg?"

"It's fine." I look down and the bruise isn't pretty, but at this point it hurts less than my ass, which is still tender. "No worse than walking into a table corner. I just can't believe she kicked me."

"Me either. Well." Pilar lets out a heavy breath. "If I have major plans that involve people outside of this relationship, I'll tell you beforehand. And I am hearing what you're telling me. You want more."

"I'm sorry."

"You don't have to apologize for that."

"I don't want you to think I'm ungrateful. Today was bad, I know. I just love being with you."

"I know, baby." Pilar takes another spoonful of ice cream before she says, "You can stay up another hour and then it's time for bed. Tomorrow we start fresh."

I almost tell her that I think I may be in love with her, but instead I say okay. I want to, but I don't argue when she puts me in my own bed. I'm starting to understand about the wanting.

❖

The next day, Pilar wakes me up for a late breakfast, but before we leave my room she has something to tell me.

"I thought over what you said yesterday, and while we have our nights where we play games and our nights where you relax, we need to add a component. We'll try it today, and then tonight you tell me how it makes you feel."

"Okay."

"Go get washed up and come right back here."

I do as she asks, and when I return, she's still waiting for me with a fresh pair of flora panties with a really cute lace trim. I stand in front of her and she slips them on me. After, she has me sit on the floor so she can braid my hair. At that moment I focus on the fact that Pilar has never shied away from my hair. It's really long and thick. I've had hairdressers groan when I sit down in their chair, but Pilar's never said a word. Instead, she hums. She doesn't braid it too tight or too loose, which I really like, and when she's done, she ties my pigtails off and adds ribbons. I like this look and I like that she likes it on me. She tells me to stand up, and when I do and turn around, she hands me Frank and says, "Let's go have breakfast."

We walk into the kitchen and something tells me to stand until she instructs me to do otherwise. She's oddly quiet and a little formal. She's looking for a certain kind of submission and I want to give it to her.

She brings some cereal and milk to the table, and the fruit we didn't finish during our lunch with Bizzy and her little maniac. She pulls out the chair perpendicular to the table and takes a seat. She looks up at me. Another chance for me to take. I sit on her lap.

Apparently that was the right thing to do. She runs her finger over my shoulder and drags it down to my nipple. I shiver a little and hold Frank tighter.

"Why did you pick this little guy? You have so many toys in there."

I shrug her and give her an honest answer. "He's floppy and soft. I like floppy and soft."

"I like your reasoning." She smiles as she reaches for the spoon. "Open up." And she brings some cereal to my mouth. I let her feed me. This goes on for a little while in silence, but she watches me carefully the whole time. She takes a few bites for herself, then feeds me some more. We enjoy our whole breakfast this way, and I mean enjoy. We've fucked a number of times, but this is the most intimate thing we've done. Her bending me over the bed and banging me silly is hot, and perfect, and amazing, but Pilar's fingers wiping stray milk off my lip? That's closeness. It's what I want. I want to eat fruit or our cereal out of her hand. I want to be in her lap as often as possible. The way she drags her finger down my belly is a sign of true affection. It makes me feel special, not needy or annoying.

"We're staying in today," she says.

"Okay."

"I have some knitting to do. Do you want to keep me company while I knit?"

"Yes."

"Okay, my Suzy. Go into my sewing room and get my orange bag. I'll meet you the living room."

"Okay."

She winks at me as I stand. "Frank will keep you company."

I go to her sewing room and grab her orange bag. When I come into the living room, she's sitting in her big chair with a large pillow between her legs. "You'll sit on the floor from time to time, but I don't want to irritate your bruise or your bottom. Come sit down." I do as she asks and look up at her. She rubs my cheek before she picks up her needles.

The hours we spend before lunch are this strange sort of perfect. We watch The Food Network, and every time I say something looks delicious, she makes a small noise of approval. When I see things I think I could make, she teases that I should poison the people in my office with my experimental recipes before I try to make them for her. I like when she teases me like that because she always touches me afterward. She's knitting like crazy, but she still touches me.

I move around like a restless child, I spend some time with my head on her knee and some time lying across the floor and the pillow. Either way I'm always touching some part of her body. I like feeling her skirt against my bare skin. I like the accidental brushes of my nipples against her legs.

At a certain point I realize I have a soft square of her work hanging over my shoulder. The yarn she's using is a bright purple that fades to pink and back again.

"What are you making?" I ask.

"Blankets for little kiddies." I look up at her, a little confused. "The women's shelter downtown takes donations. They have kids in this shelter, and sometimes a blanket or a Frank is comforting when you're staying in a new, scary place. So I make these blankets for them. I try to make each one as unique as possible, so each kid gets their own special blanket."

I pick up the ball of yarn she's working from. I'm good with budgets and execution. I'm good with organization, but other than some recent sidewalk drawings, I've let a lot of my creativity go. Pilar oozes creativity. Everything about her is style or design, and then she gives that talent away in her free time to kids who are going through a rough time.

And to me.

"I'm taking a break," she suddenly announces. "Come up here." As soon as her needles are out of the way, I climb into her lap and rest my head on her shoulder. Her one hand gathers me closer, wrapping around my side and holding me to her. With her other hand, she strokes my hip. She draws her fingers down my leg. She leans down and kisses me. This is a different kind of kiss. It's probing and possessive, demanding. She takes my tongue as she squeezes my ass lightly. There's a little pain, but I like it. We kiss for a long time. I squirm in her lap, my thighs clenching together, little desperate noises seeping from between our lips. When Pilar pulls away, she's panting and her face is flushed. I can feel the heat rising under my own skin.

"Pull up my shirt," she says. Her face is composed, but her voice is raw. Her fingers drift between my legs. "I want you to suck me while I touch you."

I do as she asks and slide her T-shirt up to her chin. I pull one breast out of its satin cup and then the other. She's touching the trim on my panties where the crotch meets my thigh. I've been a little wet since breakfast, but now I feel that unmistakable slickness between my legs. She rubs me over my underwear. For a moment I think I might like her fingers on me this way more than skin to skin. Something about the firmness of her hand or the way I can feel my wetness seeping through the fabric turns me on. I look up at her face before my eyes roll back in my head. She's concentrating on my body.

I squirm some more before I lick her breast. I lick her again before I take her nipple into my mouth. She adjusts me effortlessly, and then she pulls my underwear aside.

The skin on skin is better.

Her breathing becomes heavier the more I lick and suck. I know her nipples are sensitive, but it's not going to be enough for her. She knows that, too.

Pilar tips my chin up and we kiss again. She slips her fingers inside me. She's determined to make me come, not that she's ever taken a lazy approach, but I can feel that she won't stop kissing me until I finish on her hand. I grip my arm around her neck and kiss her deeper.

I come with Pilar's tongue in my mouth. I try not to, but the aftershocks force me to pull away. I need to breathe. She strokes another orgasm out of me, but the two climaxes nearly blend together.

I finally come down and Pilar kisses me again.

"Can I eat you out?" I ask when she pulls away.

She strokes my cheek. "Yes, baby. You may."

I shuffle to the floor and in a heartbeat, my head is under her skirt. She's already wet. I waste no time licking her slick thighs. She settles back into her chair and spreads her legs wider, giving me better access to her pussy.

I use my mouth on her for as long as she'll let me. But soon she hoists me back up and captures my mouth with her lips. She seems to savor her own flavor as I rub her clit. She moans into my mouth, so I rub her harder. She scoots to the edge of the chair, so I don't stop. She's gripping my face in her hands, kissing me and kissing me as I do what she likes with my hand. She comes with what I'm starting to recognize as her groan of real satisfaction. I kiss her face and her chest. Her heart is pounding.

Pilar straightens her clothes after a moment, and then she stands me up and guides me over to the couch.

"It's time for a little nap." She hands me Frank and settles the blanket over me. "I'm going to start lunch." I have no idea how she's so calm.

But before Pilar leaves the room I say her name. This time it's "Mami" because that's what feels right.

"Yes, baby."

I weigh the options in my head. I'm deep under, my mind is floating. I don't know if Pilar will find me in a more sublime state. I might regret it. Actually, I'm positive that I'm risking a lot by saying what's really been on my mind, risking way more than I know I should, but I feel like I need to be honest.

"I love you." I thank all that is God because my tone is light and not desperate and weepy. It's anything but a light feeling for me, but I'm not sure I want her to know that. I'm fighting a smile when she comes back over to the couch. If those three words had sent her sprinting into the kitchen, I would have died right there on the spot. She squats down beside me and strokes my cheek. I can still smell our sex on her hand. It makes me squirm again.

"I love you, too, Suzy girl." She smiles when she says it. It's a genuine smile like the one she gave me the first time we met. I let myself smile back.

"You're not going to go to sleep, are you?" she asks.

I hadn't considered it, but I'm not exactly tired. I tell her the truth.

"You want to come keep me company in the kitchen?"

"Can I bring Frank?"

"You know Frank is always welcome."

I grab my stuffed puppy and follow Pilar into the kitchen.

I feel a little strange. I'm eating lunch with Liam on the bench overlooking the garden, but I don't have much of an appetite. Still, I tell him about my weekend with Pilar. I have to let him know the uniform was a success. At least I try to tell him, but I'm stuck. I'm still in my space, that's the problem. I spent the rest of Sunday afternoon and Sunday night nearly naked at Pilar's knees. We barely spoke, but I couldn't get enough of her touching me, even if it was just simple caresses. She made me sleep in my own bed, which I accepted, but in the morning my head was anything but clear. I need a cleansing of sorts. After everything that happened with Bizzy and she who shall not be named, even after my punishment and our talk and the sex, I still have emotions pent up inside me.

Forcing those feelings down so I could get through work isn't making matters easier. I'm almost twitchy. Liam notices. "If you had such a good time why do you look like you're about to cry?"

"I don't know," I say, but I suddenly feel the tears fighting to get to the surface. I can't talk to Liam about this anymore. I need Pilar. I text her.

Can I please call you?

My phone rings a few seconds later.

"Is that her?"

"Yeah," I reply, but the word almost gets caught in my throat.

Liam gets up without another word, but he rubs my shoulder before he ducks back into the office.

My voice is shaking when I say hello. But Pilar isn't alarmed. It's like she knows. Her voice is soft and patient when she asks, "What's wrong, baby?"

"I miss you."

"I know. Is everything okay at work?"

"No." I laugh mirthlessly. "But it's nothing I can't manage."

"Tell me what's bothering you."

"I—" I falter. It's hard to express what I think I need. It's hard to ask for something like this.

"I'm gonna go."

"No, Pilar. Wait!"

"Baby, I need you to think so I'm going to give you some time to do that. There's nothing I *want* to hear. Do you understand?"

I do. This isn't about me conjuring up some magic answer to please her. This is about me being honest with myself.

"I'm going," she says again.

"Pilar."

"Bye, baby."

And then she's gone. Somehow as I stare at my useless phone my tears dry up. I need her for my release, for all of it. I can't let go if she's not with me.

❖

I don't hear from Pilar for three days. I send my panty pictures like I'm supposed to. I text her. I call her, but she doesn't respond. I'm obsessed with her silence. The act of it is driving me crazy. I know there's a lesson in here somewhere, but I can't figure out what it is. I power through work, being efficient but a complete bitch to everyone. I'm on edge with Katie and the guys. My conversations with Valerie are forced and short. I'm as polite as I can be with her, but she still asks me a handful of times if I'm okay. I'm nice to Liam because he knows what gives. Still, he's understands me enough to let me have space.

On Thursday, a little after two p.m., my cell phone rings. I look at Pilar's name lighting up the screen and I consider hitting IGNORE, but I know better. I take a deep breath, and tuck in every swear word I have, and push it out of my immediate vocabulary.

"Hello?"

"Hello, baby. Is this a bad time?" I want to ask what she could possibly want now, but I don't.

"No, I can talk." I lean back in my chair. I can talk, but I won't say anything interesting for anyone in my office to hear.

"Do you have anything to tell me?" I knew it. She was punishing me for not speaking up. She had given me time to come up with the words, but instead I spent the time being frustrated and upset with her. That only added to the frustration that had been grating on me the last time we talked. Now I'm irritated that she sounds so calm and I'm nearly crawling out of my skin. When I answer, I don't tell her how much her silence over the last few days has bothered me. If she can sound cool, so can I. Still, I have no answer and that's what I tell her.

"I don't know," I say. "But I think I'm fine now."

"That's unfortunate, baby," she replies, because she knows I'm being a brat. Her tone is still light. "Come stay with me tonight. We're going to start our weekend early."

I want to say no. It's my turn to give her the cold shoulder, but I want to give her the cold shoulder for like five minutes, not a whole night. And I'm screwed if I blow her off tonight and she decides to blow me off for the whole weekend. That I can't handle. That would be the beginning of the end.

"I have to get Frank and a change of clothes."

"Bring a few extra work outfits you can leave here. There's no point in driving all the way to Koreatown if you don't have to." I say okay, and then her sudden change in tone turns my pussy to liquid.

"Baby, you come here right after you grab your things. I'll have dinner ready."

"Yes, Mami," comes out of my mouth in a near-bashful moan.

"That's a good girl. Call me if you're running late."

I practically slam my head on my desk once we're off the phone. Real cool, Suzy. Real cool.

❖

When I get to her house, I'm greeted by a completely calm and collected Pilar. Not that she would ever be frazzled. That's my job. She smiles as she says hello. She kisses me. I'm happy to see her, but my guard is up.

"Go get washed up for dinner and then we'll eat."

I don't argue, not that I'd planned to. I take a quick shower and lotion myself up. That spot on my back will just have to deal. Pilar doesn't lay anything out for me, so I join her in the kitchen naked. She smiles at me again. She touches my cheek as she sets down a plate loaded with food. She sits with her chair out from the table and motions for me to come sit in her lap. After she feeds me two bites of chicken, I'm wet. Whatever low-threat hostility I was feeling toward her is gone. She strokes my back as she continues to feed me. She asks me eventually if I'm full. I am. I wiggle a little closer and put my head on her shoulder as she continues to eat.

"How was work today?" she asks.

"It was okay. I wish there was a way to streamline some of our processes. But 21 And Up is bent on making things difficult. I can't wait 'til I finish these projects."

"And then what?"

I hesitate for a moment. "I guess on to the next project. I have some vacation time stored up."

"I suggest you use it," she says sweetly. I look up at her and she kisses me softly on the lips.

Once she's done with her dinner, I watch a little TV while she folds laundry. She doesn't mind my running commentary. I feel better because every time I look at her I get that smile again. At bedtime, I kick myself for letting that smile get the best of me. I head to my room. Pilar joins me a few minutes later. She's wearing a black satin nighty. A layer of sheer lace covers her breasts. I want to touch her. Right now. Like right now. But she has other plans.

"Take your pick, baby." She holds up the pink cuffs in one hand, and in the other, she has a weird hourglass-shaped patch of leather with straps and buckles. I gasp as I realize it's a chastity belt.

"What are the cuffs for?" I ask.

"You can sleep in the belt or you can sleep with your hands cuffed to the bed. Your choice."

"Why?" I whine.

"You decide and I'll tell you."

I think for a moment. The cuffs aren't a big deal. They're padded, but I'll be restricted to sleeping on one side. I see what she's getting at even though I'm not entirely sure why.

"The belt," I say. At least I'll be able to move around.

"Excellent choice, baby." Pilar puts the cuffs on the bed, then slips to her knees in front of me. She's quick about strapping me up in the thing. I look down and watch her work, but my mouth pops open when she reaches into her cleavage and pulls out a little heart-shaped lock. She snaps it into place, denying me access to my own pussy, and then she stands.

"Time for bed," she says with the sweet smile that I read as straight-up cruel. I flop down on my back with a level of drama, grateful at least that the leather is soft. Still it's too thick for me to get creative.

I yank my blanket up to my chin. "Why are you doing this to me?" I whine again.

As she laughs, Pilar squats down beside me and strokes my face with her crooked finger. It's impossible for me to be angry with her when she's touching me this way.

"I gave you a few days to open up to me, but you've decided that you need to hold those feelings in. Clearly, I don't know why. I'm sure it's a valid reason, but I've told you more than once that you need to communicate with me. I can't read your mind."

I don't know whether to roll my eyes or cry. I know what she wants from me, but I don't know how to give it to her.

"So, my little Suzy girl," she says. "We're not going to play until you're ready to talk to me. You won't be playing with yourself either."

"Are you mad at me?" I ask. Pilar's very patient, but I don't want to make her upset. I just don't know how to tell her everything that I'm thinking and I'm feeling. I mean, who's *that* open? Even if I could put it all into words, I can't get over the sheer terror of being that vulnerable. I can handle a spanking. I can't handle rejection from someone like Pilar.

"I'm not mad, but you might be after a few nights in this thing." She winks and pinches my cheek. After a few minutes, I'm alone with Frank. I want to text Liam, but even though she's not angry, Pilar is definitely punishing me.

I decide I need to formulate what I'm going to say in the morning. I think back to last weekend and I...

A strange moaning sound stops my train of thought. Another soft moan gets it going again. I listen a moment longer. Maybe I'm hearing things. Maybe she's watching porn, but when I hear a very familiar whimper, I know that Pilar won't be denying her own pleasure tonight.

I know for sure that I can't touch myself, but she didn't say I couldn't watch. I slip out of bed with Frank clenched in my hand and creep down to my Mami's bedroom. Pilar is in the center of her bed, above her covers. Her nightgown is hiked up around her waist and her knees are up. Her legs are spread. Both her hands are busy, one rubbing her clit and the other stroking in and out of her pussy.

My mouth runs dry, and just as I go to squeeze my legs together, I groan against the restriction of the chastity belt. Pilar glances up at me. Our eyes hold. She doesn't tell me to leave. Instead, her head drops back on her pillow. She fingers herself deeper. Leaning against the doorjamb, I hold Frank tight and I watch. I've gone marathon sessions before. I've lost chunks of afternoons and evenings touching myself in the middle of my bed and sometimes on my living room floor. I know how what I'm seeing feels like.

I think Pilar means to tease me, at first, but I realize after her first and second orgasm she's not teasing me at all. She's not even thinking about me. She comes with a high whimper, her head lolling on her pillow. Her arms lie limp on her thighs. Her fingers are still between her legs. Suddenly, she sits up and reaches for something on her nightstand. Two somethings. Now I think she's trying to kill me. My Mami wants me to expire from lusty, horny, no-touch death. The moment she simultaneously slides the dildo between her lips and flips the switch on her high-speed, plug-in vibrator placed right over her clit, I feel my heart preparing to take its final beats.

It's inaccessible, but my pussy is throbbing so bad. I consider touching nipples, as I brush my left tit with Frank's soft fur. My light moan has Pilar lifting her head again. I freeze. She watches me for a dozen heartbeats, her hands still moving the toys to her pleasure, before she lies back on her pillow.

I love how vigorously she likes to fuck herself. It's vicious and brutal, the way she pumps the dildo in and out of her pussy. The way she angles the cock, I know it's hitting the right spots. The vibrator is loud, pulsing in the almost-silent air between us. Almost because I can't help the way I'm breathing, and Pilar's sounds of ecstasy are anything but controlled.

Her hips start to jerk. I've reached this point on my own before. I've come so many times that I've aroused myself all over again to a point that feels nearly insatiable. It's one long orgasm or many short ones looped together. If she keeps pushing herself, she'll squirt.

Pilar's hips lift off the bed in a sharp jerk and drop down just as quickly. Her movements aren't lyrical or poetic. They're frantic and honest. Pilar pulls the dildo out in another quick motion, and her cum squirts out onto her sheets. Her pussy quivers and more liquid follows. There's a large dark spot between her knees. I fight the urge to go lick it up. At this point in my own private play, I black out or give up for real, flopping uselessly on my bed until I muster the energy I need to at least move my toys out of the way so I can sleep. But Pilar is a different creature. She jumps out of bed with a renewed energy that has me straightening with surprise. The look of anger on her face has me taking a step back. I'm too afraid to make a real escape.

She takes me by the arm and leads me back to my room with hurried steps. Short of forcefully putting me under the covers, she gets me back in bed.

She leaves the room and returns seconds later with something in her hand. She's moving so quickly in the dim illumination from my nightlight it takes a moment for me to realize that they're Band-Aids. The Hello Kitty kind she keeps for me above the sink. She covers my nipples with two strips on each breast, pushing the hard peaks down. I've only had a few nipple orgasms in my life, but if I'm desperate enough…Well, it isn't an option now.

"I hope you enjoyed the show," Pilar says as she grabs my arm again. She pulls me onto my side and delivers a firm, painful smack to my butt. I yelp in protest, but she doesn't care. "Go to sleep."

Soon I'm alone and, honestly, I'm confused. I don't know if she's mad at me for watching or mad at me for enjoying it. I am pissed at myself for pushing her, no matter what the reason. The sting has faded but not the memory of her swat on my ass. I pull Frank tight to my chest and try not to cry as I fall asleep. There's no way I'll have an answer for her in the morning. I hope I have an answer before the weekend's over.

CHAPTER SEVEN

I'm still spooked the next day. Pilar releases me from my chastity belt after a neutral "Good morning." I dress quickly for work and consider skipping breakfast. I force down some juice and some eggs because I'm in no mental condition to take her on. Pilar leans against the counter the whole time I eat. Her eyes on me aren't helping. I stand when I'm finished and face her.

"Um...I should get to work."

She lowers her coffee from her lips. "Okay. I'm off today."

"I'll still send you the panty pic." Today's pair are a plain light blue, with a cartoon frog face right above the crotch.

She nods slightly. "I would hope so."

I glance at the floor before peeking up at her through my eyelashes. "You still want me to come over after I get off?"

A smile touches the corner of her lips. She puts down her coffee. "Come here, Suzy."

I cross the room and stand in front of her. She tugs me closer by the front of my pants. Her lips brush against my cheek. "I'll see you tonight."

Mitch is doing card tricks next to my desk. He's gathered a little bit of a crowd. They won't shut up, so I stop trying to work and wheel my chair into the commotion. We don't have time for this.

We're all up to our asses and elbows in work and deadlines. I'm worried that I haven't heard back from 21 And Up yet on the header for the landing page of the mobile site. But we're all so stressed that this break's necessary. My stomach growls. After I watch this next trick, I'm going to politely bug Valerie about bringing on more people. Then I'm going to grab some food.

"Suzanne, pick a card."

I reach forward and draw the queen of spades from the middle of the deck. Mitch launches into some story about the queen raiding a neighboring castle, but I'm not listening.

I grab my phone and text Pilar.

Can I see you? Like now.

She texts right back. *Sure, baby.*

I send her the address to our building.

"Suzanne, look." I'm suddenly surrounded by smiling faces and Mitch is holding up the queen of spades.

"That's genius," I say, forcing a smile.

"You think I don't know that," he says with huff, then a wink. "Okay, who's next?"

Pilar texts me again. *I'll be there in ten minutes.*

By the time I make it downstairs, I'm almost shaking. Pilar finds a meter out front. I don't mind if people see us together, but I'm ready to talk. I don't need my co-workers seeing me cry. We cross the street and slip down another block between two buildings with vine-covered walls and a little bit of cracked-up asphalt.

It's hot out, but we're in the shade. Pilar waits.

I take a deep breath.

"I don't know how to say it." She comes over here and I still can't spit it out. She reaches out and draws her finger over my lips.

"Just tell me how you feel."

"I feel like it's not enough. Like we have this perfect time together and I want more. I want more time, more submission, and it's messing with my head when we're apart."

Her eyes soften with concern. "Messing with you how, baby? Tell me." She's listening to me. She cares, but I'm still a little afraid.
"I feel like I can't tell you."
"Why?"
"Because I'm afraid of how you'll react."
"Baby, please tell me."
"I want you to spank me more. I want more time naked on your lap because it makes me feel closer to you."
"Those things make me feel closer to you, too. What aren't you saying?"
"I love you."
Pilar looks confused. "I know, baby. You told me over the weekend. I love you, too."
"No, I mean I actually love you, not 'little girl loves Mommy' love you. I actually love you."
"I know."
"You don't think that's a problem?"
Pilar lets out a heavy breath. "Why do you think it's a problem?"
"Because we just got together. Because I can't—" The tears spring up then. I can't stop them. "Because I can't separate those feelings from my submission. I don't know if I'm obsessed with the fantasy or if I really love you. I don't know—"
"You don't think I really love you. That's the problem, isn't it? You think that I can't see Suzanne? That I'm so focused on possessing Suzy that I don't care what Suzanne needs?"
I cover my face as I nod. I don't want her to see the tears running down my face. Thank God for waterproof mascara. I feel her step closer to me, but I don't drop my hands. She speaks softly now. "You think I only care about having a little girl I can parade around and not spending time building a relationship for us."
I nod again. Her arms come around my waist and I crumble on her shoulder.
"Do you remember what I asked for on kinklife?"
"Yeah," I whisper.
"Tell me what I asked for."

The post popped up clear as day in my mind. "You said you were looking for a long-term, monogamous relationship."

"Don't you think that would involve falling in love?"

"I don't know," I say. God, Laurel's tentacles run deep. I don't have any feelings for her anymore other than a slight twinge of hate, but I can just hear her telling me she didn't expect me to get so attached. So quickly.

"You do know," Pilar says as she strokes my back. "Tell me."

"I was just trained to think that falling in love was bad. Laurel accepted it eventually. Sort of, but she told me it wasn't usually the case. She said that Doms don't really fall in love with their subs. Just the idea of them."

Pilar's chest heaves against mine as she lets out a shaky laugh. "That's all I've been looking for, Suzy. I want you sweet, and I want you polite and obedient, but I want you."

I pull back a little and look her in the eye.

"Every relationship is different, but I want to love my little girl completely, not just the parts that are agreeable." She kisses my cheeks. "I love talking to Suzanne. I love hearing about her clients. Suzanne has explained to me exactly what a web architect does. Suzanne kept me company after my nephew's accident."

"Suzanne also talked back to you in front of Bizzy," I reply.

"No, that was Suzy," she says with a smile. "You think I'm not looking after all of you, but I am."

"So it's okay? That the way I feel about you is making me feel nuts?"

"You're not nuts, and yes, it's okay. But you have to talk to me like this or these outbursts will keep happening."

"You hate when I act like this, don't you?"

"No, baby. I don't hate it at all. I hate that your ex or whoever has you thinking that expressing your feelings is something you should be punished for. Emotionally. That's not how I function. I operate on honesty. I want to know how you feel. I want to make you happy, and I can't do that if you keep all this bottled up inside. You can tell me anything. You can *trust* me with anything. Promise you'll work on it."

"I will."

"Good. I don't think you want to wear the belt another night."

"Oh God, no."

Pilar's smooth laugh vibrates between us, again. She takes my face in her hands, and then she kisses me. Her soft lips aren't enough to completely erase my insecurities, but her kiss helps. It helps a lot.
It's hard for me to go back to work. Pilar and I grab a quick lunch. Being around her makes me feel better. At the cafe down the street, we run into Daisuke and one of our quality-assurance guys, Simon. Pilar is friendly to them, of course, but takes care to guide me to a table at the other end of the patio when our food is ready. I'm not sure they can tell I've been crying, but I need a little more time before I can put my professional face back on. After we eat, I walk Pilar back to her car.

"Liam is going to be so pissed he missed you." I can just hear his screech of rage when he finds out Daisuke and Simon got to meet her first.

"We'll have him and his boyfriend over for dinner sometime."

"Really?"

"I've been known to dine with vanilla people from time to time."

"That would be great. He's been dying to meet you."

"Then I'll be sure to put on my best performance." She pulls me close with two firm hands on my butt. She kisses me. "Get back to work, my Suzy girl. I'll see you tonight." I remind myself that tonight is only hours from now. Still, it takes some effort to pull myself away.

Valerie has mercy on us and insists that anyone that doesn't absolutely have to work overtime this weekend leave by five thirty. I take that offer at face value and find myself at Pilar's door at five fifty. When she opens the door her expression stuns me. She's all business.

"Hi," I say tentatively.

"Come inside."

I obey, and when she closes the door, I find myself pinned between her and its cool surface.

"Put down your bag," she says quietly. I let the strap slide off my shoulder and place it on the floor.

"That's a good girl. Now get down on your knees." I do as she asks, and just as I drop to the floor, she lifts up her maxiskirt. Her body smells fresh, like she's just showered. I want to dive in, face-first, but I wait for her next command.

"Hold up my skirt," she says.

I gather the fabric in both my hands and grip it against her hips. I look up and see that she's gazing back down at me. Not at my eyes, but at my mouth, I think. Or my breasts.

My eyes slide closed and I whimper as she fists her hand into the roots of my bun. She holds my head in place until I open my eyes again. Her other hand she uses to spread her lips. I'm already hot and buzzing, but a wave of searing heat rolls through me as she slowly exposes her clit. I lick my lips and move my head forward. She jerks me back.

I whimper again, louder this time, and not because she's hurting me, not even close, but because I want her so bad. The teasing is mean and unfair. I want a taste.

She rolls her fingers over her clit, stroking the small bud to a hardened tip. It's so clear, close up in the summer sun that still floods in through her living-room window.

"You know how to eat, don't you, baby." Her tone does me in. I have no job, no friends, nothing outside of this house but what's between her legs. I jerk back again before I answer, fighting her hold because I can't control my arousal. But she steadies me again in her grip. She's not angry at my restlessness. She knows what she's doing to me. I close my eyes as a painful moan bubbles in my throat.

"You do, don't you," she says. "You know how to eat Mami just the way she likes it."

"Yes." I answer even though it sounds more like I'm begging.

"That's good, baby. That's exactly what I like to hear." Her voice is a little strained now, but just barely.

She makes me wait. And watch. She teases herself some more with her fingers, drawing slickness up and around her clit, fingering its hood. I wonder how long she's been wet like this, how long she's been wanting to take me this way, but I can't think of anything other than the treat just inches from my face and how badly I want to bury my fingers in my own cunt once she lets me begin.

Pilar lets out a short breath before she pulls my head back one more time. I look up into her dark-brown eyes.

"You're a good girl, aren't you, Suzy?"

"Yes, Mami."

She rubs her wet fingers against my lips. And then, with her hand still gripping me by the hair, she brings my face between her legs. I know well enough now how she likes things. I lick her clit gently just twice before I rub my whole mouth over her slit.

She's in control, directing the motion of my head, pushing my face tight against her body, but I suck and suck until her legs start to shake. I slip back on my knees, putting my butt as close to the floor as possible. She follows my motions, angles my head so she's nearly sitting on my face. I shove my tongue inside. That seems to be enough. Pilar braces her forearm on the door over my head. I keep a solid hold on her hips, but I know what it's like to feel myself slipping. I know the moment when my legs are no longer willing to cooperate.

I kiss her deep, then slip my tongue out and grind the surface against her most sensitive tip. She likes this kind of pressure. Her hips start to jerk. She grips my hair tighter. My pussy nearly hurts, but I'm not complaining. I like pleasing my Mami. She comes with a long groan, higher pitched than her typical sounds of ecstasy.

She keeps a firm hold on my head, but she gently pushes my hands aside, lets her skirt slip back down to her feet. She tilts my head up.

"Nicely done," she says. I just stare back with wide eyes, waiting for her next bit of instructions.

"You're going to make yourself come for me. Right now. Do you understand?"

"Yes, Mami."

"Good. Stand up, baby." I do as she asks. She unbuttons and unzips my slacks. "Take off your shoes." I do as she asks and lose the inches that almost put us eye to eye. She glides my pants down my legs. "Over the back of the couch," she says. "Leave your panties on." I do exactly as she tells me, but once I'm in place I realize I'm on my own. I turn my head toward Pilar. She leans against the door, watching me. This time, I know I won't last long. My pussy is swollen and hot. I slip my fingers under the damp cotton. Pilar's already seen them on me, once this morning and again when I followed through with my daily chore.

Now I imagine she sees my butt up in the air, the edge of the pink underwear riding up the brown skin of my ass cheek. My fingers are down front, probably blocked from view by the roundness of my thigh. I brace myself with my arm in the top of the couch cushion and rub my fingers over my clit. Pilar's still breathing heavy. Her legs still look weak. This is the real start to our weekend, now that I've come clean, now that we're on the same page. I don't know what else she has planned, but I don't want it to involve this many feet of hardwood floor between us. She's been amazing, but like always, every time she's near me, I'm impatient.

"I want to come," I say. "Please don't make me wait."

"No one said you had to wait, baby. I said I wanted you to come."

My next step is to beg her to help me. I'm no good without her hands on my body so this, with her so close, is the real challenge. I want to make her happy so I let that be my focus. I focus on her body, the way her skirt falls below her hips. On her breasts, how I want to suck them until she comes again. Maybe if I'm really good she'll let me do just that. She licks her full lips as my knees start to weaken. I want to know so I ask. I'm blunt and to the point while I'm moaning and arching against the couch. She smiles at me.

"If you're a good girl."

I come. All over my fingers. Before I can really see straight again, Pilar has me upright. She unbuttons my blouse, then slips my bra off my breasts. She pinches my nipples, hard. I almost come again. "You have a surprise waiting for you in your room," she says.

"I do?"

"Mhm. Get cleaned up for dinner. Fresh panties and just pigtails this time. No braids. Come into the kitchen when you're ready." Pilar pats me on my butt and sends me toward my bedroom.

❖

I read the note twice because I'm having a hard time believing my eyes. There's a new oversized bear on my bed. This one's brown, and beside it there's a neatly wrapped box. The note is from Holly.

I'm really sorry about what happened. I hope we can still be friends. xo—Holly

I open the wrapped box and find a new Hello Kitty tea set. It's a bit redundant considering I only needed to replace one cup and I don't actually use it, but I'm intrigued if not slightly moved by the gesture. Most of all I'm a little confused.

I take a quick shower, then do my hair the way Pilar told me to. I join her in the kitchen and wait by the table on my knees, note in hand. Pilar's back is to me as she appears to be loading our dinner onto a tray.

"Do you like your gifts?" she asks.

"Permission to speak freely?" I say. Pilar turns her head to look at me. She sees the note.

"Permission granted."

"Did Bizzy write the note?"

"I don't think she did. The bear was Holly's part of the gift."

"There's another part?" Replacing what she defiled was not something I expected at all. Additional parts to her apology were not something I would consider.

"They've invited us to Disneyland tomorrow night."

"Oh." I can't hide my disappointment, but Pilar seems to ignore it.

"We'll eat in front of the TV tonight, baby. Go set yourself up on the floor."

I leave the kitchen and make myself comfortable on the floor in front of the couch. Pilar joins me a few moments later. She doesn't give me much time to think, but it's long enough for my stomach to churn.

"I'll tell you why I didn't bring this up earlier. We're going to Disneyland no matter what, but Bizzy asked that we give Holly another chance."

"Permission to speak freely again," I ask, trying my hardest to be polite.

"Sure, baby. Just watch your language."

"I'm not comfortable with Holly. Like, at all."

"I understand. If you're okay with her apologizing in person, Bizzy asked if they could come by tomorrow morning. If you feel like you can accept her apology then we can go together. If not, you and I go without them, and Bizzy can take Holly another time."

"I feel like I'm being put on the spot."

"I understand, *but* right now it's just me and you. If you don't want to speak to her at all, after we eat I'll call Bizzy and tell her no. There's no pressure."

"What do you want me to do?"

Pilar is quiet for a moment. I like to see this side of her. She's in control and she's thoughtful, but she's not above showing that even she needs to take multiple factors into consideration. I think now she's factoring in her relationship with Bizzy and her relationship with me.

"I want you to be happy, and I don't think you will be if you ignore this. I think you want some closure."

"Can I talk to her alone? She's a different person around you and Bizzy."

"I think that's an excellent idea, baby."

"If she's genuine, I can think about forgiving her. If not, you'll show them the door?" I say with a serious scowl. "Preferably with a boot up Holly's butt?"

Pilar laughs because I am being a little dramatic. "If Holly is at all out of line, come right to me and tell me. You can whisper it in my ear. Don't worry about being rude to Bizzy. I'll handle the rest from there."

"Okay. I'll talk to her tomorrow."

"That's very mature of you."

"Thank you. Now feed me, Mami," I say as I flop against her leg. "I'm famished."

She leans down and kisses my forehead. "Such a silly girl."

❖

The next morning Pilar means for me to sleep in, but I'm wired. I try to weasel my way into Pilar's shower to help calm my nerves, but that mission fails. I shower on my own, dress in an adorable pair of overall shorts and braid my hair, and then I wait for Holly. I sit on the couch fidgeting, eager for Pilar to finish getting ready.

The doorbell rings. I put on my game face, and then I take it down a notch. I know what Bizzy means to Pilar now, and I don't want to offend her. "Remember, just come get me if you need me," Pilar says as she walks through the living room.

"I will."

I stand when Pilar opens the door. Bizzy looks amazing again. No leather jacket this time because it's an easy eighty-five degrees outside, but her white T-shirt shows off her perfect arms. Her dark-blue jeans frame her thighs nicely. Holly's appearance is toned down. She's wearing jean shorts, a Minnie Mouse tank top, and a humbled, doe-eyed expression. She's already hoping I'll forgive her. We exchange hellos and then Holly steps forward.

"Mistress Pilar? Is it okay if I speak to Suzy?"

Pilar turns to me with a patient smile. I like that she puts the decision in my hands in front of our company, even though we already have a plan.

"Let's go to my room."

Holly follows me down the hall. I leave my door open just in case. I sit on my bed and pull Frank into my lap. I don't say a word. She lets out a deep breath and sits down at my table. She drops the facade, stretching, and shaking her head and hands. I'm ready for the worst of some serious bullshit. She lets out another breath.

"Suzy, listen."

"I'm listening."

"I am really sorry. Have you ever dealt with sub frenzy?"

I shake my head. I know what I like and what I've experienced, but I'm far from a walking BDSM dictionary.

"It's basically when a sub loses their fucking mind."

Okay, she got me there. I chuckle little. "I think I might know a little something about that." Especially after my own freak-out this week.

"Bizzy just let me run wild, and run wild I did. The district is cutting jobs like crazy. I was stressed when Bizzy told me to act on instinct. I let out the stress from every shitty parent-teacher conference, every smart-ass kid, every second of teaching to an unrealistic standardized test. When we came over here I was already out of control. Bizzy is the sexiest, most powerful top I've been with. I let that go to my head."

"What changed?"

"Her method is to let a sub react naturally, and then she corrects and trains. When we got home Bizzy asked me what really happened. I thought I had her wrapped so tight around my finger that I spit out the truth. And then she proceeded to spank the daylights out of me."

"Oh, wow."

"Yeah. You've seen her biceps. She wasn't joking around. Today is my first day off punishment."

"So you're apologizing to me because you don't want to be punished anymore?"

"Yes, and I'm apologizing because what I did was truly fucked up. I can't believe I kicked you." She looks up at the ceiling, shaking her head. "You did not deserve that and I totally understand if you don't forgive me, but I am sorry. Part of my punishment has been listening to a lot of Bizzy's lectures. She explained that I need to express this side of myself, but she refuses to let me disrespect Pilar or anyone in her care. We talked about the difference between being bratty and being a complete shithead. She said she wouldn't tolerate me being a jerk, and I saw that she was right."

"Took a little fear though, didn't it?"

"I think that's the only thing that would have worked."

"I was punished after you left for my little outburst," I reply.

"Punished how?" There's a glint of arousal in Holly's eye, and in this weird way it's what starts turning my opinion of her. She's a little sick, but so am I. She wants to share; she wants someone to talk to. So do I, but we have one more thing to clear up.

"You basically said you'd try to steal Pilar from me if things didn't work out with Bizzy. I really didn't appreciate that."

"I'll level with you. Pilar is hot. Extremely hot, but Bizzy is the right person for me, and even if we did break up, I think being with someone close to her would be a really bad idea." She lets out a little snort of laughter. "I'll probably move to a different state."

"I know a mistress in Phoenix."

"What?"

"Nothing. Thank you for the bear and the tea set. I would like it if we could get along, but you know, fool me once."

"I get it. I totally get it. I am in no way looking to piss Bizzy off like that again, and even though you might not believe me, when I see that I've made a mistake I rarely repeat it. I don't enjoy hurting people either, and once she set me straight, I saw that I'd hurt you. I am sorry." I think she's telling the truth, so I accept the olive branch.

"Pilar paddled my ass purple, and then when I had my own little sub frenzy meltdown, she made me sleep in a chastity belt, and then she spanked me again."

"Oh, that's brutal. Bizzy likes the paddle, too. My ass is still sore, and she pushed my crib out in the hallway. Do you know how awkward it is sleeping in a crib when it's in the middle of a hallway?"

Okay, so I laugh this time. "I can only imagine."

Holly nods toward my new bear. "I was serious about humping the bear. It feels amazing."

"I'll run it by Pilar. You ready to go to Disneyland?"

Holly springs to her feet with a smile. "Yep."

The drive to the theme park isn't too long. Bizzy drives. Holly and I sit in the back and talk about work. Well, Holly does. I'm half listening because I'm watching Bizzy and Pilar out of the corner of my eye. I'm intrigued by their relationship now that I know something of its roots.

Bizzy reaches over and touches Pilar's denim-covered knee. "You look great, kid," she says. The top buttons of Pilar's polo are open so I imagine Bizzy catches a glimpse of her cleavage as she glances away from traffic.

Holly taps my hand and startles me out of my staring. She waves me over to her side of the backseat.

"Don't worry. They're just friends."

"I know." I try not to sound defensive or naive.

"You want to hear my plan for the day?" she says. I glance quickly toward the front seat, and when I see that my Mami and her Daddy are still focused on each other, I nod.

She leans closer and whispers her little scheme in my ear. I'm nervous at first, but once I hear her out, I think Holly is onto something.

"What are you two whispering about back there?" Bizzy asks.

Holly shrugs and sweetly bats her eyelashes. "Nothing, Daddy. I swear."

"Mhmm. Suzy, don't let this one talk you into anymore trouble."

"I won't," I say. "I promise."

Pilar reaches back and squeezes my knee.

The park is packed. It's Saturday and schools are finally out. Pilar takes my hand and we follow Bizzy and Holly through the sea of people. When we finally hit a patch of pavement that isn't filled with kids and stressed parents, we decide to get in line for our first ride. It's a long line.

Bizzy is well distracted by Holly, and by the look on Holly's face it seems like Holly has put her plan into action. She catches my eye and winks.

There are kids around, but I don't see much wrong with draping my arms over Pilar's shoulders. Her eyebrow goes up as she gazes down at me.

I rise up on my tiptoes and whisper in her ear.

"What would you do to me if all these people weren't around?"

I look her in the eye, just to see if she's willing to play along. She is.

"Well, my Suzy. If we were home it would be time for your nap."

I lean back, scowling at her. "That's not what I meant."

She spins me around so we can move forward a little in the line. Pilar nips my ear with her teeth.

"Why don't you tell me what you'd want me to do?" she whispers.

To our left, three teenagers are very interested in Pilar's hands on my stomach. I wait until we move a little more before I turn around again.

"I want you to spank me and I want to play with your nipples."

She doesn't say a word. Her silence tells me she's turned on. She spins me around again and marches me toward the first ride. I know I've got her. The rest of the afternoon and evening goes this way. For Holly and Bizzy, too. Everywhere we stop they have some quiet exchange. Bizzy has Pilar's same eerie control, but a few times I catch her looking at Holly like she'd risk getting booted from the park just to bend Holly over to put her money where her mouth is.

Pilar lets me rattle off fantasies as we move around the park. At first it's for my own enjoyment, but as a series of unfortunate events start to plague Pilar, I keep dropping hints to cheer her up.

First, a little girl dressed as Princess Belle comes sprinting toward us, ice cream in hand. Pilar almost dodges the kid, but only enough to end up with a smashed vanilla cone pressed into her thigh. The girl's mother is too busy cleaning up the girl to even apologize to Pilar.

We stop for dinner and Pilar orders a chicken dish that tastes a little south of fresh. She tries to eat half of it before Bizzy and I both encourage her to send it back.

By the time we make it to the fireworks, I can tell Pilar is ready to go home. Apparently the universe decides it's tortured Pilar enough and moves on to me. Always the friendly lady, as we wait I find myself having some mindless chatter with a toddler on the shoulder of a man in front of us. We're discussing the finer points of nonsense when the kid sneezes on me. More accurately, in my mouth.

My shriek of disgust is part laugh, part display of horror. Thank God the boy's mother whips out a pack of wipes and gives me enough to scrub down my whole body. Though I wish I hadn't heard her say, "Jim, I told you we should have stayed home. He's been sneezing all day." She hands me a miniature bottle of water anyway, to help me wash out my mouth. Still, the damage is done.

Holly is trying not to laugh beside us, but I don't blame her. Pilar and I are a mess.

The fireworks are an amazing spectacle, almost worth the trek back to the parking lot. Holly is suctioned to Bizzy by the time we make it to the car. Pilar rides in the back with me. I follow Holly's cue once more and nuzzle my head into Pilar's lap as soon as I get into my seat belt. Her thigh still smells like vanilla.

When I wake up, we're pulling up Pilar's street. We say a quiet good-bye to Bizzy because Holly is dead asleep.

Inside, Pilar tells me to get ready for bed. We both shower in our own bathrooms. I brush my teeth like four times. When I find Pilar in her bedroom, she doesn't look so hot. She's sitting on the edge of her bed, still wrapped in her towel.

"Mami, are you okay?" I ask from the doorway.

She looks a little pale as she glances over at me.

"Yes, baby. I'm fine. You're going to sleep with me tonight."

There's no way I'm arguing with that invitation, so I hop onto the bed and wait for Pilar to shut down the house. When she joins me under the covers, I spoon her back because she seems like she needs it. She doesn't argue. She also doesn't say anything about my hand resting firmly on her boob. I go to sleep happy.

CHAPTER EIGHT

I wake up confused. Pilar's not in bed with me. I hear her in her bathroom, puking her guts out. I jump out of bed and run to check on her. She's a sweaty mess, bent over the toilet. I brush her hair off her face as more comes back up.

"It was that chicken, wasn't it?"

"Yeah," Pilar says on a short breath. "Baby, go into the kitchen and get the bucket from under the sink. I think this might be coming out of both ends soon."

"Oh, shit. I mean. Okay. Sorry. Bucket. Got it."

I find a big yellow bucket right where she said it would be. I run it back to Pilar, who has made her way to leaning against the sink. I see it on her face; there's about fifteen seconds before her composure slips.

"Where do you want this?" I ask.

She holds out her hand and takes the bucket from me.

"Thank you, baby. Now get out. You don't need to see this."

I leave her alone, closing the door behind me, and then I call home.

My dad answers. I ask him if he has any home remedies for food poisoning. He suggests a dispensary down in Venice. I tell him I'm not asking Pilar to smoke weed. He says he'll ask my mother and call me back.

When I get off the phone, I know Pilar needs her privacy, but I can't sit still. I go throw on a T-shirt, then pace around the living room. Finally, my mother calls me back. In her heavily accented Patois, she asks me who Pilar is, then gives me the third degree as to why I didn't tell her I have a new girlfriend. Eventually, she tells me just to wait it out, that I should crush some ice to help Pilar rehydrate. She says she'll text me a recipe for some soup that'll help when she's keeping food down again. She tells me to take her to the hospital if things get worse.

I know I sound helpless, but I've never been sick like this before and it's hard to see Pilar so done in. I'm a little scared. I thank my mother and then I wait.

Pilar is in the bathroom for a long time. When she finally comes out, she looks terrible. I encourage her into bed even though she refuses my physical assistance. When I go back into the bathroom to clean up, I find that she's already washed out the bucket.

I join her back in bed, keeping my distance because she isn't in the mood to be touched. Twenty minutes later, she's sprinting back to the bathroom.

It's a long day. I get her to drink some water and suck on some ice. I'm caught unawares when Joanna pops up at the door and asks if I want to come play. I feel bad for saying no, but I'm in Suzanne mode. Suzy's not home right now.

Liam comes through again and drops off some soup, clear soda, crackers, and miscellaneous medicine. My mother's recipe is complicated as hell, and once I read the ingredients, I remember the smell from my youth and I'm sure the aroma will make Pilar puke all over again.

By the time eleven p.m. rolls around, though she hasn't gotten worse, it's clear she isn't getting much better. I already make plans to work from Pilar's house the next day.

By the next afternoon, she's starting to improve. She keeps down a whole bowl of soup and only finds herself in the bathroom once in the course of some hours. She insists on changing her own sheets and tells me to shower and eat something myself. I tell her that I have no appetite, and that lack of appetite holds strong right through the following morning, when Pilar seems back to one-hundred percent and *I* have a raging fever.

In some very superficial way, I think I want to die. I've never felt so shitty in my entire life. My whole body hurts, and I'm developing a nice coating of sweat. I wrack my brain thinking of how this could have happened to me. I don't think food poisoning is contagious. But during one of my rambling fits amidst a quest to find a comfortable position on my side, Pilar reminds me that I had a kid sneeze in my mouth. I realize then that I'm probably going to die from the plague that little brat has given me.

I hold up my head long enough to make a feverish call into work. Valerie feels bad for me, or at least she sounds that way. She offers to handle 21 And Up for me until I'm back on my feet. I thank her even though I'm kicking myself. Catching up with that shit is going to be a mess.

I hear Pilar tell me to stop swearing before I slip into a fitful sleep.

I'm out of the office for the rest of the week.

On Thursday, the cabin fever sets in. Pilar moves me to the couch because I can't stand another minute of looking at just the four walls of her bedroom. She's taking great care of me, and I will freely admit that I make a much whinier patient than she did. I want to get out and walk around. I want a burger, but it's obvious, even to me, that I'm still sick.

Friday afternoon, I snap. I'm still feeling crappy, but my fever has lifted. I've been at Pilar's for over a week, and it's been almost a week since we've had sex. I need her to touch me before I go completely insane. I excuse myself to the bathroom, and when I come back, I'm in my favorite pair of lace-trimmed panties and nothing else. I crawl across the floor, regretting it immediately, but I won't let the light-headed feeling stop me from getting to Pilar's lap.

She puts down her knitting and looks at me as I make my way to her with a false sense of confidence. She lets me get close enough to raise myself up with my forearms on her thighs. She smiles down at me. "Would you like to tell me what you're doing?"

"Please. I'll die if you don't touch me. Please." I flop my head down on her lap. Maybe she'll have some sort of mercy on me. She rubs my forehead, then cups my cheek.

"You're still a little warm and congested."

"I know, but I'm so horny. And I've heard that orgasms help boost your immune system. Please."

Pilar is quiet for a moment before she stands up. "I'll be right back. Sit down. I know you're light-headed even though you're pretending you're not." I keep my excitement under control as she slips out of the room. When she comes back, she has her vibrator. I move so she can take her seat back in her big chair. She pulls me into her lap with my back to her chest.

I press my luck because I'm feeling a little bit more like myself and a little bit desperate. I turn a little toward her.

"Can I play with your nipples?"

"No," she says. "Turn around and no pouting or this is not happening." I sigh and settle back into place.

She starts with her fingers. I was really horny in my head, but I'm not wet until she touches me. She slides her hand into my underwear and spreads my lips over my clit. She bites my neck.

"When you're feeling better I'm going to shave you down here. I want to see what you look like bare."

I shiver in her arms as I nod in agreement. My mind flashes to her licking my pussy. I can't help but squirm. She cups my breast, massaging gently. I squirm some more, trying to get her fingers a little farther down. She licks my cheek.

"Stop moving or I won't let you come." I hold still and feel her cruel huff of breath against my skin. "That's what I thought."

I don't know what I'm thinking when I propose these things. I don't know what's going through my head when I think she'll give me exactly what I want, right when I want it. Then again, she seems to know me so much better now. She knows coming isn't all I want. She knows I want her to torture and tease me. Getting off is merely the end of our transaction. I want everything that she's selling and I'll pay with my acquiescence. I do my best to relax. Pilar can feel it across my skin. She holds me tighter and slides her fingers lower. She kisses my jaw, then drags her tongue over my skin, down to my shoulder.

"Mmm, I've missed touching you, baby," she says.

"I've missed having your hands on me."

She slides two fingers inside of my pussy. My hips lift on their own. She pinches me lightly. I whimper, but I do my best to hold still. She kisses my shoulder again and starts to fuck me harder.

Once I'm close, she pulls her hand away and reaches for the vibrator. It's the high-powered plug-in. My own of the same style is a go-to when I'm in a hurry. Knowing Pilar, she'll use it as a torture device. I'm right. She shoves my underwear down my thighs, then puts the rapidly vibrating head right on my clit. I arch in her arms, coming hard. Her arm snakes around my waist and holds me to her chest. I come again and again, and I realize she's not going to stop until she's ready. And she's not ready until long after I'm pleading and squirming. She's not ready until she's subdued me with two fingers in my mouth. She's not ready until I'm limp in her lap with my come coating my thighs and her pants. She's not ready until I have nothing left to give. I'm breathing easier once she turns the vibrator off, though I can barely lift my head. She puts the cruel toy to the side and then she pinches my nipples.

"You know what, baby?" she whispers in my ear. "I think it's time for your nap."

Even though I'm feeling better, Pilar makes me take it easy for the rest of the weekend. Sunday she shaves me as I sit on the edge of her tub. I'm completely turned on by the time she's done, but she puts me to bed aching for her touch. In the morning she wakes me for a full, balanced breakfast to help me face the day. If had a choice, the first full week I stay over at her house wouldn't involve either of us becoming violently ill or having fever dreams about being trapped in an amusement park, but if I had to get sick, I'm glad Pilar was willing to take care of me.

As I pack up to leave, a feeling of dread creeps up on me. I need to get back to work. I'd like to step outside, but I'll miss Pilar the moment I drive away from her house. I know it.

She walks me to my car. Before I can climb in she pulls me into her arms. "Thank you for taking care of me," she says.

"Are you kidding? You were paid vacation compared to my fever-ridden behind."

"I don't know about that, baby. They're releasing my nephew from the hospital this weekend and my sister's throwing him a party. I want you to come with me."

"Really?"

"Yes. I think we should invite Liam and his boyfriend, too."

"Really?"

Pilar laughs. "Yes, baby. What do you say?"

"I'd love to come and I know Liam will, too. There will be food, right?"

"Tons of food."

"Gary wouldn't miss it then. Thank you."

"Thank you, baby."

"I think this week is going to kick my butt, but I'll text you when I can."

"I understand. Just make sure you get some rest. I don't want that flu to sneak back up on you." She kisses me good-bye.

On the way to work, I think about the coming weekend and how I'm not looking forward to the time between now and then.

I'm at my desk not three minutes and my phone starts to ring. I have to push Pilar to the back of my mind.

I have so much catching up to do. Part of that happens during a three-hour status meeting with 21 And Up. Valerie has really covered my ass, but I still have to get up to speed with what I've missed and mentally prepare myself for the new round of bullshit the client will throw my way.

I send my panty pic off to Pilar late in the afternoon. She texts me back, but I'm on a call and don't get to check it for another hour. I don't leave the office until seven thirty. Part of me almost expects Pilar to invite me back over, but I remember what she said about the wanting and the needing, and then I remember that I haven't emptied my mailbox in over a week. I stop and pick up a fairly nutritious dinner from the store and liberate the mountain of grocery fliers from my mailbox. By the time my food is ready, I'm exhausted. I barely finish eating before I text Pilar good night and collapse into bed with Frank. I wake in the morning to two texts from Pilar and one picture of her pussy. It's a perfect way to start the day.

Back at work I'm feeling more myself. Aside from a long call with Clear Vision regarding a six-month-old invoice their accounting department just now decided to rectify, I think I'm back on top of 21 And Up. Liam's been up to his ass in work, too, but we plan to sneak out for lunch. Before I can go wrangle him, Valerie calls me into her office. She's pacing around, at the tail end of a phone call, so I wait just inside her doorway. When she hangs up she leans over her desk and looks at something on her laptop. "We really missed you last week. How's it going today?" she asks. I can see down her shirt. Okay, I look. I can't help that I like boobs.

"Fine. This paper-doll page is really ambitious, but everything Felicia showed me this morning seemed great," I reply. She looks up just as I stop trying to decipher the color of her bra in its shadow. She smiles at me just 'cause she does that sort of thing.

"I think the whole thing is ridiculous," she says as she walks around her desk.

"What do you mean?" I ask.

Valerie leans against the front of her desk and crosses her legs. "I think they're missing their market. Young girls like to play dress-up."

"Hey." I do my best to sound offended. "I like to play dress-up."

"Ah, but there's a difference between a woman with style and that woman spending hours on a retail site, trying clothing on a model that looks nothing like her. This is catered more toward young girls. Their market wants the clothes, and they want to get on with their day or get on with their night."

"You have a point, but far be it from me to tell our client this feature is off the mark." Valerie is right. The further we go into the project the more I see that the paper-doll feature will be more of a pain in the ass to legit shoppers than a feature that will draw new customers. Pages like this are popping up all over the Internet. Get the customer to interact, but 21 And Up is failing to see some things. A retail site has basic rules, and complicating those rules often does more harm than good. Luckily, the success or failure of the actual application of the feature is on 21 And Up.

"The redesign is gorgeous, even if the components don't all work together to their desired effect. Either way, I've already talked to Simon about the QA. We'll do it together."

Valerie's expression flashes with a pleasant shock. "I like to hear that, Suzanne. You're really taking this account by the balls."

I smile at her praise. "Yes, ma'am. That's the only way to do it."

Valerie grins back. "That's a good girl."

She says the words and it's like something instantly grips my stomach. It's a coincidence. My boss has no idea that a simple few words are utterances I associate only with pleasure. She has no idea what the slightest verbal cues do to me.

My skin is heating as I blush, and I realize a moment too late that *I've* reacted to those words. I cough and straighten my posture. It's nothing that anyone would catch. My sudden arousal and residual embarrassment are my own fault, but for some reason Valerie notices. She considers me strangely for a moment, her eyes narrowing just the slightest bit, but I notice. I clear my throat again and try to relax my hands.

"Suzanne, are you happy here?" she asks. Her tone is slightly off. It's personal, but I don't know exactly how to read it.

I answer her truthfully.

"I love it here."

"Good." She seems to relax and folds her arms across her chest.

"I could do without a few of the client-related headaches, but yes. Very happy here."

"Good. I'm very glad to hear that." She walks toward me and I know she's showing me out. We meet near the door. "I think next week we'll start interviewing to replace Josh."

"Sounds good," I say. And then I freeze. Her hand is on the back of my neck. It's a light touch, practiced almost. I quickly remind myself that she doesn't know what she's doing. She doesn't know what I am. She has no idea. That doesn't stop the goose bumps from spreading out over my skin. I smile at her, trying not to seem nervous.

"I'll let you get back to it," she says. She watches me carefully. I try not to squeak. "Okay."

I do my best to walk back to my desk at a normal pace. Liam is waiting for me. I don't even care that he's going through the pictures on my phone.

"You ready?" he asks.

Without a word, I grab his hand and drag him out the door.

"Okay. Tell me what's going on." I ignore Liam and order my sandwich. He huffs, but he knows me and my need to build suspense from time to time.

We sit and he stares at me while I mess with my over-oiled greens. "You want to come to Long Beach with me this weekend?" I ask.

"Dear God, no. I don't do the 405. You know this."

"Pilar's family is having a party for her nephew. She invited you and Gary."

"We're there. I have to meet this woman."

"What about the 405?"

"I'll make Gary drive."

I shake my head at Liam. "You are so mean to him. I hope he meets a sexy Mexican guy at this thing and dumps your ass."

"Shit, I hope *I* meet a sexy Mexican guy at this thing. You know I love him. Shut up. Is that what's bothering you?"

"Oh, no." I shiver violently. "I think Valerie came on to me."

"What! What did she say?"

"Well, she didn't come on to me verbally." I stop and consider how I want to say this. "You know when you're talking to someone and then you just become super aware of each other. Like you're actually looking at each other?"

"Oh, yeah. That's why I loved fucking with Josh. He used to look at my mouth all the time. So she just eye-fucked you?"

"Not exactly. It was more something she said and how I reacted and then how she reacted."

"What did she say?"

I squeeze my eyes closed, embarrassed all over again. "She said I was a good girl."

"And that's what made you sick? Made you upset?"

"Not exactly."

"It gave you a lady boner, didn't it?"

I cover my face with my napkin. "Yes."

"I fucking love how kinky you are. God, you and your foxy Mami must have the best time."

"Well, yeah. We do, but…I don't know. I feel like Valerie knew it turned me on."

"Are you truly skeeved out?" he asks.

"No. It was just weird."

"Hey, you're cute and you're working your ass off. You can't be all that surprised if she at least checks you out from time to time. And she's only human. Sometimes the breeders can't help but drool a little."

"She is a breeder, huh," I reply with my own dismissive chuckle. I hate that term, but Liam does remind me that we'd come to the conclusion a while ago that Valerie was pretty straight. Last I heard she was happily married to a sheepish accountant.

"I wouldn't worry about it unless she really crosses a line. And then you sue her fucking ass." Liam slams his fist on the table and almost knocks over my water.

"All right," I say. "Let's calm down."

"Sorry."

"So this weekend, you'll come?"

"I said I'm there. I think someone needs to talk to your Mami about this Valerie situation."

"I'll kill you." I consider throwing my water on Liam when he starts cackling.

❖

Over the next day and a half things with Valerie are completely normal. But in thinking of her that way, my time apart from Pilar becomes harder to deal with. She knows how I feel, and now it's just a matter of being patient and hoping that she rewards that patience when I can see her again.

When I get off work on Wednesday, Pilar tells me to call her once I'm ready for bed. By nine I'm ready to climb between the sheets for some crap TV and some z's. I call Pilar as soon as Frank and I are settled. She answers right away. She lets me whine for a few minutes about missing her. She tells me to hold off on touching myself. She wants her fingers to be the next to feel me wet. Of course that makes me hot as hell. We eventually get off the phone, and I'm left wondering what she'll have in store for me this weekend.

I ask Frank. He has no idea. I start to accuse him of a surprising lack of investigative skills when my doorbell rings.

I look at Frank. No one "stops by" my place. It's either our security guard doing a random walk-around, a lost pizza delivery guy, or someone come to murder me. I tiptoe to the front door and check the peephole, ready to grab a knife if the latter is true.

What I see almost kills me. I open the door for Pilar. She's standing in the hallway wearing a knee-length trench coat, red stilettos, and, I'm praying, nothing else. She has a large black purse over her shoulder.

I grip the doorframe to support myself. "You're so unfair."

Her eyebrow goes up. "Would you like to try that again?"

I stand up straight with my hands behind my back. "Mami, would you like to come in?"

"Yes, baby. I would."

I move aside so she can glide inside. And glide she does. I have no idea what she has in mind, but I hope she keeps the heels on. I lock the door behind us and wait for her instructions.

She looks at my couch for a moment before she turns back to me. "Let's go to your bedroom."

I lead her to my room. She tells me to strip. Once I'm naked she gets me on my knees on the edge of the bed. My head's pushed down into the covers and my butt lifted into the air. I peek back just for a moment. She has the pink cuffs out. Two sets. Once each wrist is wrapped in the padded leather, she wraps each ankle in the other cuff. Then I'm bound hand to foot. I'm breathing hard from the position and the anticipation. Pilar grabs my ass cheek.

"Yellow if you're uncomfortable, baby. Red if you want me to stop."

I exhale and shift to rub a few wisps of hair out of my face with my pillow. "Yes, Mami."

"Good girl," she says, and this time I really shiver. The next thing I feel is her spreading my ass. She kisses each cheek. Licks and bites it. She tells me how pretty I look in this position. I can only moan. I feel her fingers on me next, cool with lube as she runs a slippery glob up and down my crack. It's been a long time since I've done any ass play. I'm scared. I'm shaking a little, but I know she won't hurt me.

The tip of something hard and smooth probes my ass. I exhale another deep breath and try to relax. She slips it in farther. There's only a pinch of discomfort as she slips past my tightest spot, but I soak the pain in and lift my ass higher in the air. I say her name. I ask her to fuck me. She doesn't correct my language this time.

She slides the dildo in and out, rubbing my ass as I start to pump my hips to match her slow rhythm. My pussy is achingly empty, desperate for Pilar's fingers or her mouth or her cock. I beg so much. "Mami, touch my pussy. Please, touch my cunt."

She hushes me with a soft sound and bites my ass again. It feels so good, her teeth on my skin, but I always want more.

She slips the toy out and, a moment later, something a little wider goes in. When it hits its limit I realize it's a plug.

"We're just going to roll you over, baby."

She grips my waist and my shoulder, and with one gentle push she rocks me onto my back. I look up at her in the shifting light from my TV. She unties the belt on her coat. She is naked except for the cock between her legs. I cry out, lifting my hips off the bed, but my shifting doesn't get me any closer to what I want. It only makes things worse because my pathetic thrusting rocks the plug inside me.

She leans down and all I can see is the top of her head as she licks me. I fight against the restraints, but it's useless. They may be pink, but they're well-stitched leather attached to real steel. I'm not touching anything but my sheets.

Her mouth is enough to make me come. I'm writhing and making little noises. I tell her I'm close. She stops. Then she slams her cock into me. It would take all of my strength to hold back this orgasm, and a kind of determination I just don't have at the moment. Thank God, Pilar doesn't ask for it. I come and come, and come again as she pinches my clit. After some time, some deliciously torturous time, she grips my hip with her other hand and shudders against me. She curses before her teeth snag at her bottom lip. Her body trembles again.

Once she's regained her composure, she slips her cock from my pussy, then tosses it in her bag. She gently pulls out the plug and it disappears, too. When I'm free of her restraints, I see that her coat is closed again, and, though there's a little sweat on her forehead, not a hair is out of place.

She settles me back under my covers, leans down, and brushes my cheek.

"Can't you stay?" I ask.

"No, baby. It's time for you to go to sleep."

"Okay. Thank you for coming to see me."

"My pleasure," she says with a wink.

I watch her hips as she slips out of my room. For the fantasy I wait a few minutes after she's gone before I get up and lock the door.

Chapter Nine

It's another Friday and I'm at Pilar's front door. I know our Saturday will be full and our Sunday restful so I want to make the most of tonight. She opens the door. I catch her off guard and throw my arms around her shoulders. She's stunned momentarily, but she catches me and lets me kiss her full on her lips. I'm so happy to see her. It's been a long week at work. I've missed her, especially in the few moments when Valerie's odd behavior enters my mind. Just as quickly though, those thoughts are eclipsed by the images of Pilar, by the sound of her voice when she's calling me her silly Suzy girl. I kiss her with all of this energy that's been building up since we last saw each other. And she kisses me back.

Soon I wiggle out of her arms and take a step back. "Close your eyes and count to one hundred. And fifty."

"Baby," she warns me.

"Please."

She sighs. "I'll count to one hundred."

"Thank you." I kiss her on the cheek. "It'll be fun. I swear."

She closes her eyes. "One!"

I hobble out of my heels and drop one on the floor. Making a break for the hallway, I leave another one just around the corner. My shirt I leave in the kitchen. I'm headed for her bathroom, but in throwing off her trail I head to drop my bra in her sewing room. There I'm caught off guard. In the dark is a nearly completed dress hanging on her sewing mannequin. I flick the switch against the wall to get a better look. The skirt is fluffed out in a perfect circle, made of a hot-pink tulle. Above the tutu-like lower half is a wide black sash, centered in the middle with a big bow. The top of the dress is white, but I don't know what kind of fabric it is exactly. The petal collar is incomplete. What's there, though, is adorable.

Pilar's up to eighty-eight, but I'm too focused on what's in front of me. I take a step closer and touch the edge of the skirt and then the bow. I want this dress.

Pilar yells, "One hundred! I'm coming to find you."

"I'm in here," I shout back.

A few moments later I feel her behind me. Pilar's fingers cup my shoulders. She kisses my cheek. "You're terrible at hiding," she says.

I think of the dress Holly was wearing, and even though it wasn't made for her, I think of how jealous I was of the girls who were given a chance to don one of Pilar's unique creations. The dress Holly wore was cute, but this dress is *me*. "Is this for me?" I ask. I don't even bother to mask the hope in my voice. I'll pitch myself in a sobbing heap in the backyard if it's not.

"It *is* for you."

I turn to Pilar. "How long have you been working on it?"

She winks at me. "That's between me and the mannequin."

"I really love it."

"You can wear it in a few weeks."

"Are we going somewhere in particular?"

"We are. There's a little party I'll be taking you to. But we'll talk more about that later." She looks down at my skirt and my bare feet. "You're almost ready for dinner. How about we get you all the way there."

"Wait, we were playing a game. I was going to hide in your bathroom and we were going to have sex on your sink. And I still think we should."

"And you stopped in here to be nosy, so now you're going to strip off the rest of your clothes and march that cute butt into the kitchen because, my little Suzy girl, dinner is ready."

"Can we have sex in the bathroom after dinner?"

"I'll think about it."

I glare at her.

She glares back. It only takes a moment, but I lose our staring contest.

"I'll get ready for dinner, but..." I say, scowling with a little more intensity. She needs to know just how angry I am. I unzip my skirt and let it fall to the floor. I'm wearing a pair of white panties with a black cartoon kitten on my butt. "I'm going to remember this. This will be the night that you ruined a perfectly good game of 'Chase Suzy until you find her in your bathroom and then have sex with her on your sink.' Big mistake, lady. Real big mistake."

"I'm sorry you feel that way. I was hoping you'd remember this as the night that your Mami picked up your favorite ice cream and fucked you senseless on the couch."

I whip out my most apologetic shrug. "We can still do that."

"No. Dinner then bed." She points toward the kitchen. "March."

I start walking, but I still look over my shoulder. She's following me. "But I love you. Please reconsider."

"I can't believe you just called me 'lady.'" She swats me on my butt. I yelp and take off running, but she catches me in the kitchen and takes me over her knee in her favorite chair. Oh, does Pilar ever spank me, but I'd be lying if I say I don't like it. Each strike lacks the weight of a true punishment. She's reminding me who's boss, who's in control. She's letting me know how much she loves me. When she swings me back upright, I'm breathing heavily and my hair is all over the place. My pussy is throbbing from all of the squirming I did as she held me down. I shove my hair off my face. I'm ready to sass talk some more because I like this new game we're playing.

When our gazes meet she stares back at me with equal fervor. I think she's about to lecture me on back-talking. Instead she takes my chin in her hand and kisses me. Her other fingers slide into my underwear, and the moment I start to open my legs she rubs my clit. I try to shuffle to straddle her lap, but she holds me in place with a firm hold on my hair. By the time I'm whimpering in her arms, ready to offer my forfeit, our dinner is cold. Neither of us cares, though. We kiss some more as the microwave twirls. She swats my butt one more time before we eat. I'm pretty sure I asked for it.

❖

Though we have an early start to the next day, our breakfast is light. Pilar tells me if her family has their way, I'll be eating all day. I have no issue with this plan. I've texted Liam. He has the address of the park we're headed to and instructions to swing down whenever they get their day started. We hop in Pilar's car and hit the grocery store for an ungodly amount of beer and this gross-looking tomato juice. I don't question either. Instead I help her load the car and we're on way west to hop on the 405 South.

I'm nervous. I can't seem to help it. Pilar lets me wear my own clothes. I know I look cute as all hell, but I keep fidgeting with the hem of my cutoffs. One of my Jordans is tucked up under me on the seat and it won't stop shaking.

"You look very cute today, baby." I look up to see Pilar smiling across the seat at me. Self-consciously I adjust the Lakers T-shirt hanging off my shoulder. My hair is braided up into a bun. It's too hot to wear it down. Pilar is wearing this flowing purple maxidress. I just want to climb under her skirt the next time we're alone.

"You don't think I should have covered up more?" I ask.

She reaches over and touches my cheek. "What did I just say?"

I look down again. It's been so long since I've worn my own stuff on the weekends. Short shorts, high-tops, and crop tops are sort of my thing, one of the ways I'm able to throw off the shackles of corporate oppression. Liam tends to go for more eye makeup. For a moment Valerie crosses my mind and I think maybe she wouldn't mind the short shorts at all. I shiver even though I don't mean to. Pilar takes my hand.

"You okay?" she asks.

I squeeze her hand back. "Yeah, I'm fine. Just anxious."

"There's no need to be anxious. Just be yourself." I nod, but my foot won't stop shaking.

She looks forward and I gaze out the window. I reflect on the flow of traffic for a few good seconds, and then for some reason Valerie pops back into my head. My stomach turns over again. I close my eyes and try to think of something else. Pilar must sense that I'm really on edge because her hand moves to my bare thigh. I feel like I'm keeping something from her, but I don't really know how to raise the subject. And even if I do, what would I say? That my boss just happened to say something that turned me on, and I think my boss noticed just how turned on I was? Yeah, that would go over like a loaded bag of shit and bricks.

I slide my fingers over hers. "When did you come out to your parents?"

"I didn't. My mom just knew. She came to me crying after Mass one day and asked me. I didn't have a hold on my feelings yet, but I told her the truth."

"How old were you?"

"Seventeen."

I think of how I told my own mom and how she reacted. She screamed a lot even though she has a ton of gay friends. I was twenty. She came around after my dad and my brother talked to her, but those were some tense weeks at our house. It was a long summer. "How long did it take her to accept it?"

"Not long. She was just really confused, but she didn't want to drive me away. I'm her youngest and I think I'm her favorite."

I laugh. "Oh my God. Your poor brother and sister."

"All parents play favorites no matter what they say. I think my sister resented me for a little while because of it. I got a lot of our mom's attention."

"I get it. I'm a total daddy's girl and Thomas is a total mama's boy. Split, nice and even. Do you have a favorite out of these eight hundred and four nieces and nephews?" I'm teasing her.

"Yes. My niece Erica. I'm not sure if she's coming today, though. She spends a lot of time with her girlfriend."

"She's gay, too?"

"Yeah, and if you ask my sister-in-law, she'll tell you it's all my fault."

"Oh. It's one of those situations? She thinks your gay rubbed off?"

"Yes, she does. Just ignore her, though. She has something to say to everyone about everything," she says.

"Anyone else I should look out for?"

"No. Everyone will love you. Just be your adorable, lovable self. If you can manage it." She teases me back.

I stick my finger in her face. "Listen, lady—" She bites the tip. "Hey!" She has my hand in hers before I can pull away. She kisses my palm. She's already forgiven me.

"I know, baby. You're loveable all the time."

"I know I am!"

She laughs and kisses my palm again.

As we continue down the highway, Pilar gives me a clearer picture of what to expect from her family, though by the end of the day it's clear that nothing she said could have prepared me for the real thing. By the time we've arrived at the park and my every thought is focused on trying to remember the names of all of her nieces and nephews, her brother and sister, her parents and her cousins, I'm nervous again. We find a space and already I see smoke coming off grills set up on the other side of a baseball diamond where a rec game is in full swing.

Pilar and I meet around the back of the car, and I wait for her to pop the trunk and start loading my arms with beers. Instead she pulls me into her arms. I go willingly, shivering a little as she wraps her hand around the back of my neck.

"Are you going to be a good girl today?" she whispers against my temple.

I make this desperate noise and lean against her chest. "Why do you do that?" I look up into her deep-brown eyes and swallow as that smile touches the corner of her lips.

"Because I can." She pulls me closer and kisses me. I know she won't kiss me like this for the rest of the day, not in front of her family. This kiss is a reminder and a promise. No matter what happens before we return to her house, I belong to her and she wants me to remember. Only she can make me this hot, this weak. When she pulls away, I take a deep breath and lick my lips before I open my eyes.

"I promise. I'll be a very good girl today."

She takes me lightly by the jaw. "And stop calling me 'lady.'"
I try not to giggle. She's not really angry.
"I'll think about it, Mami." She kisses me one more time before
she lets me go. I watch her as she walks around to my side of the car
and grabs her knitting bag out of the backseat.
She holds out her hand for me.
"Let's go."
"What about the beer?"
"That's what nephews are for. Come on."

It's after midnight when we get back to Pilar's house. I'm
exhausted, but pleasantly intoxicated with the way the day went.
There is definitely something to be said about good food and good
company. I love Pilar's family, all but her asshole sister-in-law.
They all welcomed me with ease, made me feel like I belong with
them and with Pilar. I'm her girlfriend to them, of course. Not her
little girl, but they recognize that we're crazy about each other. Her
niece, Erica, is a personal favorite of mine. She's so pumped to have
another lesbian couple in attendance. And for her part in our perfect
day, Pilar is amazing with Liam and Gary. She lets Liam ask her all
sorts of questions about her life as a Domme. Though she barely
answers them, she playfully steers the conversation back to their
relationship and encourages Gary to get Liam up in some rope and
a gag as soon as possible. They both see the appeal in the idea, Gary
more for the gag.
As we walk through the front door, it occurs to me why the day
meant so much. I can't imagine Laurel treating me this way, opening
up her life to me like this. I think she had a sister somewhere. The
topic of her parents, like the rest of her life, was practically off-
limits. I didn't see how much that had hurt us, how I needed more
than her affection. I needed a complete sense of belonging in her
life. But little by little, Pilar gives me that. She gives me everything.
Even a slow dance by the makeshift DJ booth and a devastatingly
deep kiss toward the end of the night. She makes me *feel* loved.

Pilar stays just a few steps behind me as she orders me to her bedroom, then into her bathroom. She leans against the sink. I stand near the tub.

"Strip," she says, just before I almost drop to my knees. I'm not sure what kind of show she wants, but my best guess is that she just wants me naked. I leave my clothes in a neat pile next to the toilet, on top of my sneakers. She steps closer and reaches around me. The shower comes on, but I'm looking at the smooth skin on her shoulders. It's just a little darker than it was this morning.

The water heats up quickly. I don't move, though. Not until she tells me to. She's not looking in my eyes when she trails her finger across my belly. I swallow and try not to shake. Her gaze is still on my skin when she speaks.

"What was your favorite part of the day?"

"Watching you," I say.

"Watching me do what, baby?"

"Do anything. I liked watching you talk to your sister. I liked seeing you bond with your nieces. I love watching you knit."

"Do you?"

"Yes. Did you have a favorite part of the day?"

"I did, baby." Finally she looks me in the eye. "Get in the shower. Wash yourself."

The water is perfectly hot. I use her rose-scented scrub, and now I take my time washing my breasts, my ass, and between my legs. I turn so she can see. As I'm rinsing my face I'm startled by Pilar's fingers on my back. She's in the shower with me, suddenly naked. I can feel her hot skin against the back of my legs. I turn even though she didn't tell me to. She admires my breasts.

"Hands behind your back and leave them there or I'll spank your butt."

"Yes, Mami." I do as she asks and lock my fingers behind me. She roughly grips my breast. She pinches my nipple and then she slaps it. The sensation is jarring. A sting of pain, met by a sudden cooling and another rush of heat as the water runs over my shoulder. I close my eyes and suck my breath between my teeth. She smacks one breast several times with the same aggressive strokes. My hips rock forward. I moan.

She switches to the other breast. When she stops I can barely breathe. My chest is stinging, hot, but I want more. She turns off the water and motions for me to step out of the tub. She's behind me again, a hand on my wrists, holding them together, and a hand on my throat. Her grip is just tight enough to control, never to hurt. As she guides me into her bedroom her tongue traces my earlobe. "I like watching you, too."

When I'm settled on Pilar's bed, I'm cuffed facedown to her headboard. My skin is still wet, though it's quickly drying between the air and Pilar's bedspread. She steps away from the bed, and when she comes back I feel her hands, cool on my ass. She spreads the lotion around. I try to hold still as she moisturizes my whole body, but it's so difficult. I want to come. I want to come right now.

"No, baby. You're gonna wait."

She turns me just enough to lotion my front. She spends more time torturing my nipples with hard pinches from her lotion-slick fingers. I fidget, rubbing my legs together. She smacks my thigh. She doesn't have to tell me to hold still.

Finally, I'm settled on my back, breathing in the lingering scents from our shower. She strokes the damp hair at the base of my neck. I squirm again.

"You're gonna stay here awhile. Okay, baby?" My only objection being that I'm horny as hell, I nod. "I'll be back in a little bit. Just try to relax."

There's no way relaxing will happen. I can feel my heart beating inside my clit, but I say okay and try to focus on being patient. I stare at the ceiling, slightly unnerved by its stark whiteness.

Pilar gave me a day of freedom and now she needs to reclaim what's hers, on her terms.

I wait as long as I can. I have no idea what she's actually doing, but at the moment I'm just not strong enough to play her head game. Controlling my tone is tough, but I call Pilar's name. When she doesn't respond right away, I call her name again. My tone is louder, more frantic. I lift my head once she appears in the door. I don't notice my tears at first, not until a few streak from the corners of my eyes.

"Come back," I plead.

"I thought I told you to wait."

I don't answer. I know I'm being disobedient, but I don't know how to rationalize my freak-out. I've been tied up and left before. The idea of sleeping cuffed to my bed here at Pilar's didn't produce this amount of fear. Now though, I can't handle it.

She's back by the side of the bed, wiping away the tears that run down the side of my face. "You don't want me to leave you alone, do you, baby?"

"No. I want you to stay."

She climbs on the bed and straddles my stomach. I'd give anything to have my hands free. I want to feel her soft hips. I want to touch her breasts.

"Do you still want to know about the best part of my day?"

I nod frantically.

She leans down and kisses my face, my cheeks, and my chin, and then she licks my lips. I'm shaking, I want her so bad. There's nothing I can do but wait. She moves down to my throat and sucks my skin. "The best part of my day," she says, "was dancing with my little girl."

My sigh of relief is high and yearning.

"We're doing this my way. Okay?"

I manage to squeak out my okay.

Pilar releases the cuffs just long enough to secure me on my stomach.

"Oh, Suzy. You look so pretty this way."

"Thank you, Mami."

She's on me again. This time her hands are braced on my hips, her slit spread on my ass cheek. She starts to fuck herself on my skin. Every motion grinds my pussy into the sheets, rubs my clit against my lips.

"You feel so good," she says.

I whimper in reply. Her thigh separates mine. She lifts me off the sheets and her leg replaces her bedding as the friction against my cunt.

I groan. "Fuck me. Please."

"Say it again."

"Fuck me. Please!"

Pilar grips my hips and pounds into me. We're all juices and skin, clits and wetness. I lose my breath against her pillows and she gives it back to me on the next thrust. I grind back on her, crushing myself against her thighs. My orgasm comes hard. I'm shaking, still shaking when she soaks my skin with her own cum.

Catching her breath, Pilar lies down in the sheets beside me. Flopping to face her, I look her in the eye.

"Untie me," I beg.

Pilar looks at me for a moment before she kisses my mouth. She frees me from the cuffs, then rubs my wrists and my shoulders. When she lets me go I throw my arms around her waist. I don't want to let go. She strokes my back. She kisses my forehead. "I love you too, baby," she whispers against my skin. I finally stop shaking.

I'm deep in my submission for the rest of the weekend. Pilar lets me stay in her bed Saturday night. She feeds me Sunday morning and keeps me naked on my knees, by her side all day long. When she puts me to bed that night, I'm feeling loved and precious. The last thing I want to do is go back to work. The thought strikes me as I'm getting dressed. I could be Pilar's little girl 24/7. If only things could work that way.

Pilar comes into my room just as I'm stepping into my heels. "Another long week?" she asks, sitting on my bed.

"Yeah. We launch the mobile site next Monday. We have to QA all week, and that's just the mobile site." I sigh. I can't wait to hop on this vacation time.

"Have you named this guy yet?" She pats the head of Sir Bears-Alot's replacement.

"For now I'm just calling him Bear."

"I see how you've gotten so far in marketing," she says before she laughs at the glare I shoot her. "I want you to take him home with you."

I freeze with my earring halfway through my lobe.

"Uh, okay."

"I'll tell you why when it's time."

I swallow nervously.

Once I finish getting ready, Pilar helps me shove the oversized bear into the backseat of my Jeep. I have a sinking feeling that I won't see my Mami before the end of the week.

"I'll text you," I say.

Pilar kisses my lips. "I'll see you soon."

At the office, I give myself five minutes to connect with the real world before I'm swallowed up again by 21 And Up's bullshit. Junk e-mails fill my personal in-box. There are a few event announcements from kinklife, but I delete those, too.

For the first time in ages, opening my Facebook account brings a smile to my face. I'm glad to see my brother and his girlfriend had a great time at a friend's wedding over the weekend. The pictures are adorable. I like and comment accordingly, but it's the handful of friend requests from Pilar's nieces and nephews that I get a kick out of. There's one from Pilar, too. That's the request that really makes me smile. I accept it immediately. Erica's tagged me in several pictures that I love. One in particular of Pilar and me dancing. We look so happy, and instantly I remember how it felt swaying in her arms. God, I want out of this office. I check my in-boxes and find two more surprises. A message from Josh and one from Laurel. The message from Josh is short, but curious.

Hey, Suzanne, I'm sorry I bounced without telling you, but Val and I weren't seeing eye to eye on some crucial things. I had to move on. I hope things are going all right now.

Maybe the issue wasn't with the job after all. I shudder, thinking about my own run-in with Valerie. I know Josh's problems were of a strictly professional nature, but I feel bad that it was something between them, something procedural, that drove him away and not an issue with a client. Or maybe he wanted a raise she didn't want to give. Ready to rip the scab right open, I click on Laurel's message. It's over a week old.

Hey, sweetie. I just wanted to see how you are doing.

I think of something petty and snide to reply with, but in the end I just erase her message. I'm happy now. There's no need to prove that to someone who found me clingy and annoying. I send Erica a message to thank her for the pictures, and just as I hit send, my office phone rings. I check the number on the display. 21 And Up is ready for another round.

Chapter Ten

I work overtime for the next three days. I send my panty pictures to Pilar, of course, but we barely have time to talk. She texts me, which helps, but I'm so stressed our exchanges don't last long. Thank God, she understands. Wednesday night, she texts me and tells me to check my e-mail. I find her message buried in a stack from Monday afternoon. I open it, cursing myself for not checking it sooner.

Hello, baby, I know you're busy, but you need to do one thing for me.
I want to see you with Bear. Tape yourself on your webcam. Here's some inspiration to get you going.

There's a link and a picture of Pilar lying on her bed completely naked. Her breasts and her curves are simply mouth-watering. I click the link and a video of a girl in nothing but a pair of white panties starts to load. I hit play and watch the girl as she moves around her room. She adjusts her cam so it's facing her bed, covered in stuffed animals. She grabs a large white bear from the bunch and centers it on her bed. She climbs over its fluffy, round stomach and settles down.

This is different from watching Holly. It's hot. My clit starts to throb and my wetness starts to drip. I'll be saving this link. I wonder if I can do what Pilar wants. I know I can. I've humped pillows before, been strapped to a Sybian for Laurel's amusement. I've even rubbed myself against the side of my mattress as a horny kid, but can I do this? It's so…embarrassing. This is something I would do, but I'd keep it a secret, evidence of my private desperation.

The idea of disappointing Pilar pricks my throat. I can do it. It might take the edge off from work. It's late, but this also might be exactly what I need to help me fall asleep.

I look around my bedroom. Bear is still in my car. I go down to the parking garage and get him. Back in my apartment, it takes me another ten minutes to get ready. I strip down to my panties and braid my hair. I watch the video again. It's another few minutes before my laptop camera is situated across from my bed.

I give myself a silent pep talk and then I hit record. The girl in the video rubs her nipples and tugs on her breasts, but it's clear her focus is on getting off. At first, I imitate her moves, but after I few thrusts of my hips, my pussy makes its needs more than evident. I grind myself against the rounded plush stomach, holding myself up with my fists balled against his large stuffed head. I think of Pilar. I think of her watching me and it becomes easier. I open my eyes and look at myself moving on my monitor, and I'll confess that I look pretty sexy. I don't bother to hush my moans as I hump the bear with harsher strokes. It feels really good.

Soon, I'm coming. I hear myself saying Pilar's name. I'm coming for her. I bring myself down then up once more, orgasming again against the girth between my legs. I sag against my bed just for a moment before I jump up and go over to my laptop.

"I hope you liked it," I say as I wave to the screen. "Love you."

The next day, Pilar texts me. She liked it a lot.

I work all weekend. The mobile bugs are out of control, exactly what happens when you push up a deadline and force people to rush through coding. Valerie asks that I be on call for Leah and Simon, but before I leave on Friday I realize that on call means working.

I almost start crying as I dial Pilar. Her voice sounds so sweet when she answers, I do wipe away a few tears. "I don't think I can come over."

"Why, baby?"

"I have to work."

"Oh." Pilar sounds relieved, and it occurs to me that she thinks I might ditch her for personal reasons.

"There is nowhere else I want to be than with you."

"The feeling is mutual," she says. I can almost see her smiling. I want to firebomb 21 And Up's main offices. "Just make sure you take food and water breaks."

"I will."

My office phone rings again. Gritting my teeth, I hang up with Pilar and get back to work.

I did something wrong. I must have; otherwise the universe wouldn't be punishing me this way. It's Sunday afternoon and I've only stopped replying to e-mails and taking calls to eat takeout and sleep, and even then I'm on the phone half the time I'm eating, and I feel like I'm answering e-mails in my sleep.

I find copy errors on the checkout page. The privacy terms won't load. The shoe section insists that you've ordered the same pair of size-seven silver heels, no matter what pair you put in the cart. There are so many bugs we might as well start the fucking mobile site from scratch. Worst part is I don't have a landline at home so I can't test portions of the site while I'm on the phone. Leah, who is a perfectionist, is so pissed, but we keep reminding ourselves that 21 And Up is to blame. We need more time.

I'm on the phone with her again when my doorbell rings. I'm too exhausted to grab a butcher knife. I probably ordered food in a trendy T-shirt haze and just don't remember. I check the peephole, then rest my head against the door. I can't do this right now. But I don't tell Pilar to go away. I open the door and let her in. She strokes my butt as she makes her way to my kitchenette. I watch her, half listening to Leah as Pilar puts a few containers of food in my fridge. She passes me again with a wink and makes herself comfortable on my couch. Of course she's brought her knitting with her.

"You know the worst part about this?" Leah says.

"What's that?"

"Even after we launch, we still have to update this fucking thing every time they update their inventory."

I groan before I let a curse rip. Pilar doesn't so much as flinch, but I hang my head.

"This is the worst account ever," I say.

"For real. Okay, I'll call you back." I let Leah go so she can solve the shoe problem once and for all. Then I face Pilar.

"I'm sorry."

"For what?" She looks up from a fresh ball of yarn with a calm expression.

"I'm so stressed and I still have a ton of work to do. I can't—I..." I almost say I can't be your little girl right now. Aside from that being a completely insane thing to blurt out to a mistress that you practically want to marry, I know I'll have to do even more explaining than my brain or heart can handle. Pilar smiles. I want to cry. She understands.

"I don't want you to do anything. I came here to keep you company." She nods to the empty pizza box on the table. "And I wanted to make sure you ate something other than junk. You keep working and I'll just sit right here."

I flop down on the couch beside her and put my head on her shoulder.

"Thanks."

"No need to thank me, baby."

"I actually have a little time if you want to tie me to the TV stand and bang me out."

Pilar lets out a surprisingly loud laugh. I chuckle, too. "I didn't bring the cuffs, but why don't we try this? Come here."

Pilar motions for me to lie down in her lap. She pulls up her shirt and her bra. Her breasts practically fall into my mouth.

"Go ahead and suck me," she says, her voice sounding thick with arousal. I don't know how she does it. Still, just like that I'm in my little-girl space. I grip her breast and suck her nipple between my lips. Her skin puckers instantly, the delicate ridges and bumps pebbling against my tongue. I move my hand to her other breast and stroke her nipple with my thumb. My Mami groans and rests her head against the back of the couch. I snuggle closer, rubbing my other hand down her side.

She looks down at me again and touches my hair. "That feels good. Mmm, that's a good girl."

I squeeze my thighs together. This time Pilar doesn't scold me for squirming. She slides her hand between the fabric of my panties under my pajama shorts and my skin. I almost cheer with glee as she starts to finger my pussy. I bite down lightly on her nipple, then kiss it before I pick up with my sucking. We bring each other off, me just with my tongue and her with her amazing fingers. She lets me between her legs to feast on the juices coating her thighs, but I can't make her come again before my phone rings. She rubs my back as I tell Simon not to freak out about another bug. She rubs my feet as I get back to my e-mails. Later, though, before we eat, we find ourselves spread out across my couch, my head between her legs and her head between mine. She comes before my phone rings again.

Having Pilar spend the night helps me relax more than I expect. And I mean beyond the sex. There are times I need to be her little girl, and even though we haven't really discussed it, though she did introduce me to her family that way, sometimes I just need a girlfriend by my side to support me when I'd rather quit my job than spend another minute reviewing glitch corrections or answering e-mails. Monday morning I feel much better, even though I'm still exhausted. Pilar makes breakfast and sends me off to work, not so much prepared but at least with a reduced rage level. I tell her I have no clue how the week will go, but I won't mind if she feels the need to pop in during the next few nights to check on me. I get no promises, just a smile and kiss. Always wanting, that's the way she has to have it.

My calm turns to energized determination as I drive to West Hollywood. The mobile site goes live in an hour, and I'm almost positive we've caught every bug. I'm also strapped with a scripted list of reasons to offer 21 And Up when a customer finds the inevitable fuck-up in the site. The minute I step in the office, something feels off. People are moving around, but no one really seems to be working. I drop my stuff at my desk and then walk over to Mitch's cube.

"What's going on?"

"The servers are down."

"What?" Already, I start walking backward toward my desk.

"Yeah. Been fucked up ten minutes or so."

"Shit." I run to my phone and call Leah. She sounds terrible when she answers. I think it would be a little too much to think she has someone like Pilar to help her through the roughest patches of overtime.

"Hey, hon," I say. "You heard about the servers?"

"Yeah. Simon just called me. This is actually good."

"How so?" I say, scoffing. My other line is already beeping in. The fan is plugged in. All I need is a nice scoop of shit.

"I can run a few more bugs from this end and get them corrected, and then we can tell them the servers are up. For all they know, our servers are down all day."

I consider the idea. It has merit, but on the few occasions that our servers have crapped out, it's been one hour max before we're up and running again. "Use the time you need to, but I don't think I can stretch them more than an hour before it starts looking like we just don't have our shit together. Besides, I think Valerie will want to know about the launch as soon as the servers are back up. I can't lie to her about us needing more time."

"Don't lie," Leah suggests. "Tell her the truth. She knows what pains in the ass they are. She might be on board."

I hesitate, thinking of how I can phrase this to her. "Tell her I need more time. While the servers are down." I stand up and squint to see if I can catch a glimpse of Valerie in her office. She's not in yet.

"Go for it. I'll tell her when she gets here."

"Thanks."

I catch up with Valerie on our way into what turns out to be a three-hour status meeting with 21 and Up. They've already been informed that the servers are down. And while Alex, their account point person, assured me they understand, I am treated to a thorough chewing out by Larry, their marketing VP. When I get back to my desk, I find an e-mail from Leah. She's done all she can. I realize then that if I'm reading her e-mails the servers must be up and running. We've pushed the mobile site live, an hour late. Valerie swings by my desk to pat me on my back. Too bad I'm in no mood to celebrate.

I suffer through another late night because, *of course*, more tiny bugs are caught throughout the day. More phone calls with Alex and a promise to Leah that I'll take her out to dinner once the dust settles. I almost forget to text a picture to Pilar. I slip into the restroom and send it off, but for the first time the thrill is missing. It's not Pilar. Not even close. I love her. It's the job. Or maybe not even the job. It's the account. I can't mess with 21 And Up much longer. I would rather work on fourteen accounts like Clear Vision and Bee's Candy than deal with 21 And Up's whiny bullshit. I really hope Valerie was serious about the promotion and the raise.

Back at my desk, I text Pilar a short love note, telling her how much I miss her. She texts me back almost immediately, saying she feels the same way. That does lift my spirits, and I know if I can just make it to the weekend, we can be together again. I can be her little girl the way I want to be.

The next day, I get a brief reprieve from the madness. First thing, I have a meeting with Valerie and Donna Praiser, our president of production.

I meet Valerie in the hall on my way to Donna's office. Valerie tells me how nice I look. I take the compliment at face value, grateful she doesn't throw in a reassuring pat or stroke on the back for good measure. I'm too stressed to decode her behavior today. Once we're in Donna's office, the three of us sit at a small table Donna has overlooking the fountains in the building's courtyard.

Donna is pleasant, but I have to admit that I don't know her very well. She's Valerie's boss, and I only see her in our part of the office when something is going terribly wrong. She was at the Christmas party, too. The rumor is that she's pretty old-school and still cares only about our print and broadcast departments.

"I hear you have your hands full with 21 And Up?" she says as she smiles. She opens a manila folder on the table in front of her. Something tells me Valerie's briefed her on the status of the account. 21 And Up doesn't run a single broadcast ad, and the print ads are basically limited to teen magazines. Still, I smile back, shoring up my confidence.

"My hands are very full, but I am definitely learning a lot about producing digital campaigns under pressure. Especially with their mobile app."

"It looks fantastic. I had my assistant walk me through it this morning. Good job."

"Thank you."

Through some silent communication, Donna suddenly defers to Valerie. "Suzanne," she says. "We've hired four new producers. One to help Mitchell with Dylon Motor sports, one to handle a new account with R.J. Major's, and two to take on 21 And up."

"We signed R.J. Major's?" The chain restaurant fits in with the Chili's and TGI Friday's crowd. Their location near me looked like it was lacking in the business department.

"Full rebranding. Print, broadcast, and digital," Valerie replies.

"Valerie's informed me that it's time we moved you up."

"I—yes. We discussed it briefly," I say.

"Good. We'd like to create a position for you that's new to this office. We have several print directors in New York, and we were hoping to start you as our first junior digital director. You'll report directly to Valerie."

I'm excited for the offer, but I don't leap before I take a look. "The title sounds wonderful," I say, trying to keep my laugh even. "But may I ask what exactly the position will entail?"

"Sure." Donna slides the folder across the table. The first sheet lays out a formal job description, along with the indication of the salary. I try not to cough.

"We've been expanding a lot over the last year, and we're trying to convince more prospective new clients to consider switching to us for their digital needs," Valerie says. Which really means for all of their digital, print, and broadcast needs. "I'll need to travel more with the other department heads, and we need someone here to be able to hold down the fort. The gang trusts you. You're great with delegation and you're excellent under pressure. We think it would be a good fit."

"Wow, thank you. That's—thank you."

"Why don't you take this home tonight and read it over? If you don't think it's for you, we can talk to the new guy we've brought in for R.J. Major's."

Hell no! almost comes out of my mouth. That would mean I was stuck with 21 And Up. No fucking way. "I will. I'll give you an answer in the next day or two?"

"End of the week is fine," Donna says.

"Oh, and I was hoping to actually take my vacation after the site is up." I admit it now. It would look pretty bad if I took a promotion and then immediately went on vacation without giving Valerie a little warning.

Donna waves me off. "That's fine. Take your days. You'll be rested when you get back."

"Okay?" Valerie shoots me a hopeful grin.

"Sounds great," I say.

"Great." Donna slaps her palms lightly on the table as if we've already sealed the deal.

"I'll see you back downstairs," Valerie says.

I collect my folder and scurry to the elevator. Instead of heading back to my desk I tuck down the hall to my favorite bench. I'm breaking her rules, but I can't wait. I call Pilar.

"Everything okay?" she asks when she answer.

"Are you free to celebrate tonight?"

"Sure, baby," she replies with a slight chuckle. "Just tell me what we're celebrating."

My dinner out with Pilar and the subsequent spine-melting fuck she gives me afterward is the last of my fun for almost two weeks. I hand over my signed promotion papers after taking one last look at that salary bump. I'll start my new position, complete with a new office, with a window, as soon as the paper-doll site is launched, after a much deserved two-week vacation. Now that I can really afford it, I think about taking Pilar away somewhere. I hope she'll let me. For maybe a second or two, or like complete hours at night before I go to bed, I wonder what she thinks about moving in together, but I know it's too soon. I don't know that Mommies do this with little girls all the time, but she hasn't even mentioned collaring me yet. Every relationship is different, but I think she would do something, make some gesture before we decided to take up permanently under the same roof.

In the mornings, I'm back to work, scrambling to train two new producers, Heidi and Ryan. We've signed a new project for 21 And Up. I don't have to worry about the details because thank all that is God, Ryan and Heidi are responsible for it. In the meantime, though, I live and breathe that stupid paper-doll function. The whole thing is a walking bug, but our programmers are working so hard to get things rolling. Liam is swamped with work, too. We both work a ton of overtime and take solace in the fact that the company is paying for many a take-out dinner.

I see Pilar when I can and she does everything she can to help me relax. I don't know what I'd do without her. I spend a lot of our time together working, unfortunately, but at bedtime she's there for me with hot food and a bath. Or some ice cream, her long fingers, and her perfect mouth.

She calls me one day at my desk and tells me I need to take Saturday night off. I think we're clear enough that I'll be working late on Friday, but I make up my mind right then that Saturday night belongs to Pilar. 21 And Up and their stupid paper dolls can suck it.

"What's happening on Saturday night?" I ask her.

"I'll tell you Friday, baby. Get back to work."

I growl at her playfully through the phone before I tell her I love her. She tells me she loves me, too.

At this point, I shouldn't be surprised by things Pilar does or says, how she's able to read me or a situation so well that she meets my needs before I even know there's something to be considered.

It's Friday night. I'm running late and I'm frazzled. My Saturday and Sunday are clear, but as I walk up Pilar's front steps I'm already thinking about Monday and everything that needs to be done. With Frank tucked under my arm, I check my e-mail one last time before I ring the doorbell. I'm slipping my phone in my bag when she opens the door. I'm happy to see her, especially since she's in her robe, but I'm frustrated that I can't seem to escape work these days. My vacation days can't come soon enough.

I smile at her. I'm about to say hello. I want to tell her I've missed her, but the look on her face, an expression that is patient but determined, combined with the fact that she's blocked my entrance, tells me I should let her have the first word.

My mouth slips closed, though my eyebrows go up expectantly. I hope I haven't forgotten something.

"We're playing a different sort of game tonight, baby." She reaches across the threshold and cups my cheek. I soak in her warmth, fighting to keep my eyes open. "Until I say so, there will be no talking. Do you understand?"

"Yes, Mami."

"Good. You may come in," she says as she steps aside. I exhale as I enter her house. My mind is scrambling, trying to figure out where she's going with this, as if I could put a stop to it, as if I want to. As if her plans are a problem to be solved. Ugh, I'm still in work mode, I think as I step toward the couch.

"Let's put your things down in your bedroom and then we'll have a bath."

I turn and walk down the hall. Pilar's at my heels. This is all routine. I come to her house. I bathe and we settle into our weekend, but this enforced silence changes everything. Even though she has her rules, Pilar does let me chat a lot. I realize I have things I want to say. I want to talk about work. I need to, just to get it out of my system, but now I can't. By the time we make it to her bathroom, I'm already cataloging the things I want to say, making a mental list for when she finally lets me speak.

She dims the lights and undresses me. As the tub fills, she kisses me. It's the kiss, I think, that makes things worse. I want to tell her how much I've missed her during the week. I want to tell her how being with her makes me feel. I whimper painfully and try to pull away, but Pilar's instincts and reflexes are faster than my protests. She gathers me in her arms, kissing me harder, letting me know there's nowhere for me to go. Right now, this is where I belong.

When our kiss ends, her grip suddenly shifts from a strong arm around my waist to firm fingers on my chin.

She looks me right in the eye.

"Whatever you're feeling right now, I want you to feel it. If you're frustrated, be frustrated. If you're angry with me, be angry. If you're tired or sad, feel those things. Do not push them down. You can fight me, but don't ignore what's going on inside."

How do you know? I want to say, but of course I don't.

My nostrils flare and my lips begin to tremble. It's all of those things, and they're manifesting themselves as this ache in my chest. The tears come so fast, the kind that come so thick and hot you don't even attempt to wipe them away until your vision is already blurred. I cry those types of tears that demand so much of me I can't even close my eyes.

Pilar turns off the water and steps into the tub, pulling me with her. No bubble bath this time, just steaming hot water. She settles me between her legs, and rather than squaring my back to her chest, she lets me roll to my side so I can put my head on her shoulder. The tears keep coming, and finally she reaches up with a wet hand and wipes my face.

I let out a shuddering breath as the water runs over my lips. She has to keep touching me or I won't make it through the night. Her lips brush my forehead and she whispers, "Tell me."

I tell her everything. I tell her that I'm exhausted. I tell her that working for 21 And Up is sucking away my will to live. I tell her that I know I'm being overworked, but that our office environment has become one that no longer takes an employee's mental health into consideration. I tell her I could work one hundred hours a week and no one would think that was a little strange. I'm just a hard worker. I just love my job. I do love my job, I tell her. Or at least I used to. I love my coworkers and I don't want to let them down. I've been offered this promotion and I want to show Valerie and Donna that I can handle the responsibility, but I feel like I may crack soon. I feel like I've set myself up in an impossible situation. I feel like it's not okay for me to be done in, like it's some grand failure to admit that I'm stressed out and feeling overworked when every piece of me is screaming toward that truth.

And then I tell her how much I hate being away from her. I tell her I can't even enjoy sending my panty pictures to her because I can't let my mind stray to her long enough for my inner little girl to process even a few moments of arousal when I have another status meeting in five minutes. I tell her I never want to eat another meal in a conference room if it means not eating a dinner that is meant to be eaten with her, on her lap. I cry and cry on her shoulder, shaking and hiccupping, letting out everything that has been on my mind these last few weeks. She holds me, stroking my back and hips under the water.

"Do you want to quit?" she asks quietly. I consider this possibility seriously before I answer.

"No," I say. "But I want off this account, and I will be if I can just make it a few more weeks."

We're quiet again for some time. My tears stop, though I'm still breathing heavily. My hand drifts to Pilar's thigh, and soon the soothing feeling of her skin helps calm my thudding heart.

Without a word she starts to move and I know bath time is over. I lead the way out of the tub. Our routine continues as usual from there. She dries me off, we lotion up. This time, though, when she leads me to her bed she takes me in her arms. I'm between her legs as she leans against the headboard, back to chest, thighs against thighs. She turns on the Food Network because she knows I like the background noise. Then she rocks me in her arms.

"Do you want to know what we're doing tomorrow night?" she asks.

"Oh, yeah," I say, trying to cover a yawn. "I almost forgot."

"We're going to a play party."

I turn slightly to look at her. "Really?"

"Yes. A woman I know is hosting a Mommy/little slumber play party downtown, and we've been asked to come. What do you think about that?"

I'm nervous, that's my initial reaction. I've been to play parties with Laurel, and that was when she demanded the most of me. I always did my best to please her, and even when people complimented her on my behavior, she never seemed satisfied. Throw in the difference between your run-of-the-mill sub and the mentality of a submissive little girl, then add in a group setting? Yeah, that makes me nervous. I tell Mami and I ask her what I should expect.

I feel like she answers me honestly. "I'm expecting there to be the typical show and competition, but of course everyone will be judging each other's little girls and Mommying style on their own personal standards, but I won't really know until we get there. I'll have to assess the women there, assess their little girls, and then I'll know how we should proceed. I want you to have fun, but we'll just have to see."

I like this approach. Environments change depending on the players, and I like that Mami is coming at this with both of our interests in mind. Some Dominants are so interested in the show that they don't know when to rein things in, even when it's obvious that both they and their sub have wandered into deep water.

"Do you think you'll want me to play with other little girls?" I ask cautiously. Our first meeting with Bizzy and Holly was supposed to be just lunch and some hanging out before it devolved into a WWE match, but play parties are different. It's expected that some erotic activity will go down. I'm no stranger to exhibitionism, but I wonder if this time Pilar will want me to perform. I ask her.

She contemplates my question for a moment. "I'd like to show you off, though I really will have to assess the crowd before I know how much. But don't worry, baby. I won't make you do anything that you feel uncomfortable doing."

"Okay," I say softly. "Thank you."

"You're welcome, baby."

I thread my fingers through hers and run my thumb over her palm. "Do I get to wear that dress?"

We both shake a little when Pilar laughs. "Yes, you will."

I smile, for the first time all night. "Then I'll go."

"Oh, you've decided you'll come along with me? Is that right?"

"Yeah. It would be wrong for me to send you off alone. It just wouldn't be right."

"And what would you do if I brought another little girl home to replace you?" Her tone is as teasing as the light touch she trails down my stomach. Goose bumps spring up on my skin. I squeeze my legs together.

"Don't you think that would confuse Frank?"

"Oh, I don't know," Pilar says. "I think Frank has a lot of love to give."

"No, he doesn't. Frank is a dark, withdrawn puppy. He reserves all his love for me. But if you brought another little girl home?" I know she's joking, but my jealousy at the idea has its own flavor and texture, it's so strong. "I'd be nice to her, I guess, but she'll have to sleep on the couch or the porch or something. My bed isn't big enough for two little girls."

"I think you're right. I think you'll have to come with me then."

I sigh so heavily it almost sounds like a moan. "I guess so." She tickles me then, and I can't help but giggle and squirm. She's still tickling me when she says, "Are you wet for me, Suzy?" The heat of her tone contradicts the lightness of her touch, so much it catches me off guard. It trips me up right into my little space. I still don't understand how she does it.

I curl up onto her, hiding my face against her shoulder. "I don't know," I say bashfully, though I totally am. I've been wet since she kissed me in the bathroom. Her voice and the way she's holding me are only making matters worse. My clit is hard—I can feel it—and my lips are starting to swell.

"You don't know? Do you think I should check?"

I hesitate again before shaking my head.

"No? Well, maybe I should spank your sweet little pussy until it's ready to open up for me so I *can* check."

My eyes squeeze shut and I hold back a moan. I'm definitely wet now.

"I think that's exactly what I'll do. Lie flat and don't move."

I situate myself more completely on my back, against her lush breasts. Her arm comes around my waist and she holds me down. The first touch of her fingers to my slit is a light, teasing pat that sends the most delicious vibrations up my clit. My leg twitches, but I manage not to move much. She pats me again and again, and with each tap my hips want to move a little more. It's a struggle to stay still, but I try.

"Are you wet now, baby?" she whispers in my ear.

I shake my head. "No."

"How about now?" She delivers another tap, this one a little harder than the ones before. My hips jerk forward.

"No. I don't know yet."

"Now?" She smacks me this time. The blow is hard and perfect. A few more like it and I'll come. Pilar knows by the way I try to lunge forward, by the way I cry out. She slides her fingers lower, not even a fraction of an inch, and she can feel my juices coating my lips. She massages my labia, careful not to open me up. At times, this drives me crazier than the most intense penetration. This is one of those times. I whimper and try to roll my hips away from her exploring hand.

"Hold still," she says, her tone as harsh as it gets, still laced with affection and care. "Hold still or I won't let you come."

"Yes, Mami," I reply, my voice tight. I relax my thighs.

She kisses my cheek and then my neck. "You want me to spank your pussy until you come. Say it."

"I want you to spank my pussy until I come."

"Say it again because you know it's true. You know it's exactly what you want."

"Please, Mami. Spank my pussy until I come. It's what I want."

She licks my cheek. I turn away sharply to avoid her tongue only because I need to disobey. The hand around my waist flashes up to my chin. She holds me in place and licks me again. Then she spanks my pussy again. Her smacks are just as hard, sharp punctuations like a sensual code across the sensitive skin shielding my clit. The closer I get, the harder she hits, the more my body quakes. Soon I'm begging her, "Spank me. Oh God, spank me." And she does, building her speed and strength.

My orgasm tackles me down from my gut, causing my body to arch forward as I scream. Pilar follows me, sitting us both completely up as she shifts her grip to my neck. Always to control, never to hurt. She shoves three fingers into my pussy in one tight thrust and I come again. The little restraint that I've had is completely gone. I ride her fingers, almost recklessly, letting her grip on my neck and her lips pressed against my temple hold me in place. I've soaked the sheets between us by the time she pulls out, but she's not through yet.

I'm on my back and she's climbing on top of me before I realize this is exactly where I would have wanted her to take things next. Our thighs intertwine, and though I'm sore, I'm far from spent. I hold on with one hand on her shoulder as she fucks me into the mattress. I grip her breast with my free hand and suck her nipple into my mouth. Her restraint cracks momentarily as she tosses her head back. I trace the familiar bumps, suck and lick in the ways I know drive her crazy. And she fucks me harder. I wonder if we'll bruise from this pounding. I wouldn't mind if we did. I'd enjoy her marks on me.

Pilar rears up with her hands fisted in the sheets, her position pulling her breast from my mouth. I see her focus again. She's not stopping until I come. I close my eyes and drive harder against her thrusts, and it's only once or twice before I'm soaking her skin again. She comes on top of me with a fierce grunt and a "Suzy. Oh, Suzy. Fuck." I accept her weight gladly when she can't prop herself up anymore. I lick her shoulder, tasting her saltiness. I nibble her skin. There's no need for her to move because in a few minutes I'm going to ask her if we can do it again. I'm positive of what she'll say.

I think to myself in those few minutes when we're breathing, trying to find our sanity again, I don't know what I would do if she brought another little girl home. I'd probably run the bitch off. I love Pilar too much. There's no way I can share.

CHAPTER ELEVEN

First thing Saturday, I try on my dress. It fits perfectly, though Pilar wants to make one adjustment to the skirt. I don't want to take it off, but Pilar insists that it might be a little hard for me to, say, shower before the party while wearing it. After she's done with the quick alterations we run a few errands. I don't know why, but I'm glued to Pilar's hip throughout the day. I think it's the combination of the emotions still swirling through me from last night and my anxiety over the party. I want to go. Pilar tells me Bizzy and Holly will be there, so at least I'll see a couple familiar faces, but I'm still nervous.

I know this will be different than the parties I went to with Laurel. Those leather parties gave Laurel a chance to showcase just how much I could take. It gave her a chance to tease other Dominants with my beauty and my stamina, but there's something more. I'm different now than who I was with Laurel. We were both selfish, I think. We came together at a time when I was a little desperate and reckless. I think she's failed, in her mind, with subs before me, and I was someone she thought she could mold. We lied to each other, never answered the important questions honestly. We never brought up the important questions at all. I wanted love with my mistress. I wanted something whole and complete, a full expression of what I wanted and what I wanted to be to another woman. Laurel wanted a plaything, and I performed that role until I realized it was a part I know longer wanted.

I'm nervous because I have a feeling I'll have to interact with the other little girls. What if there's another situation like I faced with Holly's evil twin? I'm nervous, but I love Pilar. I want to make her proud. I want to anticipate and surpass her expectations like she does for me every day. I'm terrified that I'll screw something up.

She can tell I'm on edge, but she doesn't bring it up. Instead, she lets me cling to her as we hit the grocery store. She lets me take my afternoon nap beside her on the couch. When I wake up, she makes me a light dinner because there's going to be food for the little girls at the party. I shower, and then she lotions me up. She helps me dry my hair and then she braids it. For the first time, she dresses me. I hold still as she secures the small buttons running up my back, and I try not to fidget as she pulls my knee-highs up over my feet. She's on her knees in front of me, still dressed in her loose T-shirt and her skinny jeans she wore out this morning.

I stare for a moment at the part in her hair. I don't want to go to the party. I want to stay home, in her arms. "Permission to speak freely?"

"Sure, baby. Tell me what's on your mind." She doesn't look up as she speaks. She reaches for one of the new Mary Janes she's picked up to complete my outfit. I help her slide my foot inside and sit, my nerves tingling up my spine.

"Come on vacation with me. I want to take you away for bit. Like, let me pay."

Pilar sits back on her heels. I don't know how to take the sigh she lets out, but when she looks up at me, her expression is all empathy. She strokes my knee.

"I can't let you do that," she says.

My heart seems to choke on its next beat. "You can't go away with me or you can't let me pay?"

"Both," she replies, but quickly adds this before I break down in tears. "However, I would be happy to take you on vacation somewhere."

Starting this kind of evening with an argument is a terrible idea, but this is girlfriend territory. I'm offering to do something nice for the person I love. I'm suggesting that we do something romantic together on my dime, through my effort, and she's shutting me down without giving my invitation the slightest thought. I don't want to fight, but I want an explanation.

"I'm your girlfriend too, right? I mean, that's how you introduced me to your family." I'm fucking up. My tone is all wrong, but I've been thinking about this for weeks. Pilar takes a deep breath, then sits next to me on the bed.

"Yes, you are my girlfriend, and yes, I would love to go away with you, but it's not in my nature to let you plan or pay for things. I wouldn't feel right about it."

Oh, great, I think. This is about to devolve into a money fight. It's my turn to take a deep breath.

"Not that it's something I've anticipated, but I've saved a ton of money being with you. Plus, I'm on the brink of a huge raise. You pay for everything. I understand that's part of our arrangement, and as your little girl I do appreciate it, but as your girlfriend, I would like to be able to do things for you from time to time. I have these vacation days and I want to take you somewhere."

Pilar braces her hands on her knees as she looks over at me. I know she's made up her mind. "I'm touched by the thought, baby, but the answer is no. When you know when you can use those days, tell me and I'll happily take you somewhere. You can pick the when, but I'll plan the trip and I'll pay."

"But—"

"I said no. It won't sit well with me."

"Am I allowed to do anything for you that doesn't involve frilly panties?"

"I know you've had a very hard week so I'm going to pretend you're not being so rude to me. You know exactly what I want from you, and until this very moment you've been doing just fine with it."

She means my submission. I understand, but it's hard for me not to bristle at her words. For the first time I feel like Pilar is actually trying to control me, and I'm not into it.

She slips back to the floor and slides my other shoe onto my foot. I'm cooperative enough not to fight her.

"All done," she says, forcing a smile. "Stand up so I can see you." I do as she asks and turn in a slow circle. The dress is awesome and a nice distraction from hurtful words sloshing around in my head. When I'm facing her again, Pilar touches my eyebrows and then my lips with a clinical brush of her thumb. "Come to my bathroom." I follow her on numb limbs and sit still as she plucks a few stray hairs from my right eyebrow. She slaps a little bit of eye shadow and mascara on me, and a hint of blush. I look nearly doll perfect when I glance at myself in the mirror.

"Do you have that pink lip gloss in your purse?" she asks. I say yes. "Okay. Grab that and I think we're all set. I'm going to get ready. I want you to double-check your overnight bag, then wait for me in the living room."

"Yes, ma'am."

I expect her to correct me, but instead she offers a tight smile, then nods toward the door. Back in my room as I make sure I have the new pajamas she's bought me and my toothbrush, I foolishly let my anger build. I'm sure she doesn't want to ruin this night, but I have punishment coming. I can feel it. The worst thing is that her punishing me in this situation would be utter and complete bullshit. All I want to do is treat her to a nice vacation. I didn't ask her to let me be the mistress for the weekend. I didn't ask her to do anything crazy, but that need of hers for control supersedes anything I could possibly want, even though I know it would be good for our relationship. Shit, she can lead me around Hawaii on a leash and collar, naked as a baby if she wants, but she can at least let me pay for the flights and the hotel.

It takes Pilar a little over an hour to get ready. I'm settled on the couch, watching *The Wheel* when she walks into the living room. I'm upset with her all over again because she looks so damn good. Her high-waisted, black pencil skirt accentuates everything from her breasts to her hips and thighs. And when she turns around to grab her purse, I see it's doing wonderful things to her butt, too. The ruffles of the front of her short-sleeved, white blouse add inches to her already ample bosom. She's curled her hair and wrapped it up in a bun and finished the look off with light eye shadow and dark-red lipstick, and a pair of black stilettos. Oh, I want her so bad it hurts, but I'm still pissed at her.

"You look very pretty," I say matter of factly, even though I'm drooling pathetically on the inside.

Her response is terse and she doesn't look at me when she says, "Thank you, baby."

And apparently she's pissed at me, too. This is sizing up to be a wonderful night.

We don't speak in the car. I know what I'm supposed to do. Behave. And Pilar, in complete control of herself, needs only guide the way. I'm actually looking forward to seeing Holly. Maybe I'll get a chance to vent to her. The hotel isn't too far away. We pull up at the valet stand, shrouded by potted palm trees. I grab my stuff and follow Pilar inside. As we check in, I smile politely at the woman behind the desk.

"Here are your keys, Ms. Castillo. Your party will be assembling in the penthouse, room 1004. Some of the other guests have already arrived."

Pilar thanks her and I also offer my bashful thanks. I'm laying this little-girl shit on heavy tonight. The other women will think Pilar is the best Mommy in the world. We stop by the room, on the seventh floor, where Pilar drops off her overnight bag. She gives herself one final look in the mirror, checks my makeup, and then we're back in the elevator. Pilar is silent again, but when she takes my sleeping bag from me and slides her hand up the back of my neck, I know she's sorry. We just can't talk about it right now.

With the walk down the hall to the penthouse, I'm nervous again. Beyond that door lie strange Mommies and other little girls I might not get along with. I remind myself that the only person I really need to worry about is Pilar. As she knocks, I do my best to shake off my anxiety.

"You'll be fine," Pilar whispers. She gives my neck a gentle squeeze.

"Thank you."

The door flies open and a short, black woman in a tight, black dress greets us. Behind her, music filters into the hallway.

"Ah! Pilar! I'm so glad you could make it."

Pilar leans down and kisses her on both cheeks.

"Francis, this is my little girl, Suzy. Suzy, say hello to Mistress Francis."

I offer my sweetest, most demure hello. I can feel Pilar smiling at me.

"Pilar. She's darling. Come in." We enter the suite, and as the woman at the front desk said, a bunch of guests have already arrived. I do a quick scan of the room as Mistress Francis and Pilar do their quick catch-up. Across the room, by a long table lined with drink cups and snacks, is my boss, Valerie.

I've known fear before, but what I experience now, because she's looking right at me, is genuine panic. I gasp and take a stuttering step back. My feet are already in escape mode.

I vaguely hear Pilar excuse herself from Mistress Francis, and immediately she's in front of me.

"What's wrong?"

"Don't look."

Of course she looks, and she sees who I'm looking at because Valerie is still watching us. She just doesn't know why.

"What's the problem?"

I purse my lips and mutter, "That's my boss."

"You mean Vee?"

"You know her?" I think I might vomit all over my new dress.

"Yes, I know her. Bizzy introduced us a few years ago. She's been on the outskirts of our Mommy gang for a while."

"Jesus, why didn't you tell me?" I say, even though I know I shouldn't.

Pilar looks at me like I've clearly lost my mind. I sigh and then apologize. I'm scared and a little embarrassed, but Pilar's not at fault here.

She straightens her posture and gently cups my cheek, encouraging me to focus on her and only her.

"Do you want to go home?"

I scramble to come up with an answer. Rules of the game dictate that Valerie cannot approach me without going through Pilar, and knowing what she knows, it would be downright evil for Pilar to let that happen. I also know how crazy it would look if we suddenly bolted.

"No, I—I want to stay." I need to stay. For Pilar. "But this happens sometimes, right? Sometimes you just run into people and it's okay?" I scan Pilar's face for reassurance.

"It does. And she knows nothing about you or this?"

I shake my head. "No, I mean I guess she knows about this and you, but she had no clue about *me*. I thought she was very vanilla." I've just lied, but I can't take it back. "This is the last place I expected to see her." That part is the truth, but now the whole truth makes sense. The way Valerie touched me that day in her office. She knows how to read little girls like me. My stomach clenches as I picture her expression that day. She knows exactly what little girls like me like.

"Just stick by me. Okay? If she does anything out of line or makes you the slightest bit uncomfortable, you let me know and I'll have Francis handle it. Okay?"

"Okay."

"Good girl." Pilar kisses my forehead, then takes my hand in a tight grip. We're a team again. The fight's forgotten.

"Is everything okay?" Mistress Francis asks.

Pilar immediately turns the charm back on. "Just questioning whether we left a curling iron on."

"Do you need to call someone?" I feel bad, because Mistress Francis is genuinely concerned, but not that bad, because Valerie is still staring.

"Oh, no. I shut it off before we left," Pilar says smoothly.

"Excellent. Suzy, why don't you come meet my little girl?" We head toward the couches, away from Valerie, and Mistress Francis introduces us to her little girl, Sunshine. Sunshine is black as well and ridiculously gorgeous. She has a good seven inches on her Mistress, but she defers to her both physically and verbally the same way I defer to Pilar. I admire her black-and-white Lolita dress, complete with capped sleeves and white laces that crisscross down her torso. I admire the leather-and-lace collar around her neck as well before Mistress Francis tells her to show me where to put my stuff.

Sunshine loops her arm through mine and leads me to the open double doors to a large bedroom. "I'm glad you came," she says. "Miss Francis said some great things about your mistress."

"Thanks," I say back. "I'm sure we'll have fun." I drop my sleeping bag next to the bed in a pile with the other girls' things, then follow Sunshine back out to the main living area and back to Pilar's side. We both wait patiently as our Mistresses talk. More guests arrive and Pilar carefully navigates us around the room, avoiding Valerie and the two little girls she has at her side. Valerie looks good, dressed similar to Pilar in a navy pencil skirt and a white blouse, but she's wearing way more makeup than she does at the office and her hair is actually done, opposed to the simple down way I'm used to seeing. The girls with her are pretty, nearly identical brunettes in matching school uniforms: yellow and navy plaid skirts and navy sweaters. One of the girls seems bored and the other seems anxious, like she's waiting for the night to get interesting.

Finally, Holly shows up, but she's not with Bizzy. Another woman is with her, dressed plainly in jeans and a Rolling Stones hoodie. Before we can talk to them, the music is turned down a little and Mistress Francis calls the room to order.

"Ladies and gentleman," she says, flashing a smile at the one butch Daddy in attendance. A few of the girls giggle, but it's all in good fun.

"I just wanted to thank you all for coming. As you know, tonight is for our little girls." She glances at her watch. "In thirty minutes, we'll head upstairs and let them have their fun. In the meantime, I'd like to remind everyone of the rules. Please respect each other's commitments. When in doubt, differ to the Domme. In the public areas, no penetrative intercourse or skin-to-genital, genital-to-genital contact. If you would like to engage in those activities, please retire to your own rooms. Of course, spanking is allowed anywhere you see fit."

That gets a few laughs as well.

"I've asked the lovely Brooke and Di to act as our babysitters tonight." Two women, who I realize are flying solo, wave from either side of the room. "If you have any questions or requests, please ask them."

A woman across the room raises her hand. Mistress Francis nods, but she looks annoyed. "Just to clarify, you did bill this as a ladies-only event." At first, I think she's referring—in an insanely rude way—to the butch by the table, but I realize that most sets of eyes are on another Latin woman and her gorgeous Asian little girl. The woman glares back at the rude guest and pulls her little girl tight to her side.

Mistress Francis opens up with a frightening smirk. "By all means, Liz, you and Sage are more than welcome to leave if present company doesn't meet your high standards."

The little girl, Sage, tugs on the woman's arm, eyes pleading. She keeps her mouth shut.

Mistress Francis smiles. "Wonderful. Sage, we're happy to have you." Mistress Francis then has us go around the room and introduce ourselves. Well, she has the Mistresses introduce themselves and their little girls.

The "offending" couple is Mistress Zoe and her little girl, Gloria. Apparently, Bizzy had an engagement she couldn't get out of, so Holly's accompanied by her sitter, Ellee. I try not to even note their presence, but I can't help but tense up when it's Valerie's turn. Her little girls are named Giselle and Carly. Giselle has wiped the bored expression off her face and plastered on a simple smile that matches Carly's. All together, there are nine Mommies, our butch Daddy, and fifteen little girls. A woman named Melinda wields some magical pimp powers and has three little girls by her side. The party begins again as a chatty social. Pilar chats with Ellee while Holly and I carefully dissect what the other is wearing. I've never been so glad to see her in my life. Having another person I know helps keep at least a small part of my mind off Valerie. She seems to be avoiding us as well, but I do feel her glancing at me every now and then.

Soon it's time for our Mistresses to go. There are good-byes around the room, some tearful. I'm just plain old nervous. Pilar cups my face in her hands.

"I talked to Brooke. If you need me, just tell her and she'll come find me. Otherwise, just stick to Holly. She knows a lot of the other girls."

"Okay."

"I love you."

"I love you, too."

Pilar kisses me hard on the lips, and God bless her, she hangs by my side, prolonging our good-bye until Valerie has left the room. Pilar kisses me one last time, gives my side a final squeeze, and then she's gone.

Pizza is on its way up and the music is blasting. Now that Valerie is out of my sight and it's clear that her girls have no clue that we share a connection, I feel a lot better. Still, I know Valerie will be on my mind all night. I can't even think about what will happen on Monday.

Holly appears at my side again and grabs my hand. I make up my mind not to mention Valerie to her. She may be my boss and we may be in the same place at the same time, but it would be disrespectful and a little cruel to gossip about her. Hopefully, Valerie decides I deserve the same treatment. "Let's put our pj's on," Holly says.

"Oh, ah. Sure." I let her tug me toward the bedroom. She calls after Gloria as we go. A few moments later, the three of us are shut in the master bathroom. Holly pounces on Gloria, pulling her into a hug. "How are you? You look awesome."

"Thanks. So do you." Gloria beams and reaches for the top button on the front of her dress. "You wanna see?"

"Of course! Show me."

I glance curiously between them, not sure whether I should laugh or cover my eyes. Holly realizes I have no clue what's going on and nudges my shoulder in apology.

"I've known Gloria since she was Michael."

Gloria stops mid-unbutton. "Excuse me. Michael has always been a shell of what Gloria will ultimately be."

Holly cocks her head and offers an apologetic frown. "I'm sorry."

"It's okay. You lesbians still have a lot to learn." With a wink, I think Holly is forgiven. Gloria finishes unbuttoning her dress and slips out of her sleeves. Her hands drop to her waist and she tips her hips forward, showing off a pair of fake breasts.

"Holy shit. They look awesome. Can I touch them?" Holly asks.

"Yeah, go for it. I'm completely healed."

Just as Holly goes to cop a feel, someone knocks on the door. "Who is it?" she yells. Gloria doesn't even bother to cover up.

"It's Sunshine," her voice calls through the door.

"Come on in," Holly replies. Sunshine slips in and closes the door. "We're just checking out Gloria's boobs."

"Cool." Sunshine hops on the counter and crosses her legs. "I want to see."

Holly gets back to the task at hand and gives Gloria's left breast a good squeeze. "Your doctor is a fucking genius." She peeks up at Gloria's face before turning her attention back to her chest. "They feel great and they hang just right." Holly's observation is dead on. Gloria's breasts have a slightly unnatural shape. They're perfectly round, but the implants are situated low enough that they aren't touching Gloria's chin. They do look pretty good. If I wasn't staring at them I'd think they were real.

"Dr. Friedman is amazing. He did my sister's tits."

Holly squeezes her other breast, then gives her nipple a slight tweak.

"Hey!" Gloria squeals as she slaps Holly's hand away. "Slut."

Holly laughs, looping her arm through mine. "Just checking."

"My nips are fine. I promise you. You wanna feel?" Gloria asks me.

"It's certainly a way to say 'Nice to meet you,'" I reply. I usually don't grope people five minutes after meeting them, but Holly nudges me forward. "I am curious. You don't mind?"

"Not at all," Gloria says. "I've been dying to show these things off."

"Okay." I chuckle as I lean forward a little and give her boob a squeeze. "Oh, wow. I thought they'd be harder. They're kinda squishy."

"That's why I picked them. Not perfect, but pretty close."

"They're fucking hot," Holly says.

"Thank you, girls." Gloria wiggles her head like a proud peacock.

"The twig and berries?" Sunshine asks, confirming my initial assumption.

"They're staying for now. These hurt so bad. Mentally and physically, I'm just not ready to go through all of it again."

"What does Zoe say?" Holly asks.

"She's been amazing. She said whatever I want, she'll support me. I think she's going to collar me soon."

"Really?" Holly says.

"Well, she did pay for these. She might want to see her investment through."

"That's great," Sunshine says.

"What's wrong?" Holly asks me. I don't mean to pout, but the talk of paying for things reminds me of how our night started out. I don't even want to think about how far away Pilar and I are from a collaring situation.

"Oh, it's silly. I asked Pilar if I could take her on vacation. Like foot the bill," I admit. "She shot me down."

Sunshine hops off the counter and puts her hand on my shoulder. "That sucks, but I'd let it go if I were you."

Gloria and Holly seem to agree. "They need their control and so do we. You have to let her have it," Gloria says. "Or why else are you with her?"

"You make a good point," I reply. It would be easy for me to find a good girlfriend, but what I want is Pilar, as my Mistress.

"Did she say no to vacation altogether, or did she just say no to you paying?" Holly asks.

"Just to me paying. She said we could go somewhere."

"Hon, I'm not seeing the problem here," Gloria says.

"Yeah," Holly adds. "Let her take you on vacation and just enjoy it. You know you will."

"I know I could do that, but I wanted to give her something."

"Give her some real good head. She'll be thankful for that," Sunshine says. The other girls bust out laughing. I can't help but smile with them.

"If you want to get her something, get her something thoughtful, but you know nothing can come between a Mommy and what she has planned for her little girl," Gloria says. "After I got out of the hospital, I got Zoe a massage. She was so stressed out worrying about me, I knew she needed some time to relax, but she got to relax and let her guard down without me around. She said it was exactly what she needed. And then she fucked me senseless."

The girls are definitely on to something. I see that Pilar needs her control, but I don't think she would be upset if I got her a gift. "Maybe I could get her a new sewing machine or something."

"Did she make this?" Gloria asks, flicking my skirt a bit.

"Yeah, she did."

"Damn," Sunshine says, and then she laughs. "We ordered this number."

"If the woman likes to sew, then a new machine sounds very thoughtful. And then when she takes you away, eat that pussy until she can't stand anymore," Gloria says.

"Thanks. I think I will."

There's another knock on the door, and then Brooke sticks her head in. "What are you girls doing?"

"Looking at some boobs," Holly says.

Brooke blinks when she realizes Gloria's top is off. "Oh. Oh! You have to give me the name of your doctor."

"I will."

Brooke lowers her voice a little. "Let me know if Sage gives you any trouble."

"I think she'll stay away from me, but thank you," Gloria replies.

Brooke nods in understanding. "Pizza's here. So come on."

"We're just gonna change," Holly says.

"Okay. Hurry."

"I can't believe Liz said that," Sunshine says after Brooke's left us alone.

"Why did Ms. Francis invite them?" Holly asks what's on the tip of my tongue.

Sunshine shrugs and rolls her eyes. "Sage has been going through some tough times, I guess, and Liz said she needed some time to socialize."

"She should have left Liz at home then," Holly says. "Bizzy showed me the invitation. It said all female-identified persons, and at this point I think Gloria's gayer than I am."

"You are the one with the Daddy." Gloria playfully winks at Holly. "Whatever. Fuck Liz. She's just jealous of my hot Asian cock," Gloria says, grabbing her crotch in a vulgar gesture. "Maybe I'll ask Sage if she wants to suck it."

"I'm pretty sure that violates the mouth-to-genitals rule," I say. That earns another laugh from the girls. We quickly change into our pajamas and join the rest of the party.

Chapter Twelve

I have fun. After I give up watching every single move Carly and Giselle make, I have fun. It's a real slumber party, with a few differences. At one point, a girl named Faye pulls down her pajama bottoms and shows us her bruised ass cheeks, punishment for talking back to her Mommy. It was the spanking or missing the party. She picked the spanking. We eat pizza and other junk. Brooke busts out a case filled with nail polish and lets us dig in. Sunshine paints my toes while I paint Holly's. Gloria's not letting anyone touch her pedicure.

We gab about our mistresses, but the conversation on our side of the room turns more to the naughty things they have us do. I admit to Holly that I've given Bear a ride on tape for Pilar. Her "Hell yeah!" and the other girls staring in our direction has me hiding my face in my pillow. We talk a little about who's collared and who's not. It's not a pissing contest, more of a statement of facts. Mistress Francis is apparently a best-selling author who writes under a different name. Sunshine is her assistant and collared, 24/7 little girl. They've been together for five years.

Holly jokes that she's not sure she could go long enough without pissing Bizzy off to earn her collar. I keep my mouth shut. I know every relationship is different. Laurel had no plans to collar me, ever. I have no idea if Pilar even thinks you should collar a little girl. Valerie does, though. When Giselle gets changed for bed, I see a thin leather collar is hiding under her schoolgirl sweater. I do my best not to look at it. Either way, I figure it'll be a long time before

Pilar and I get to that level of commitment, even though I'm madly in love with her. Maybe we'll sort it out on vacation.

Late in the night, Sage suggests we play spin the bottle. I think about declining, but I don't think Pilar will be too upset if I exchange a few innocent pecks here and there. The game is completely silly. Some of the shyer girls plant their lips on the cheeks of their victims. When Gloria's spin lands on Holly they make a dramatic show of licking each other's tongues. It's pretty gross and hilarious.

I get kissed three times. Once by Faye, Sunshine, and Carly. I can't help but feel like Carly knows that I know Valerie, but she kisses me lightly on the lips and tells me she likes my Hello Kitty shirt. It's pretty much the only interaction I have with her all night.

Eventually, Brooke and Di get us all set up in our sleeping bags and put on a movie. It's after one a.m., way after our bedtime. I'm out cold, on the floor between Holly and Sunshine, right after the lights go out.

I have no idea what time it is when Pilar wakes me up. I open my eyes and she's leaning over my sleeping bag, touching my cheek.

"You want to come sleep with me for a while?"

I think I'm dreaming, but I say yes. I shimmy out of my sleeping bag and let Pilar help me up. In a daze, I look around the room. Carly and Giselle are in the same sleeping bag. Brooke is sitting in a chair in the corner reading something on her e-reader. Faye and Sage are gone. I reach down to grab Frank and my sleeping bag.

"Just leave your stuff. We'll come back for it." I still grab Frank and follow Pilar out to the elevator.

I'm half asleep, half hearing the questions she asks me. I ask her a few myself, like what she did all night.

"We just had a little mixer on the roof. There's a nice pool up there. You want to see it?"

"No. I want to go back to sleep."

She laughs a little as she pulls me into her arms. With her guidance I'm able to sleepwalk back to our hotel room. We climb into the large bed and I shiver against the cold sheets. I'm in Pilar's arms again and she's kissing my face. I keep my eyes closed.

"I'm mad at you," I tell her.

She kisses my lips. "Are you now?"

"Yes." My bratty verbal diarrhea starts bubbling up. I let her kiss me again. "You won't let me take you on vacation, and I bet you don't want a sewing machine either."

"Are you drunk?"

"No." The bed is warming up quickly and Pilar's boobs serve as the best cushion. There's not much time before I'll pass out again. "Good night."

The next morning, there's brunch. Sage and Liz are gone, but the rest of the ladies are there. My nerves are on a razor-thin edge again because Valerie is there with her girls. I do my best to ignore them, but it's hard. I mean it's my fucking boss. I have to think of what I'm going to say to her on Monday. I'll have to talk to Pilar first. Over waffles, Holly strikes up a conversation about kinklife, and with Pilar's permission, I swap handles with Sunshine, Gloria, and Holly. Pilar finishes her coffee and lets me know it's time to go. She says good-bye to everyone, including Valerie, who simply nods at me, then thanks Mistress Francis before we leave. I'm glad we came to the party, but I'm happy to put some miles between Valerie and myself.

In the car, I immediately turn to Pilar.

"Did she say anything to you?"

"She said you were beautiful and that I was very lucky, but she didn't say much else."

Pilar's confident grin does nothing to soothe my nerves.

"Are you sure she didn't say anything else?"

"Suzy."

"I know," I say, understanding full well that I'm stepping in it for the twentieth time in two days. "But it's my job, not just my weekends." I'm such an idiot. "Crap, I didn't mean it like that."

"I know what you meant. She didn't say anything else. I'm sure she's curious, but that's where it'll end. Don't worry."

I shudder and sink down in my seat. "Her girls were nice. I—I just—what do I do at work?"

"Nothing. You both know that the other has particular interests. It would be unprofessional for her to bring them up, and it would be disrespectful to me if you approached her about it." She's one-hundred-percent correct on both accounts. "Just go back to work, behave the way you normally would. Give it some time and it'll be less awkward."

"But not completely."

"No, but only because you have a professional relationship and now you know something private about each other. If she crosses any lines, you let me know and I'll handle it."

For once, her promise of protection doesn't bring me comfort. Pilar has no control in my professional life whatsoever. It's not like she can stand guard over my cubicle. All I can do is pretend like this weekend didn't happen.

"I'm sorry," I say again, for my tone and my approach the whole weekend.

"I know, baby. It's okay."

In this situation "It's okay" really means "Wait until we get home." When Pilar pulls into the driveway, she's quiet for a moment before shutting off the car. Her expression isn't exactly calm, but I can't read it.

"Go inside and put your things away, and then I think we should have our straight talk instead of waiting 'til tonight."

I swallow and nod and then offer up a "Yes, Mami." I know what I did was wrong, but I can't believe Pilar is this upset with me that she needs to push our weekly talk up by eight hours. I hop out of the car and wait for her to let me in the front door. A few minutes later I join her on the couch. We sit close to each other, but I can feel the tension Pilar is carrying. She might as well be on the other side of the room.

"We need to talk about your trust issues and me. And you and your need for control."

"What do you mean?"

"Do you understand what Topping from the bottom means?" I know exactly what she's getting at. She thinks that even though my role is to be the submissive, I'm trying to take away her ability to dominate me. My eyes spring wide in shock and my stomach cramps up on itself. I wish I had Frank with me, but he's in my bedroom.

"Yes, but I—"

"You have a hard time taking no for answer, even when I explain why I'm asking you to do something. Especially when my plans go against what you want personally. Let's talk about this vacation." I do my best not to groan, but my eyes kinda-sorta roll. I'm over the vacation thing. We don't need to discuss it again. Just as quickly, Pilar taps my thigh. She's pissed now and she has my attention. I swallow and try to explain myself instead of offering another apology. I'm fucking up so bad.

"I understand what you're saying. You're in control. When you said you didn't want to go I should have dropped it. I just wanted to do something nice for you."

"No. You just wanted to do something nice for yourself, and you wanted to bring me along." The cramp in my stomach moves up to my chest, and my eyes start to sting. Pilar goes on before I can argue anymore. "You do realize that I'm on vacation right now, don't you?"

"I—yes." Of course she is, and she's been spending every minute of her free time being supportive of me while I struggle with the worst account ever.

"This is a break for me. This, well, not this conversation, but this time between seasons on the show is relaxing for me. I'm doing what I want and spending time with the people I want to see. I don't need or want you to take me on vacation. My job isn't stressful. But you are stressed out and you do want a break from the city, so instead of just telling me that you need a break and you would like to get out of town, you suggested that you take me away and then got offended when I said no."

"I didn't think of it that way."

"I thought this was about your need to control certain situations, especially since you're feeling so helpless at work, but in the car it occurred to me that this is about trust. I don't think you trust me to do the best thing for you."

"I do!" I dropped to the floor without even thinking and put my hands on her knee. "I trust you more than anyone." Pilar's expression finally softens and she strokes my cheek. I lean into her hand.

"But what does that mean if you don't trust anyone? I don't have to tell you anything that goes on between me and another Mommy or Daddy, but I told you what happened between me and Valerie, and you didn't believe me. You didn't trust me to tell you the truth so you kept pushing until you knew I wasn't going to give you the answer you wanted. You're scared that Valerie said something to me. Instead of believing that she really didn't say much at all, you choose to believe that she said something that you needed to hear and placed the blame on me for keeping you out of the loop."

"That's not what I meant," I say quietly.

"But it's what you said and it's what you did. Intentions only get us so far, Suzy." I don't know what else to say so I apologize again. I'm not sure Pilar accepts it. It's like there's this muddy hole and I keep slipping deeper and deeper to the bottom. She sighs and strokes my hair. I don't want to cry, but I hate the way she's not looking me in the eye. She's looking at the floor beside me. She's somewhere else, thinking of what to do with me. I forced her to do that. I forced this distance between us.

"What can I do to make it better?"

Pilar tortures me with nearly a minute of silence before she answers. When she does, the tears I've been fighting break their hold. She wants to know what she's doing wrong. She wants to know if she's letting me down, if there's some way she can earn my trust. I spring up on my knees and clutch both of her hands. I tell her, nothing. She's done nothing wrong.

"I don't just love you, Suzy," she says. "I care about you and your happiness and well-being, but we have an agreement and I need your trust for this agreement to work. Do you want this to work?"

"Yes. I want to be with you. I want this to work. I'm stressed and paranoid and worried that this thing with Valerie will become an issue at the office. But I trust you."

"What we have between us, it's beyond the point of selfishness for me. I feel like I understand you pretty well now. I feel like I understand what's best for you, but I would help you find another Mommy before I kept you for myself if I felt that's what you needed."

"No," I say. "I want you."

"Well then, baby. I know we've already talked about this, but you need to keep the lines of communication open with me before things get this far. Way before you feel the need to push back and way before you start confusing my needs and wants with your own. They are complementary, but they aren't the same."

She's right. I tell her so. I want to climb into her lap and beg her to hug me, but I stay put right there on the floor. I've already pushed my luck with her too far.

"Valerie thinks you're a very pretty girl, and I will be more than happy to take you on vacation. Okay? That's all there is to it."

"Okay, Mami."

She leans down and kisses me then. She asks me if there's anything I need to tell her or anything I want to get off my chest, but I've got nothing. I'm just mad at myself for, once again, making the wrong call, for being too afraid to let her lead me the way I want her to. And for letting my fear of Valerie supersede my love for my Mistress.

Pilar kisses me one more time, then tells me to go change. We spend the rest of the afternoon on the couch, both of us snoozing with the TV on. Me in her arms where I need to be. She feeds me dinner and helps me with my bath. I only get a kiss at bedtime, and a light one at that. Although I think I'm forgiven, I go to sleep with the worst feeling in the bottom of my stomach. Something is still off between us, and the next day I'll have to face Valerie. Frank is there to soak up my silent tears, but still, he's of very little comfort.

❖

Monday morning, I know I'm out of line. I know it's tacky, but I have to tell Liam what happened. I have to tell someone. We offer to grab lattes for a bunch of people, then power walk down to Hearth Cafe. Liam almost drops his coffee when I dish the whole story.

"You are fucking kidding."

"No, I'm not."

"And she has two little girls? Why is everyone's sex life more interesting than mine? I'm the double-jointed gay guy. *My* sex life should be making headlines."

"This isn't exactly headline worthy."

"But it's pretty damn juicy. What are you going to do?"

"Nothing. I can't bring it up. She shouldn't bring it up. Plus, I already got in trouble with Pilar for making such a big deal about it. I just have to live with the fact that Valerie is an active Mommy Dominant."

"You know what I'm thinking, right?"

"No..."

"She was sizing you up that day."

"Oh, shut up." I'd give Liam a little shove, but my hands are full of latte. Instead, he lets out his evil little laugh and just bumps my hip.

"No, you're right. I'm sure that was just a coincidence. You've just made it so easy to fuck with you."

"Thanks."

"I say you don't worry about it. It's awkward, but it's not like she wants it getting out. Though, now you have a little leverage in case, say, you need a reason to blackmail her."

"You really must be bored, huh?"

"Yesss."

"We need to get you and Gary into a bondage class pronto. You need something to do."

On edge doesn't come close to describing my mood that day. I wait and wait and wait for Valerie to walk by my desk. I almost crave the moment where we have to face off and exchange that look that says, "Oh, I know what you did this weekend, you little freak," but the moment doesn't come.

At eleven, we get an e-mail that she'll be out for the day. My imagination goes back into overdrive. Is she sick? Or is she taking extra time to spend with her little girls? Thinking of her with them makes me feel weird. It's a bit of a turn-on. She's not an ugly woman, after all, but she's just not who I expected in that role. But knowing her in this other way? There are just things about people you'd rather remained a secret. This is one of those things. I'm not sure I'll ever be able to look at her the same way. It's too much to consider the ways she might be thinking about me. Or Pilar.

As the e-mail stated, I don't see Valerie for the rest of the day, but first thing Tuesday morning she's there for our status call with 21 And Up. I almost gag when she walks into the conference room, but her demeanor hasn't changed. I don't know, maybe I expected her to wink at me or give me that knowing nod, but she greets us all in her regular fashion, and then we hop on the call. I'm hypersensitive to everything she says and does during the meeting, but from the way she only looks at me while I'm speaking and sometimes not even then because she's making notes, I realize that Pilar was right; Valerie knows where the professional line is and has no interest in crossing it. I should have listened to her.

By the end of the call, after ten or so snide comments from the 21 And Up reps about how long it's taking us to get the paper-doll function up, I've forgotten all about Valerie. The weekend is definitely over, and work is waiting not so patiently to swallow me whole.

Late that night, I get a frantic e-mail from Katie about the paper-doll banners. 21 And Up has requested ten more. I'm too tired to think about it. It's more code, more flash design. I'll just have to deal with it in the morning.

I wake up tense and a little miserable because Pilar and I haven't actually spoken since Monday morning, and our Sunday conversation is still sloshing around in my head. When I get to work,

I find that in her frantic scramble to find out when the banners can be ready, Katie has CCed Valerie on our e-mails. She calls me into her office. I quickly scan the chain of e-mails sent while I was trying to sleep, then grab a notepad and head to her office. Valerie's leaning over her desk, as she often does, clicking on her mouse.

"I will handle the banners," I say just as I cross the threshold.

"No doubt in my mind that you will." She takes a seat and leans back in her chair. "Why don't you close the door?"

I freeze halfway to her desk, and that moment arrives. We stare each other down. There's no wink, no evil smirk, but the shift occurs right then. I can flee and make an ass out of myself if she really just wants to have a closed-door meeting about 21 And Up, the kind of meeting we've had before. Or I can wait for Valerie to cross that line that almost seems tangible and I can defend myself. Either way, I turn and close the door. The smile on Valerie's face when I step back to her desk tells me exactly the way this meeting is going to go.

"Put down your notepad and come here."

What I feel next can't be expressed in words, rather in temperatures and reactions from my skin. I walk to the side of her desk, just next to her chair, fear dictating my every step.

She touches my leg first. I regret wearing a skirt. I close my eyes and try not to react to the change in her tone—that practiced, precise tone that a vulnerable submissive is hard-pressed to resist.

"Did you have fun this weekend?" she asks.

I don't reply. I can't. My whole body is burning hot, and if my skin could actually crawl, it would be trying to escape. My heart pounding against my ribs is the only thing keeping my whole stomach down. I can feel her in my neck that is strained so tight I know it will be sore later.

She trails her finger down to my knee. I don't know what to do. "Answer me."

"Yes. I had fun."

"Carly says you're quite the kisser. Did you enjoy kissing my little girl? Look at me when I talk to you, Suzanne. Or is it Suzy?"

My eyes snap open. "It's Suzanne, please." I can't control my legs. It's like my feet have turned to Jell-o, but that name belongs to

Pilar. The wider the cruel smile on Valerie's face stretches, the more I realize she knows who I'm defending.

"Suzanne, then. You haven't answered my question."

"I don't know."

Her eyebrows go up, but her tone is soft and playful. "You don't know? What kind of answer is that?"

"It was fine. She's very nice."

"Carly *is* a very nice girl. How did seeing me with my girls make you feel?"

"Uh...nervous. Anxious." Terrified, with justifiable reason.

"Seeing you made me feel anxious, too. I didn't know how you'd react here in the office, but you know how to keep a secret, don't you, Suzanne?"

"Yes."

"I see that. You lied to me when I asked if you were seeing someone. Your Mommy sent you those flowers, didn't she?"

I tell her yes.

"She's sweet, but she's wrong for you. We talked about you, you know?"

"Yes. She told me. She told me it wasn't much of a conversation."

She laughs a bit. "I bet she did. How long have you two been together?"

"Almost two months." Her hand is still moving up and down my leg. She strokes my calf.

"Oh. Not long at all. No wonder she hasn't collared you. I like to claim what I want right away."

"Then why haven't you collared Carly?" The words are out and Valerie's reaction is just as swift. She smacks me lightly on the thigh.

"You've got some mouth on you. I don't plan on keeping her, that's why." She looks me up and down slowly. I feel my nostrils flaring. I can get through this, I tell myself. Just get through this. Though I have no idea what will happen next. Her palm rubs up and down the length of my thigh, all the way up.

"Lift up your skirt," she says. My response is automatic because I don't know what else to do. Sometimes you can't run from a barking dog; you just have to wait for it to attack. I grab the hem of my skirt and pull it up. My panties are especially girlie today. White with little ladybugs on them. They're new. Pilar hasn't seen them on me yet. I stare out the window now, tinted from the inside so no one can see in, and try to ignore the perverse look of approval on Valerie's face. When her finger brushes my slit, I do everything I can to shut my body's reactions down, but it doesn't work. I'm trembling, it feels like, but really I hold perfectly still. She takes her time, finding my clit through the fabric. Her touch is gentle, but her fingers are slimmer than Pilar's, I distantly know. Just another difference that sets them apart.

"Your mouth could use some work, but look at that control. You're very obedient."

I close my eyes again and wait.

"I think we have ourselves an interesting situation here," she says. "In a few weeks you'll be working directly for me. More private meetings. I might even take you on a pitch meeting here or there. I have some plans for you, but I should talk to your Mommy first, I think."

My eyes snap open then, but my voice is barely a squeak above a whisper. "Please. I—"

"Shh, Suzanne. Let me finish. I've already talked to Pilar about a trade. Carly is a very good girl. Pilar would enjoy her company. And it seems like you could use a little more discipline, discipline I could give you."

A defense of Pilar and our relationship comes rushing to the surface, but it's immediately halted as Valerie pulls my panties to the side. Her fingers stroke along my bare skin. I want to beg her to stop, but my words come out as a pathetic whimper.

"Son of a bitch." She sucks in a breath through her teeth. "You have a gorgeous pussy, Suzanne. And look how wet you are."

She holds up her finger, glossy with the evidence of my arousal and terror. I think I might pass out. Her fingers go back between my legs. She strokes me again.

"Pilar loves me," I manage to say. "She's not interested in a trade."

"And how do you know that? Is that what she told you?"

"Yes."

"And why wouldn't you believe her. Such a good little girl. Let me tell you something. Pilar wants to keep you happy while she has you, but do you really think she's planning to keep you forever? Even if she collared you, it's not like a piece of leather is legally binding. If things aren't working for her, she will move on. Or if something better comes along for you. It's a conversation, one conversation. I explain what I want, make her see what she really wants, and it's done."

"I want to be with her." My voice is shaky, but it's the truth. I want Pilar.

"Sometimes it's not about what you want. Sometimes it's about what you need. You need more discipline, more structure, a little more training. And I need a little girl that I can have access to during business hours. Carly and Giselle are great, but I only get them on the weekends. I want more and I think you do, too. Imagine all the time I could spend spanking you right over this desk. All the afternoons you could spend right here between my legs. I think Pilar would want that for you. Along with a little attitude adjustment."

She stands and pulls down my skirt, even though my slit is still exposed. "I think I'll call her tonight. In the meantime, you can keep a secret, can't you, Suzanne?"

I say yes because any argument will only keep me in her office longer.

"Good girl. Now why don't you head back to your desk? I know you have work to do."

I turn calmly on my heels, reminded instantly of how my underwear is bunched against my thigh. I grab my notepad and do all I can to walk, not run, back to my desk. Air is rushing in my ears, but the whole office is oblivious to the sound. Phones are ringing. Keyboards clicking. I hear Mitch laughing. I have to go. I pack up my laptop and grab my keys. No one seems to notice that I have all of my stuff as I slip out the door.

CHAPTER THIRTEEN

I miraculously make it back to my apartment without wrecking my car, but I fail to hold off a complete breakdown until I get home. I think this is the panic attack I've been waiting for. I'm prepared to hide my face and my tears from my neighbors, but the elevators are empty as I head up to my apartment.

I know what I need to do. I need to call Pilar. I need to tell her what happened, but I can't. I can't tell her that I let Valerie touch me. I can't confess that I had a real sense of what she was capable of doing. I can't admit that this isn't the first time that Valerie has stepped out of line with me. Pilar was right. I didn't believe that a short conversation between them was all that transpired by the rooftop pool. I blamed her for my omissions, and now I've trapped myself in this horrible corner.

I have to call Pilar, but not yet. I'm not ready to yet.

I e-mail Liam.

Went home sick. Tell Katie.

And then I dial the dispensary. I'm too overwhelmed. I need my parents. My voice cracks when my mother answers the phone. It's her accent when she says hello and the way she switches to Patois the moment she realizes it's me.

"What's wrong, my princess baby?" she asks. I would do anything to be back home with her right now. To be back with her and my dad, mixing edibles and working out plans for next week's deliveries. Anything to be somewhere other than this place I'm in now. I tell my mother something happened at work. She asks me what. I can't say the words. I'm almost thirty and I can't say that my boss sexually harassed me because I know I could have stopped it. Her mother's intuition kicks in and suddenly she's asking all the right questions. The truth comes out, though not the word-for-word details because I can't repeat them. It's too hard.

"You hold on. Let me talk to your father." I hear muffled voices and then my dad is on the phone. He asks me about the circumstances of my promotion. I swear to him that from my end, this had nothing to do with it. He tells me he knows. It's Valerie's motives he questions. I finally start to question them, too. I tell him I'm scared. He tells me they're going to speak to their lawyer, and then I'm even more frightened. I beg him not to because I know somehow this is my fault. I'm not ready to face the professional consequences.

I tell him that HR might not even believe me. It's tricky, I explain, because we're both women. I'm out to my immediate office friends, but I don't know how seriously the heads will take a claim of female sexual harassment from the black lesbian. I tell him it's more likely I'll suffer. He relents then.

I'm drained by this point, but they won't let me off the phone until I promise them both that I will call them back that night. They don't like the fact that I'm dealing with this alone. I realize I shouldn't have to handle this on my own, that I don't have to. I hang up with my parents and then I text Pilar.

I'm too chicken to call her just yet, even though we're in emergency territory. I text her and ask her to call me as soon as she can.

I puke twice in the shower. When I'm out of the bathroom and dry, and the ladybug panties are down the trash chute, I brave a look at my phone. Tons of e-mails from work, but those I ignore. A text from Katie saying she hopes I feel better and a text from Liam.

What's going on?

He knows something's up from the way I disappeared. I don't answer his texts and I don't answer his calls. I need to talk to Pilar first. But as the afternoon goes by and I hear nothing from her—no texts, no calls, no replies to my frantic messages—I consider getting back to Liam. More e-mails and missed calls clog up my phone. Still nothing from Pilar. I'm not surprised when Liam knocks on my door. It's early evening when he shows up. I open the door, and the look on Liam's face reflects exactly how I feel. We park it on my couch and I tell him what happened. Somehow, it's easier to tell Liam the whole truth.

"Oh, God. I shouldn't have joked about her like that."

"No, you were right," I say.

"So were you! You said she gave you the creeps and I turned it into a joke."

"That's not it." My phone vibrates in my palm. It's not Pilar. I groan. Liam asks what I'm gonna tell her. I tell him, the truth. He stays a while longer. I cry a little. I don't sob, but I can't seem to keep my face dry. Liam hugs me. I'm freaking out about what Pilar is going to say. I hope she understands. I tell him I can't believe Valerie. I liked her. I liked working for her.

"I wonder if she fucked with Josh," Liam says. It's definitely a good question. Especially with the way he split so abruptly.

"You know how in all those movies, you see that girl getting harassed by some douche or smacked around by her husband and you think 'Oh, I'd kill him' or 'That shit would never happen to me. I'd kill him.'"

Liam lets out a light chuckle. "Yeah."

"It's not like that in real life."

He pulls me closer and rests his head on mine. "I know, sweetie."

Just then my phone rings again. I don't know the number, but I feel like I need to answer it. I say hello, my voice unsure. It's Bizzy. She wants to see me. Now.

❖

I convince Liam I'm fine to go see her alone, and then I head to Bizzy's house in Brentwood. It's a long drive. One of those long drives where the scenery starts to change and you feel like you're in a whole different state by the time you've arrived in a different part of town. I park in Bizzy's driveway like she told me to. My hand is shaking when I knock on the door. A nearly naked Holly answers it. All she's wearing is a pair of panties and a pair of thigh-high athletic socks. She pulls me inside.

"I have no idea what happened, but Daddy's been on the phone about *you,* almost all day," she whispers.

"Shit."

Holly squeezes my hand. "Good luck."

I follow her through the house to Bizzy's office. It reflects her style. Cool, masculine, a little dark. She greets me with a smile and tells me have a seat on the couch. She sends Holly to get us something to drink.

"How are you?" she asks while we wait.

"I'm okay. I've been much better."

"Don't worry," she says. "We'll figure this out shortly."

I'm not sure what that means, but I don't like the sound of it.

Holly comes back with a glass of water for me and a green blended something or other for Bizzy. Of course she juices. She's in great shape. Holly's sent to watch TV. She kisses her Daddy and offers me a sympathetic smile before she leaves me to my doom. Bizzy takes a sip of her drink, then joins me on the couch.

"Tell me what happened today."

I sigh and the tears start leaking out again. I tell her everything. When I get to the part with Valerie's inappropriately busy hands, she asks me a strange question.

"How did it make you feel?"

"What did you mean?" I say. "I hated it. I didn't want her to touch me at all."

"I don't think Valerie should have approached you that way. What I'm trying to figure out is how it made you feel."

"Awful. She made me feel awful."

"And why was that?"

"Because she did it at work. Because she's my boss. Because she's not Pilar." I'm trying not to raise my voice at Bizzy, but it's hard. I know I messed up, but I didn't ask for it. I didn't want it.

"I talked to Valerie and Pilar today. And they've spoken to each other."

I actually gulp. The knot in my throat is huge. "They have?"

She touches my knee lightly before pulling her hand away. "You're not in trouble."

I don't believe her.

"Why am I here then?"

"Because I felt I needed to get involved as an impartial third party."

"But you love Pilar. You care about her. How can you be impartial?"

Bizzy smiles a bit and shakes her head. "My feelings for Pilar don't blind me to the fact that she's human. I suggested I could help and she agreed."

I understand, but I'm still confused and terrified about what I'm doing at her house and why Pilar couldn't at least text me back. Bizzy explains. "Pilar is having some doubts."

"About me?"

"About herself. Valerie called her this afternoon and told her about your exchange this morning. She proposed that she take you on. Pilar said no, but she called me because she saw some valid points in Valerie's argument. Maybe you need someone different."

This is what terrible feels like. Pilar is dumping me via her former Dom, and the thought of it, the thought of being without her makes me feel worse than I have ever felt before.

"I don't want someone different." I sob then. I can't hold it in any longer.

Bizzy hands me some tissues. "I'm not here to make you cry, Suzy, and maybe this is where it is impossible for me to be completely impartial, but I want what's best for Pilar. When she loves, she loves very deeply, and I don't want her to end up in a situation she can't recover from. At the same time, I'm pretty fond of you. Holly loves you. She won't stop talking about you. I think with a situation as young as your relationship is with Pilar, it's not too late. Between myself and Miss Francis—You like her, don't you?"

"Yeah. She's pretty nice." I sniffle and wipe my face.

"We can help you find someone who better suits your needs."

"But I..." I hiccup and then stop trying to make her see that I don't want someone.

"Tell me about your last Mistress. Tell me about Laurel." I didn't expect her to go there, but I answer her request. I tell her everything about Laurel. Once I get started I find I can't stop. I tell her things I'd forgotten about, stuff I'd intentionally pushed to the back of my mind, like the time Laurel made me fuck one of her friends that wasn't even in the scene, just because she knew I would do whatever she said.

I tell her how Laurel refused to meet my brother when he came for New Years, how she used a cane on me one time even though it was one of my hard limits, and I tell her about the one time she ignored my safe word. It wasn't anything painful, just some scary sensory-deprivation stuff I wasn't ready for, and she went there anyway and ignored my pleas for her to stop. Her aftercare had been better than usual that night so I'd let it slide. And I tell Bizzy how it ended and how she'd even messaged me a few weeks ago. I tell her I didn't reply.

"Did you love her?" Bizzy asks.

I shake my head. "No, but I think I wanted her to love me. Clearly she didn't."

"You're probably right. Suzy, I want you to think about what you want and what you need." She holds up her hand as I try to interrupt. "After you've had some time to calm down and can think more clearly, I want you to really consider your role in this lifestyle. Laurel tried to determine that for you, and you see what happened there. A Dom can guide and control and help you explore and hopefully open your eyes to new, positive experiences, but if you are going against your own desires it won't work. Without your trust and true consent any relationship you have with any good Mistress won't work. Do you understand me?"

I do. I say so.

"Pilar needs a little time to think as well."

I might kill Valerie. It's a distinct possibility.

"Why couldn't Pilar tell me that?" I ask.

"Because she understood that she was too upset to have a productive conversation with you."

That actually makes sense. I agree to give Pilar that space, and in the meantime I'm to think of what it would really mean to be with Pilar long-term and what it truly means to me to submit.

I'm a complete wreck so Bizzy lets me spend the night. She doesn't think it's a good idea to send me home alone. I text Liam and let him know I'm okay. I resist the urge to text Pilar. I think about how she might not even want to hear from me at all. I break down crying again while Bizzy makes dinner. She lets Holly and me stay up watching movies.

Before we go to bed, I ask Bizzy if I can use her computer. It takes a few minutes to find the right e-mail addresses, but no time to type up what I want to say. I quit my job and let Donna and the head of HR know Valerie and her sexual-harassing ass are the exact reason why. She might not even get a slap on the wrist, but at least she won't fly under the radar as a predator because of me.

I hate that I won't be working with Liam and Katie and the guys anymore, but it had to be done. Thanks to my time with Pilar and the vacation I'm not taking her on, I have enough money to hold me over until I find something new.

The rest of the week goes by in a bizarre haze. I find the bottom of that muddy hole. My feet sink in and I wonder if I'll ever get out. Liam grabs my work laptop for me so I don't have to go back to the office. He tells me the place is abuzz with gossip, but Valerie is still employed by Reach Advertising. When I change my work info on

Facebook, Josh sends me a message saying he might have a spot for me at his new agency. He didn't hate marketing after all. He just hated working at Reach. I thank him and send him my résumé. I call my mother every day because she's freaking out. It becomes a part-time job just convincing her and my dad that I'm fine. I lie when they ask about Pilar. I tell them we're fine, too. My mother will drive down here if she thinks I'm going through all this crap on top of a breakup.

I cry a lot. I force myself to eat and bathe. I develop a love/hate relationship with Frank. I need him, but he smells like Pilar's house. It's hard to be around him. I keep looking for work and spend time with Holly and Liam and Gary. I hear nothing from Pilar. I still wear her panties every day, because I've tossed all the pairs she didn't buy me. By Friday night, I understand that this really might be the end for Pilar and me.

Finally I do what Bizzy asked me to. I start to think about what I want and what I need. It's hard to separate Pilar from the equation, but I try. I think of what the ideal relationship based on domination and submission would be like for me. I think about what ways I want to be challenged and what type of woman I would want to push me in those ways. That's when Pilar pops back into my mind. I always want that woman to have her soft touch and even her stern voice when I'm getting on her last nerve.

I want that smile, that body. I most definitely want those breasts. But something does occur to me. If I have a trust bone in my body, it's certainly broken. I don't think Pilar is capable of hurting me, but I'm expecting her to let me down. I think of our first weekend together and how she told me to learn to manage my expectations, and I realize that my expectations are so fucked. They aren't about joy and satisfaction. My expectations are built on disappointment and pain.

I'm waiting for Pilar to hurt me even though I believe her claims of love. I'm waiting for her to decide that she can do better. And that stunted our growth as a couple. But Valerie, that shithead just compounded our problems. I make a vow to confront her if I ever see her again. No violence, of course, but I will definitely let her know that even without Pilar, she would never be enough for me.

❖

Sunday morning, Pilar calls. Her voice sounds strange. She's trying hard to be distant, but I detect a lot of emotion when she asks me if I'd be willing to come over. It bothers me that she asks. I miss her direct instructions. I don't say anything about that, though. I just tell her I'll be there soon.

On the way there I decide it's a great idea to drive myself a little bit crazier. I think about how this is it. I'm just going to Pilar's to pick up the clothes I've left over there. This is the last time I'll see her. Or worse, I'll see her again, but I'll be pathetically single again and she'll have her new little girl by her side.

I force the jitters down and ring the doorbell. The light smile of welcome on Pilar's face isn't enough to hide the bags under her eyes. We've both had a rough week. She invites me in and I follow her to the kitchen. On the table is a white leather collar with pink accents, a silver bracelet, and a set of keys. She tells me to have a seat. I keep quiet as I eye the objects in front of me. She gets right to the point.

"I want to say I'm sorry. I knew you were having trust issues, and the last thing I should have done was push you away. We should have talked this out the other day, but I was in a bad place and I think I would have hurt your feelings. I didn't want to do that."

I clear my throat. "I understand. Bizzy explained that."

"Good. Do you want to be with Valerie?" she asks. I'm sure Bizzy passed on the details of our conversation. Still, I understand. Pilar needs to hear it from me.

"No. Absolutely not. I told Donna that she harassed me and I quit my job. I never want to see Valerie again unless it's to punch her in the face."

Pilar snorts and covers her laugh a little. "I might beat you to that. I don't think she should have talked to you that way, but she *never* should have touched you. I wish I'd heard about your interaction with Valerie from your lips and not from Valerie and Bizzy. I'm sorry for that, too."

I absolutely accept that apology, though I cringe to think of the way Valerie must have phrased that confession.

She goes on. "I wanted to give you some options when it comes to me and us, based on what I think I can handle and what I can give you. Does that sound fair?"

"Very." Fair and frightening.

"Option one would be that we go our separate ways. I say that because I don't know how you're feeling, but I did screw up, and I understand if you want to move on." I want to object, but I let her finish. She picks up the keys. "Option two is the girlfriend option."

"What's the girlfriend option?"

"We could date. You can have my keys. Hopefully you'd give me a set of your own and we could simply be together. We know we like sleeping together. We enjoy each other's company. We could be a vanilla couple, and if things get kinky from time to time, then great. But no pressure."

"And option three?"

Pilar picks up the collar. "You would be my little girl. You'd wear this every moment we spend together." She hands me the bracelet. There's a break midway around and a small hex screw that would secure it around my wrist. "You'd wear that always."

"Are you saying you want to collar me?"

"Yes. I would be open to the idea," she says, her voice nearly emotionless. It hurts me that she's trying so hard to school her features and her tone, that Pilar is focusing on keeping her feelings under control.

I examine the bracelet a little closer. There's an inscription. *Mami's sweet, silly, little Suzy girl.*

My heart trips and flutters. I take a deep breath. I remember what Bizzy said. I think about myself.

"Can I tell you what I need if we do option three?"

"You need more. You need to be my little girl all the time."

I nod. "I felt selfish and foolish before, but it's what I wanted almost from the beginning."

"The weekends and the occasional weeknights aren't enough."

"Right. I didn't know that I could be this way. I thought it was a bad thing to want to be submissive all the time, but it's not. It's what fulfills me. I think that's why I liked working for that—" I skip the "bitch." "That not-nice lady. Before all this, I could sense her dominating personality, and it made me feel comfortable to be around that energy."

"You should have gotten that from me."

"I would've liked that. But you were right. I was pushing. I wasn't trusting. I was making a mess of things."

"So you need that consistency," Pilar says. "But I think you need more than that. You need to experiment with more kinks and fetishes. You want me to push your physical boundaries further."

I nod again. "You're right. I love how gentle you are with me, but I feel like I have a masochistic side that I've been denying. Laurel was trying to hurt me. Like actually hurt me, but now I want to cultivate my relationship with pain. And even bondage and deprivation."

"I can do those things with you."

I put the bracelet down on the table. It sucks to ask the next question, but I have to.

"Is that what you want? I know you *can*. I don't doubt your abilities in any aspect, but I don't want you to push you outside of your comfort zone just to make me happy."

She nods back and flashes me the most devastatingly sexy smile. The fear inside me instantly turns to molten lust. My pussy starts to pulse with moisture. I flex my thighs and shift in my seat. Pilar notices. "Trust me," she says. "I know what I want and what I can handle. I think I was trying to be careful with you. I didn't want to push you too far. You're an emotional girl, but that doesn't mean you're weak. We can do more. Much more."

"Okay." I bite the inside of my lip. I've made up my mind. "Can I have a few minutes to myself? Just to think."

"Of course. I'll be in the other room. Call me when you're ready to keep talking." With a gentle brush of her fingers across my shoulder, Pilar leaves me alone.

I'm giddy for a few moments. I did what I needed to do. I stuck up for myself. I stopped letting Laurel-related fear get the best of me, and I told Pilar exactly what I wanted. And she agreed. Still, I force myself to take a step back. I stand and walk over to the counter. Do I want this? I ask myself. I want her. At the very least the sex is too damn good to give up. At the most I would marry her, no questions asked. I would grow old with her. Make home improvements together. Get a dog. I would do all that shit. Easily. But if I'm being completely honest with myself, I'm not just someone's girlfriend. I'm something different.

I take a few breaths, then call Pilar back to the kitchen. She finds me by her chair, on my knees, naked except for a pair of her pink-and-purple-plaid panties with tiny bows on the hips. I have the collar in my hand. She sits down with ease and confidence, but her eyes give her away. She's all business. She's a little nervous.

Pilar takes the collar from me. "Are you sure this is what you want?"

"Yes, Mami."

"You want to be my little girl, with me, always under my rules and my instruction and my care?"

"Yes, Mami. I belong with you, always. Naked at your feet. I want to be yours."

She runs her fingers over my hair, then smoothly runs her fingers down my cheek until she grips me lightly by my chin. The start of arousal turns to a full gush as she leans closer. "I made a mistake. You needed me, and instead of being there for you, I hid. I ran away. When your trust was fragile, I pushed you away. I will never do that again. Ever."

Her thumb brushes a few tears from my cheek. "Thank you, Mami." I say. "I'm sorry I didn't tell you about Valerie sooner. I was scared."

"All's forgiven." Pilar smiles, that genuine, gorgeous smile, and like that I'm Suzy puddle right there on her kitchen floor. "You

can keep your place until we square things away, but you'll stay
with me."

"Of course, Mami. Always." I smile through my tears now.

She buckles the leather around my neck. Not too loose, not too
tight. I love the fresh smell of it, but I can't wait until it smells like
me, like us. My sweat and her rose-scented perfume. "Just so you
know, Valerie didn't force my hand. I ordered this and your bracelet
last week, but I wanted to wait until you took some time off work."

"Well, I'm off work now," I say with a cheeky cock of my
head. Pilar tweaks my nose as I giggle.

"Francis is dealing with her."

"She is?"

"Uh-huh. Give me your wrist, baby." I hold up my hand and
watch as she secures the shiny metal around my wrist. It's perfect.
Elegant and strong, just like my Mami. She touches my cheek again.
"Francis and Bizzy have deep connections in the community. People
have been warned about her, and she'll never bother you again."

I almost breathe my thank you. I think for a second that I don't
deserve Pilar's love or Bizzy's and Francis's protection. But I do,
and I'll earn and take them every day of the week.

"I love you, little girl." Pilar leans closer and brushes her lips
against mine. I love her, too. I tell her. She kisses me deeper and I'm
lost, swimming in the shallow waters of my little space, anxious to
go deeper. I want to ask what's next, but I don't have to.

Pilar guides me off the floor and across her lap. She pulls my
underwear down around my thighs. I shiver as she strokes my ass.
My collar gently presses into my skin and I breathe deeper.

"This is a spanking to cleanse. I didn't know you needed this
before, but you need it now. And I will spank you like this often.
This is for my pleasure and for your release."

"Thank you, Mami," I gasp.

Pilar starts to spank me—firm, repetitive strokes with her hand
until my skin is hot and tender, until I'm sobbing across her thighs.
It's exactly what I need. What I never got from Laurel, but what I
want only from Pilar. She encourages me to tell her how I feel. I tell
her I love her, that I need her, that I need her hands on my body in

this way. I thank her over and over. By the end, I'm breathless, with tears streaking my face. Pilar pulls me upright and hugs me tight to her chest. She kisses me all over. She tells me she missed me, that her nights were horrible without me. I tell her the same. She tells me that once I calm down a bit I'm going to make her come. I tell her it will be my pleasure.

I wrap my arms around her shoulders and kiss her neck. "You need to be more strict with me too, Mami. You let me get away with murder."

She pulls me closer and pinches my butt. She chuckles softly in my ear.

Later that night, after some interesting bondage play in the kitchen, Pilar sits me down and we make a list of the week's chores on my Hello Kitty stationery. She understands that I need different types of balance in our relationship, so she's wrapped that balance up in my submission. I do chores, and once I'm working again, I'll help pay some of the bills like the cable and the water. Once a month I get to plan a date. It's her idea, but I appreciate it. I like doing things for her, too. And still I'm hers. No longer pathetically single or lost in what I'm looking for.

Before bed, we both log into our kinklife accounts to make some changes. Pilar's picture stays the same, but her status changes. I change my avatar to a cute 160 x 160 picture of me wearing my Mami's collar. Beside that it reads: *submissive to, little girl of, collared by Mami-P.*

About the Author

After years of meddling in her friends' love lives, Rebekah turned to writing romance as a means to surviving a stressful professional life. She has worked in various positions from library assistant, meter maid, middle school teacher, B movie production assistant, reality show crew chauffeur, D movie producer, and her most fulfilling job to date, lube and harness specialist at an erotic boutique in West Hollywood.

Her interests include Wonder Woman collectibles, cookies, James Taylor, quality hip-hop, football, American muscle cars, large breed dogs, and the ocean. When she's not working, writing, reading, or sleeping, she is watching Ken Burns documentaries and cartoons or taking dance classes. If given the chance, she will cheat at UNO. She was raised in Southern New Hampshire and now lives in Southern California with an individual who is much more tech savvy than she ever will be.

You can find Rebekah at letusseeshallwe.blogspot.com.

Books Available from Bold Strokes Books

At Her Feet by Rebekah Weatherspoon. Digital marketing producer Suzanne Kim knows she has found the perfect love in her new mistress Pilar, but before they can make the ultimate commitment, Suzanne's professional life threatens to disrupt their perfectly balanced bliss. (978-1-60282-948-0)

Show of Force by AJ Quinn. A chance meeting between navy pilot Evan Kane and correspondent Tate McKenna takes them on a roller-coaster ride where the stakes are high, but the reward is higher: a chance at love. (978-1-60282-942-8)

Clean Slate by Andrea Bramhall. Can Erin and Morgan work through their individual demons to rediscover their love for each other, or are the unexplainable wounds too deep to heal? (978-1-60282-943-5)

Hold Me Forever by D. Jackson Leigh. An investigation into illegal cloning in the quarter horse racing industry threatens to destroy the growing attraction between Georgia debutante Mae St. John and Louisiana horse trainer Whit Casey. (978-1-60282-944-2)

Trusting Tomorrow by PJ Trebelhorn. Funeral director Logan Swift thinks she's perfectly happy with her solitary life devoted to helping others cope with loss until Brooke Collier moves in next door to care for her elderly grandparents. (978-1-60282-891-9)

Forsaking All Others by Kathleen Knowles. What if what you think you want is the opposite of what makes you happy? (978-1-60282-892-6)

Exit Wounds by VK Powell. When Officer Loane Landry falls in love with ATF informant Abigail Mancuso, she realizes that nothing is as it seems—not the case, not her lover, not even the dead. (978-1-60282-893-3)

Dirty Power by Ashley Bartlett. Cooper's been through hell and back, and she's still broke and on the run. But at least she found the twins. They'll keep her alive. Right? (978-1-60282-896-4)

The Rarest Rose by I. Beacham. After a decade of living in her beloved house, Ele disturbs its past and finds her life being haunted by the presence of a ghost who will show her that true love never dies. (978-1-60282-884-1)

Code of Honor by Radclyffe. The face of terror is hard to recognize—especially when it's homegrown. The next book in the Honor series. (978-1-60282-885-8)

Does She Love You? by Rachel Spangler. When Annabelle and Davis find out they are both in a relationship with the same woman, it leaves them facing life-altering questions about trust, redemption, and the possibility of finding love in the wake of betrayal. (978-1-60282-886-5)

The Road to Her by KE Payne. Sparks fly when actress Holly Croft, star of UK soap Portobello Road, meets her new on-screen love interest, the enigmatic and sexy Elise Manford. (978-1-60282-887-2)

Shadows of Something Real by Sophia Kell Hagin. Trying to escape flashbacks and nightmares, ex-POW Jamie Gwynmorgan stumbles into the heart of former Red Cross worker Adele Sabellius and uncovers a deadly conspiracy against everything and everyone she loves. (978-1-60282-889-6)

Date with Destiny by Mason Dixon. When sophisticated bank executive Rashida Ivey meets unemployed blue collar worker Destiny Jackson, will her life ever be the same? (978-1-60282-878-0)

The Devil's Orchard by Ali Vali. Cain and Emma plan a wedding before the birth of their third child while Juan Luis is still lurking, and as Cain plans for his death, an unexpected visitor arrives and challenges her belief in her father, Dalton Casey. (978-1-60282-879-7)

Secrets and Shadows by L.T. Marie. A bodyguard and the woman she protects run from a madman and into each other's arms. (978-1-60282-880-3)

Change Horizons: Three Novellas by Gun Brooke. Three stories of courageous women who dare to love as they fight to claim a future in a hostile universe. (978-1-60282-881-0)

Scarlet Thirst by Crin Claxton. When hot, feisty Rani meets cool, vampire Rob, one lifetime isn't enough, and the road from human to vampire is shorter than you think... (978-1-60282-856-8)

Battle Axe by Carsen Taite. How close is too close? Bounty hunter Luca Bennett will soon find out. (978-1-60282-871-1)

Improvisation by Karis Walsh. High school geometry teacher Jan Carroll thinks she's figured out the shape of her life and her future, until graphic artist and fiddle player Tina Nelson comes along and teaches her to improvise. (978-1-60282-872-8)

For Want of a Fiend by Barbara Ann Wright. Without her Fiendish power, can Princess Katya and her consort Starbride stop a magic-wielding madman from sparking an uprising in the kingdom of Farraday? (978-1-60282-873-5)

Broken in Soft Places by Fiona Zedde. The instant Sara Chambers meets the seductive and sinful Merille Thompson, she falls hard, but knowing the difference between love and a dangerous, all-consuming desire is just one of the lessons Sara must learn before it's too late. (978-1-60282-876-6)

Healing Hearts by Donna K. Ford. Running from tragedy, the women of Willow Springs find that with friendship, there is hope, and with love, there is everything. (978-1-60282-877-3)

Desolation Point by Cari Hunter. When a storm strands Sarah Kent in the North Cascades, Alex Pascal is determined to find her. Neither imagines the dangers they will face when a ruthless criminal begins to hunt them down. (978-1-60282-865-0)

I Remember by Julie Cannon. What happens when you can never forget the first kiss, the first touch, the first taste of lips on skin? What happens when you know you will remember every single detail of a mysterious woman? (978-1-60282-866-7)

The Gemini Deception by Kim Baldwin and Xenia Alexiou. The truth, the whole truth, and nothing but lies. Book six in the Elite Operatives series. (978-1-60282-867-4)

Scarlet Revenge by Sheri Lewis Wohl. When faith alone isn't enough, will the love of one woman be strong enough to save a vampire from damnation? (978-1-60282-868-1)

Ghost Trio by Lillian Q. Irwin. When Lee Howe hears the voice of her dead lover singing to her, is it a hallucination, a ghost, or something more sinister? (978-1-60282-869-8)

The Princess Affair by Nell Stark. Rhodes Scholar Kerry Donovan arrives at Oxford ready to focus on her studies, but her life and her priorities are thrown into chaos when she catches the eye of Her Royal Highness Princess Sasha. (978-1-60282-858-2)

The Chase by Jesse J. Thoma. When Isabelle Rochat's life is threatened, she receives the unwelcome protection and attention of bounty hunter Holt Lasher who vows to keep Isabelle safe at all costs. (978-1-60282-859-9)

The Lone Hunt by L.L. Raand. In a world where humans and praeterns conspire for the ultimate power, violence is a way of life... and death. A Midnight Hunters novel. (978-1-60282-860-5)

The Supernatural Detective by Crin Claxton. Tony Carson sees dead people. With a drag queen for a spirit guide and a devastatingly attractive herbalist for a client, she's about to discover the spirit world can be a very dangerous world indeed. (978-1-60282-861-2)

Beloved Gomorrah by Justine Saracen. Undersea artists creating their own City on the Plain uncover the truth about Sodom and Gomorrah, whose "one righteous man" is a murderer, rapist, and conspirator in genocide. (978-1-60282-862-9)

Cut to the Chase by Lisa Girolami. Careful and methodical author Paige Cornish falls for brash and wild Hollywood actress Avalon Randolph, but can these opposites find a happy middle ground in a town that never lives in the middle? (978-1-60282-783-7)

CPSIA information can be obtained
at www.ICGtesting.com
Printed in the USA
JSHW021424101022
31507JS00001B/21

9 781602 829480